THE
FALLEN
HERO

ALSO BY KATIE ZHAO

———

The Dragon Warrior

THE
FALLEN
HERO

Katie Zhao

BLOOMSBURY
CHILDREN'S BOOKS
NEW YORK LONDON OXFORD NEW DELHI SYDNEY

BLOOMSBURY CHILDREN'S BOOKS
Bloomsbury Publishing Inc., part of Bloomsbury Publishing Plc
1385 Broadway, New York, NY 10018

BLOOMSBURY, BLOOMSBURY CHILDREN'S BOOKS, and the Diana logo
are trademarks of Bloomsbury Publishing Plc

First published in the United States of America in October 2020 by Bloomsbury Children's Books

Bloomsbury books may be purchased for business or promotional use. For information on bulk purchases
please contact Macmillan Corporate and Premium Sales Department at
specialmarkets@macmillan.com

Library of Congress Cataloging-in-Publication Data
Names: Zhao, Katie, author.
Title: The fallen hero / by Katie Zhao.
Description: New York: Bloomsbury Children's Books, 2020. | Series: The dragon warrior; book 2
Summary: Determined to prevent the war her brother, Alex, is provoking, twelve-year-old
Faryn Liu and her half-dragon friend, Ren, seek help from the New Order, warriors
based in Manhattan's Chinatown, and from the Monkey King.
Identifiers: LCCN 2020007744 (print) | LCCN 2020007745 (e-book)
ISBN 978-1-5476-0197-4 (hardcover) | ISBN 978-1-5476-0198-1 (e-book)
Subjects: CYAC: Adventure and adventurers—Fiction. | Demonology—Fiction. | Dragons—Fiction. |
Gods, Chinese—Fiction. | Racially mixed people—Fiction. | Chinatown (New York, N.Y.)—Fiction. |
New York (N.Y.)—Fiction.
Classification: LCC PZ7.1.Z513 Fal 2020 (print) | LCC PZ7.1.Z513 (e-book) | DDC [Fic]—dc23
LC record available at https://lccn.loc.gov/2020007744
LC e-book record available at https://lccn.loc.gov/2020007745

Book design by Danielle Ceccolini
Typeset by Westchester Publishing Services
Printed and bound in the U.S.A. by Berryville Graphics Inc., Berryville, Virginia
2 4 6 8 10 9 7 5 3 1

To find out more about our authors and books visit www.bloomsbury.com and
sign up for our newsletters.

To all the friends I made on the journey to publishing my stories. This is cheesy as heck, but I couldn't have done it without you.

———

CHAPTER

1

Ba," I whispered.

The man I could've sworn was my father blinked and squinted. Confusion darkened his features. "Who are you?"

My stomach dropped. "Faryn Liu. I'm . . . I'm . . . I'm your daughter?" *The daughter you left behind at the Jade Society in San Francisco's Chinatown eight years ago. Remember?*

I hadn't imagined reuniting with Ba this way. We stood among rubble and ruins, the remains of Manhattan's Chinatown. Torn red paper lanterns scattered across the streets and hung limply from buildings. Nearby, produce stands had toppled over, spilling fruits and vegetables onto the road. And instead of welcoming me into his warm embrace, apologizing for abandoning me and promising we'd stay together forever, my long-lost father stared at me with no recognition in his eyes.

Something awful had happened to Ba along his journey, costing him his memories. That was the only explanation. He couldn't have *really* forgotten his daughter. Right?

"I'm sorry, girl," Ba said, shrugging helplessly. "I'm not your father. I-I'm afraid I don't have any children. Would you like me to help you find him?"

"I . . . N-no. That's okay." Embarrassment burning my cheeks, I turned away. My heart sank into my stomach with dread. A nightmare. This had to be a nightmare.

"I'm sorry, Faryn," came a quiet voice.

I turned toward my friend Ren. The wind ruffled his white hair. His eyes, one green and one black, flickered from me to Ba and widened with sympathy.

Great. Why did Ren have to witness this shameful scene—my own father not remembering me? I shook my head to indicate that this conversation was over. This wasn't the time or place to explain to Ren all my family-related troubles anyway. Around us, the battle had died down, but the threat of danger still hung in the smoky air. I turned my gaze to the crowd of warriors behind Ren. Dirt-smeared men, women, and children stood before me amid rubble that layered the street. Some of the warriors held swords and shields in their hands, and others held bows and arrows. One confused kid had a Nerf gun. The warriors stared at Ren and me in near-silent awe.

No, not at just Ren and me. At *us*. The deities of legends

surrounded me—Nezha, the boy god; Guanyin, goddess of mercy; Erlang Shen, warrior god.

We'd just landed in Manhattan's Chinatown after fleeing the gods' banquet on Peng Lai Island, where we'd learned about the Jade Emperor's plans to destroy disloyal humans. It looked like we'd come a little late. The demons had already destroyed much of Chinatown.

"Warriors of the New Order," Guanyin said with a grim smile, "you've fought bravely today to protect the people of Chinatown."

"It's the gods," gasped a silver-bearded old man. He dropped his sword and shield and knelt. Weapons clattered to the ground as everyone behind him did the same. "Help is here. We're saved."

"You may rise," said Guanyin. In a scattered, clumsy motion, the crowd obeyed. "I'm afraid we come bearing bad news, brave New Order warriors. The Jade Emperor will not be sending reinforcements."

"*What?* Why not?" demanded a tall, beefy-looking man.

"Mr. Wan! Show respect for the gods," hissed the short man beside him. Slowly and reluctantly, Mr. Wan inclined his head toward the three gods in a display of respect.

An old man stepped out from the crowd, carrying himself with the confidence and poise of a god. His long white beard flowed down to his belly. He wore a gray robe, and a sword dangled from its belt on his waist as he bowed. "My name is

Xiong," he said in a deep, soothing voice. "I am the master of the New Order. What brings you to our society, gods?"

I thought the reason was obvious, but maybe Xiong wanted to be polite. Like, "I'm pretty sure you've come to help us win the war but maybe you're just dropping by to say hi" polite.

Guanyin, Nezha, and Erlang Shen exchanged glances.

Erlang Shen spoke next. "We three—I, Erlang Shen, along with Guanyin and Nezha—will help you vanquish these demons. Our combined forces are enough to stop the demons from rampaging. We need not involve the Jade Emperor himself."

Ren twitched and turned toward me, his eyes full of confusion. I knew why: the gods were withholding important information—the Jade Emperor wasn't only *not* sending reinforcements, but he was also actively *using* the demons to get rid of all the pesky, "disloyal" humans. I guess the gods figured sharing this information with the warriors right now wouldn't exactly boost morale.

Erlang said his piece with such conviction that even I almost believed it. Plus, the god's threatening sneer told us that if we *didn't* believe him, the demons would quickly become the least of our worries.

"Warriors." Nezha pointed toward the crowd with his flaming spear. "The battle isn't over. You must do your ancient, sworn duty and protect the people of this Chinatown." He raised his weapon high.

In a clumsy wave, the warriors pointed their weapons

skyward, too. I didn't stop watching Ba. My heart clenched when his sword came up last, as though he wasn't quite sure what was going on.

A roar ripped through the street. Gasps and screams rose from the crowd. A huge, black, bearlike demon flew out of a collapsed building and leapt straight for the chariot—straight for *me*.

I reached into my hair to pull out the hairpin that could morph into my trusty spear, Fenghuang. My fingers met thin air.

Then I remembered. The powerful weapon was gone. My brother, Alex, had taken it, leaving me defenseless in the face of the demon. Worse—there was no *way* Alex could pull off that hairpin look.

"*No!*" My father's voice rang out loudly and clearly, like he'd shouted in my ear. A second later, hands shoved me out of the way.

"Oof!" I careened into the other end of the chariot, and pain shot through my rib cage. I opened my eyes. Ba lay on the ground, unmoving. Before I could scramble over to him, several other demons charged out from behind the first, scattering the warriors. Nezha and Erlang Shen were on them in a flash. They batted demons out of the way left and right, as easily as if they were made out of paper. Guanyin floated high above, clearly intending to take care of the largest demon that had tackled Ba.

A demon with red skin burst out of nowhere, headed straight for—Ba. Instinctively, I leapt forward to defend him.

"*AUGHHHHHHHHHH!*" From the fore of the crowd, a tall boy dove in front of us. It looked like he was going to take on the demon by himself.

"Jinyu!" someone screamed. "*No!*"

I watched, paralyzed, as the demon swatted away the tall boy like he was nothing. Jinyu flew into a building and then crumbled to the ground, motionless.

The demon turned its eyes back toward Ba and me. The gods and warriors were busy with their own battles. We were on our own.

Panic numbed my senses. But strangely, my thoughts were clearer than ever. My father was defenseless. A boy might have just *died* in front of me. And if I didn't want there to be any more deaths, I had to bring down the demon myself.

My mind and body entered overdrive. I grabbed Ba's sword from the ground, drew it back, and let out a battle cry. The demon charged straight at me. It swiped a great paw so close to my face that I felt the sting of claws just barely missing my skin. The demon roared and drew back its paw for another attack. I didn't think. Didn't pause. I lunged forward and drove the tip of my sword's blade upward, through the neck of the beast.

The demon let out an ear-piercing scream of pain, a ghastly, inhuman sound that nearly tore my eardrums.

I collapsed onto the pavement. Stabbing sensations shot up my palms and knees. Ba's sword skittered away at the foot of a food cart, at least three feet out of reach. I tried to stand to retrieve it, but a horrible pain tore up my right foot. The pain escalated until all I could do was bite my lip and hope the tears stinging my eyes didn't spill over.

"Finish the demon off!" a warrior shouted nearby. "It's almost done for!"

The warriors roared and surged forward in a wave toward the downed demon. Then the world grew blurry around me and disappeared.

Someone touched my arm and shook me. Ren's concerned face peered down. Dimly, I registered Ba's motionless form still lying inches away.

Before I could reassure Ren I was fine—or, at least, still alive—the world faded to black.

CHAPTER

2

Six Months Later

I was having those strange dreams again, the same ones I'd had ever since arriving at the New Order. I found myself up in Heaven among the gods without a clue as to how I'd gotten there. I couldn't speak or move, and nobody was ever able to see me. But I could see *them*.

I dreamed of my brother wearing his new black battle armor. Sometimes, Alex was alone. Sometimes, other Heavenly soldiers accompanied him. Once, I'd even seen Alex using the power of my old weapon Fenghuang, a mighty white-tipped golden spear that gave the wielder the power to lead all dragons. He commanded a whole crowd of dragons in a vast garden.

This vision was the clearest yet. I stood in an enormous

hall. Alex paced the red carpet right in front of a golden throne, holding his battle helmet under one arm. I wanted more than anything to run up and hug my brother, even if he'd hate that. Too bad I still couldn't speak or move.

From the throne came a woman's dark, silky voice. "Heaven Breaker, you seem disturbed today."

My heart slammed in my chest. Even though I couldn't see the speaker from the shadows, I'd recognize that voice anywhere: Xi Wangmu. She was the Queen Mother of the West and wife to the Jade Emperor, the ruler of the Heavens. She also happened to want all demons destroyed and didn't care if that meant wiping out humanity in the process. Really charming, that one.

"Those pesky Jade Society warriors are stirring up trouble," Alex reported.

The Jade Society in San Francisco—where I used to live with Alex and our grandfather Ye Ye. Last I'd heard, they were still in recovery mode from the near destruction of the society during the Lunar New Year. Hope bloomed in my chest. Were the warriors growing stronger?

"I put a stop to their antics, though." Alex stopped pacing and stood up straight, puffing out his chest. "I went down to Earth and threw their ringleader—Zhao Boyang—into Diyu, where he'll await punishment by King Yama."

Oh no. Back when Alex and I had lived in the Jade Society, Mr. Zhao had been one of the only adults who'd treated us with unconditional kindness instead of questioning our half-warrior parentage. I pictured the man's crinkled eyes and gentle smile and shook my head.

Alex had thrown Mr. Zhao into the Underworld so easily. When had my brother become so cruel?

"Your old society, soldier," Xi Wangmu said softly. "Your old ally Zhao Boyang. Don't you feel terrible for punishing him so?"

"No." Alex's reply was swift. Cold. "Those who interfere with our plans must be punished. No exceptions."

"Excellent. Truly excellent, my Heaven Breaker." Xi Wangmu said *my Heaven Breaker* like she was tasting the term on her tongue. It made me want to puke. "Speaking of plans, for the upcoming Hungry Ghost Festival, we will—"

"*Faryn!*"

A familiar voice awoke me from the dream with a jolt.

"Alex?" I sat up straight, knocking the side of my head against something solid—the wall. "Ow!" Rubbing my head, I looked up. A towering pile of books was stacked on the table in front of me, bookshelves lining the walls. My gaze landed on a confused-looking boy, around eight or nine years old. He was slightly chubby. He had short, stubby black hair, and there was chocolate smeared on his mouth—from the Choco Pie he held in his right hand, probably.

"Ah Qiao. What're you doing here?"

"Looking for you. I knew I'd find you in the library. You're in here a lot these days!" Ah Qiao chomped down on his Choco Pie. Crumbs spilled onto the table.

"I'm researching something." Since realizing Ba had lost his memories, I'd done my best to try to find a cure. I'd gone through every memory-related book in the library at least three times but still hadn't found a satisfactory answer. The weathered book I'd fallen asleep reading—*Restorative Potions*—seemed the most promising. Only problem was, the chapter titled "Memory-Restoring Elixirs" was mysteriously blank.

"Researching? But you're always sleeping here. Don't you have your own bed?"

"I am not always sleeping here," I said defensively.

Ah Qiao pulled his phone out of his pocket. "I have pictures. Wanna see?"

"No! Hey, don't you have homework, or training, or someone else to bug—?"

"Faryn!"

I jolted, sure that this time I'd heard Alex's voice. But no. The person who'd arrived at the door was Ren. Not my brother, who'd betrayed us and was plotting gods-knew-what with Xi Wangmu. Ren, my friend, who could sometimes turn into a fifteen-foot-tall dragon. You know, just normal puberty stuff for an average thirteen-year-old kid.

The hope of seeing Alex had briefly bloomed, but now it disappeared. I swallowed my disappointment.

Get a grip. Alex is gone. He chose *to leave you. Just like Ba. Just like how everyone else in your life has left you.*

Every day, I thought about Alex and how he was a top contender for the Worst Little Brother Ever award. Six months ago, during the Lunar New Year, when little brothers were supposed to give their older sisters compliments and nice presents, *my* little brother had decided to give me the gift of utter betrayal. While I saved the world from the wrath of the fearsome nián demon, Alex decided to become an evil turd. Guess who *didn't* get a hóng bāo, a red packet of money, for good behavior.

"I heard you in the hallway," Ren said. "You were yelling pretty loudly. Something about a demon-Alex. I thought maybe the library was under attack or something." He raised his hand so I could see he'd drawn his sword.

"Of course the library wasn't under attack." I frowned. "The demons have been gone for six months now, remember?"

The combined forces of warriors and deities had helped to beat back the demons in Manhattan's Chinatown—for now, at least. We'd heard hardly a peep of any demon activity since the end of the Lunar New Year. The warriors had different theories. Some believed the demons were gone for a good while. Some believed the demons were regrouping for an even bigger attack in the future.

"You're lucky you *weren't* under attack," Ren said. "I would've been the only one around to help you."

"Why? Where'd everyone else go?" It was rare for the New Order apartments to be empty. The warriors took up all the rooms in a six-story apartment complex right outside Chinatown. As the Elders had explained when we'd first arrived, the building was guarded with ancient magic that made it look like a doctor's office to any outsiders. This meant the warriors were very safe, because *nobody* ever wanted to go inside a doctor's office.

The New Order was the Jade Society 2.0. Clearly, the New Order warriors had gotten a much bigger chunk of the budget the gods had allotted warriors for building their societies. The apartment complex was way bigger on the inside than it appeared from the outside. It had everything a warrior could possibly need: a training ground in the basement, apartments on the first and second floors, a dining hall on the third floor, a library on the fourth floor, a game room on the fifth floor, and even a spa on the sixth floor.

"Everyone's gone to the temple, of course," Ah Qiao said loudly. "Don't tell me you forgot what day it is."

In the aftermath of my dream about Alex, it had slipped my mind. "July 31st. It's the day before the Hungry Ghost Festival."

One of the biggest celebrations of the year, the Hungry Ghost Festival was a time for the living to reunite with their dead ancestors and friends. It was more of a formality now, since the warriors were no longer powerful enough to *actually* summon the dead. Still, the holiday always reminded me of the family I'd never known—Mama, my mother; Nai Nai, my grandmother; Gu Gu, my aunt; Jiu Jiu, my uncle. They had all passed away before I was born. This year, my grandfather was also on my mind. Ye Ye had passed away during the last Lunar New Year and now lived as a deity in Heaven. The thought brought a pang to my chest.

Every warrior needed to be alert for demon activity during the Hungry Ghost Festival, just like on every holiday, when the demons grew stronger—and especially this year, the wake of the demons' attack during the Lunar New Year. And I'd almost slept through the prefestival ceremony. The worst part was, Xiong, the master of the New Order, was just about the strictest guy on the planet. He once made me run ten laps around Chinatown because I forgot it was my turn to sweep the dining hall floors. I guess a guy named Xiong, which literally means "fierce," is bound to be one tough cookie.

"Xiong's speech starts soon. Ah Qiao, you should get going. I need to speak with Faryn."

"No! I don't wanna go to the dumb—"

One hard, penetrating stare from Ren was enough to silence Ah Qiao. The little boy gave me a sullen look, as though asking for backup. I just looked at him.

"Fine," Ah Qiao grumbled. He tossed his crumpled-up Choco Pie wrapper into a nearby trash can and ran out the door.

"We should head over to the temple, too." I stood up.

"Wait. First I have . . . something important to . . . to think about," Ren mumbled, shifting his bag.

"More important than the New Order's preparations for the Hungry Ghost Festival? Do you *want* to run laps for Xiong? 'Cause I'm telling you right now, it's not fun."

"I-I've been summoned," Ren confessed. "To the palace of the Dragon King of the Center Sea. For training. The Dragon Kings sent me a vision in my dream. I saw the palace. This dark, ugly cloud surrounded it, and—and the Dragon Kings told me if I went to the palace, they'd train me for battle."

My heart sank at the thought of Ren leaving me on my own. We hadn't spent a day apart for the past six months. "Oh. What . . . what are they training you for?"

"Apparently, word of my—uh—special situation has spread pretty far. The Dragon Kings are worried that without their training, I'll be a danger to those around me."

"Th-that's ridiculous," I spluttered. "You haven't hurt a single soul since arriving at the New Order!"

Ren still appeared hesitant. "Not *yet*. I'm sure it's because the gods have been strangely quiet, so all the dragons—mine included—have been quiet, too. So have the demons. I don't like it. I don't like it at all . . ."

"Yeah, I prefer war," I said sarcastically.

"I didn't mean it that way. All I'm saying is, things have felt *too* peaceful lately. Feels like . . . something big is about to happen."

Ren's words reminded me of my dream about Alex and Xi

Wangmu. I shivered. It had only been a dream. A vivid dream, maybe, but still just a dream. No way would Alex actually throw Mr. Zhao in the Underworld. Right? But the Hungry Ghost Festival did start soon and the demons were bound to grow stronger. Maybe that had caused Ren's restlessness.

"I hate the feeling of waiting around," Ren continued. "I want to train. Properly."

"The New Order has been training us properly," I insisted. "*More* than properly. Those guys practically have it out for us!"

At the New Order, every warrior took training seriously. Ren and I rose with them at five in the morning to jog three miles, and that was *before* the actual training of the day. In the evenings, we received lessons in math, science, history, English, and Chinese from world-class instructors, right in the apartment complex.

Ren shook his head with a sad smile. "I'm half-dragon and half-warrior. No warrior society is fully equipped to train someone like me."

I knew Ren was right. In our time at the New Order, he'd kept up with lessons—better than most of the other warriors, in fact—but he hadn't transformed into his dragon form. There was probably nowhere safe for him to do that, except in the presence of other dragons.

"There's something else, too." Ren suddenly seemed shy. "The Dragon Kings told me that if I go to them . . . I might be able to find my mother."

"Your mother?" I blurted out. "You're sure she's there? I mean . . ."

Ren's expression fell. During the Lunar New Year, we thought we'd found Ren's mother, a Mandopop singer named Cindy You—only to discover that a demon prince had taken on her appearance instead. Talk about bad karma to start off the New Year.

"I'm sure she is," Ren said softly. His forehead scrunched up. "Well, like, eighty percent sure. Rounded up from fifty."

The steely glint in Ren's eye told me that his mind was made up, and nothing I said would change it. I'd been in his shoes—I would go to the ends of the world for Ba, too.

"So you're . . . leaving? Just like that?" I tried to sound casual, but my voice trembled.

"I was going to . . . but I don't know," Ren confessed. A shadow crossed his face. "I don't even know if we can trust the Dragon Kings. The other gods believed that the Dragon Kings would side with the Jade Emperor, remember?"

I thought back to what Guanyin, Erlang Shen, and Nezha had speculated during the Lunar New Year: that the Dragon Kings would fight alongside the Jade Emperor—and against the humans.

Ren stood up straight. In the past six months, he'd grown taller and lankier, so much so that he'd had to buy all new clothes. He shouldered his bag more firmly. "Maybe I should leave. Nobody here would miss me anyway."

"I'd miss you," I blurted out and then blushed. Ren's cheeks turned pink, too. "And—and so would Ah Qiao!"

The little eight-year-old boy had taken to hero-worshipping Ren, for whatever reason. Trailed him everywhere with hearts bursting out of his eyes. I think the kid just really liked Ren's white hair.

A small, rare smile broke out across Ren's face. But as quickly as it came, it vanished. "I don't think anyone else would miss me."

I couldn't argue with that. Judging by the fearful looks many New Order warriors still gave Ren, they wouldn't miss him at all.

Ren was my only true friend here, though. Unless I counted the lady who gave me extra sesame balls whenever I went into my favorite dessert shop in Chinatown. I couldn't stand the thought of Ren leaving.

"I won't leave," Ren said quietly. "If it'll make you happy, I'll stay."

A grin stretched across my cheeks. "Really?"

"Yeah. I'll stay. Don't look so relieved just yet, though," Ren warned. "We gotta get to the temple for Xiong's speech. And we're late."

"You're right," I groaned. I pushed aside the stack of books but tucked *Restorative Potions* into the black backpack I'd brought with me. I had a feeling it would come in handy. Then I followed Ren out of the library, hoping there was still time to sneak into the temple before Xiong noticed we were late.

CHAPTER

3

I arrived at the Chinatown temple in true Faryn style: late, with a hair comb stuck in a giant knot in my hair. Unsurprisingly, Ren and I were the last warriors to arrive. As they had with the New Order apartments, the gods had used their magic to craft the temple to be even bigger than it appeared from the outside. The ceiling was so high above my head, I had to crane my neck to see it. The echoes of Xiong's deep, stern voice reverberated around the space.

On the central table, golden statues of several major deities, like the Jade Emperor and Xi Wangmu, stood alongside the newly placed statues of Erlang Shen, Nezha, and Guanyin. Food and candles, offerings for the gods, filled the surface. On side tables stood the statues of minor deities, like Mazu the sea goddess and Leigong and Leizi, the god of thunder and goddess of lightning.

I couldn't even look at the statues of the Jade Emperor or Xi Wangmu without my stomach turning.

The Jade Emperor ruled Heaven and Earth, making him the ultimate boss man of all the gods. His wife, Xi Wangmu, was powerful in her own right—which she'd proven during the Lunar New Year, after revealing that she'd been controlling me when I was the Heaven Breaker. Oh, and minor detail, they were planning to erase both demons and disloyal humans from the face of the planet so the gods could reclaim their old power.

Yeah, those two were real fun at parties.

The air buzzed with nervous energy in anticipation of the Hungry Ghost Festival. Growing up in the Jade Society, I'd helped with preparations every year. The warriors of the New Order likely planned to light incense; then they'd burn lots of paper money so our ancestors could buy some flat-screen TVs for broadcasting Netflix with all their dead friends.

The men, women, and children stared as the red temple doors swung shut behind us.

"Everyone's looking," Ren whispered unnecessarily.

"Really? Hadn't noticed." I shuffled out of sight behind the large statue of the warrior god Erlang Shen, with his three eyes and a wicked, gleaming double-edged spear. I grabbed Ren's sleeve and pulled him toward me. Maybe nobody would notice us back here chilling with Erlang, and—

"You're late, Jade Society warriors."

I flinched. Ren groaned. A couple of teenagers snickered.

Over the heads of the crowd, Xiong's black eyes pierced into mine. Xiong wasn't the tallest man in the New Order or even the strongest-looking one. But his presence commanded attention from everyone, from the smallest child to the most muscular warrior.

Xiong was an old man with a white beard long and luscious enough to rival Santa Claus's. He was the leader of the Elders and took charge of everything that happened in the New Order. Xiong reminded me of Ye Ye, my tough-as-nails grandfather.

"I'll speak with you two about your tardiness later," Xiong declared.

"At least he isn't making us run ten laps around Chinatown," I whispered to Ren.

He gulped. "Not yet."

"Right now, we have more important matters at hand," Xiong continued. "I've just returned from the Yuē Huì with the other warrior societies."

The masters of the three warrior societies across the United States—in Chinatowns in San Francisco, Manhattan, and Seattle—had an annual meetup, or Yuē Huì, to discuss the state of their societies. Until I'd arrived at the New Order, I'd had no idea about any of this. Mao, the mistress of the Jade Society who'd dedicated her existence to making Alex and me miserable, had kept the warriors in the dark about the meetup. It was her way of denying that the demons had been growing stronger in recent years and that the warrior societies needed to band together once more, as they had in times of old.

There had once been a fourth warrior society in Chicago's Chinatown, but according to Xiong and the Elders, it had been buried by corruption and the loss of tradition. No warriors remained in that city—which really did seem to be the case, since we'd visited it during the Lunar New Year and found no sign of warriors.

"During the Lunar New Year, we warriors defeated the demons soundly enough that they've stayed quiet for the past six months. But they won't be out of commission forever. The other society leaders and I agreed to tighten defenses against the growing threat of the demons." Xiong gazed around at us with a warning look on his face. "Today is the day before the Hungry Ghost Festival. Tomorrow, and for the next two weeks until the fifteenth of the month, ghosts and demons will grow stronger. It's been many, many years since our prayers have summoned our ancestors, but given the return of the demons, this may also be the year that the spirits become strong enough to roam the earth once more. If so, we'll welcome our ancestors back into our midst—and solidify our protection around Manhattan's Chinatown."

Whispers broke out among the crowd. Across the room, I made eye contact with an all-too-familiar face—my father's. Ba gave me a smile and nod, like acknowledging a friend, before turning away.

I returned the smile a little sadly. Six months had passed since I'd arrived at the New Order, and Ba still hadn't regained his memories. After he'd protected me from the demon's attack when I landed in Manhattan's Chinatown, I'd hoped that deep down, Ba still remembered me. At least once a week for the past half a year, I'd made it a point to visit Ba just to talk to him.

Two of the warriors closest to me turned to each other, and when the light hit their tan skin and black hair, I recognized Ashley and Jordan Liao, siblings around the same age as Alex and me. They stood slightly apart from the crowd—also like Alex and me, always hovering on the outskirts of their warrior society.

"You think we'll get to see Jinyu again?" Ashley whispered.

My heart stuttered in my chest. *Jinyu.* Xiong's son, and the boy who'd died six months ago—to save me.

"Probably. Everyone else is coming back from Diyu, right?" Jordan's voice cracked, and he turned away from his younger sister. "I still can't believe . . ."

". . . That he's gone?" Ashley supplied sadly.

"Yeah. I mean, it's been six months already." Jordan swallowed hard. "But Jinyu was the last guy any one of us would've thought would just . . ."

"Jinyu was the best fighter out of all of us," Ashley agreed. "Nobody saw it coming."

Even though I'd never had the chance to meet Jinyu, I'd

heard so much about him that I felt like I'd known him anyway. If the stories were all true, the kid had brought down a huge demon by himself when he was just eight years old. Some of the rumors had to be exaggerated. Especially that bit about Jinyu's favorite food being Brussels sprouts. *Nobody* likes Brussels sprouts. Jinyu had died during the Lunar New Year, at the too-young age of fourteen.

And it was your fault, Faryn Liu, a voice whispered in the back of my head. *His death is all* your *fault.*

A warm hand touched my shoulder. Ren. "Hey. You okay? Those guys—are they bugging you again?"

I shook my head. The siblings—well, Ashley—had demonstrated resentment toward both of us, but mostly me. I didn't want Ren to think I was weak, so I usually just shrugged off their comments. This was nothing compared to the years of bullying I'd endured at the Jade Society. "Everything's fine."

"Jinyu should be alive." Ashley's voice grew louder. Colder. "It was only because that Jade Society warrior couldn't hold her own during the battle that he had to step in, and then he—he—"

"Shhhhh!" Jordan turned around and glanced at me. My attempt at hiding behind the statue of Erlang Shen hadn't worked at all. "Hey, Faryn. Hey, Ren." He waved.

I managed a small smile and waved back. Ren just stared until Jordan got uncomfortable, coughed, and turned around.

Jordan had made it a point to be friendly and invited Ren and me to a bunch of events, but I knew what Ashley and a lot of the other younger warriors thought of me. They'd never see me as anything but the outsider who'd taken their friend away from them.

Ashley's dark-brown eyes narrowed when they met mine. I looked away quickly, trying to ignore the guilt that rose in my chest.

Ashley had every right to be furious with me.

I could never forgive myself for what I'd done—or, rather, failed to do. That day often repeated itself in my nightmares: Jinyu leaping in front of me, slashing the huge black demon with his sword. Jinyu lying on the ground, broken, the light already faded from his eyes.

I clenched my fingers into fists. I wouldn't cry. Not here. Not in front of Ashley, Jordan, and the others.

"Looks like the ceremony is starting," Ren said.

The adult warriors in front of me were so tall that I had to stand on my tiptoes to see. Craning my neck, I glimpsed flickering smoke from incense and heard low murmurs as the Elders prayed to the gods.

A sudden movement and creaking noise caught my attention.

I looked up—and shrieked.

"King Yama's drawers!" Ren cursed.

"What is it now, Faryn and Ren?" groaned Xiong.

"You cannot continue disrupting such a sacred cerem—AIYAHHHHHH!"

Slowly, the statue of Erlang Shen came to life, a golden light washing up his body from the tips of his black boots to the top of his helmet. Ignoring the shouts and cries of the New Order warriors, the warrior god flexed his fingers and smirked. His eyes landed on me, and familiar flames danced in their depths. He nodded. "Hello, Heaven Breaker." Next, he gave Ren a nod of acknowledgment. "Dragon boy. Looking jumpy, you two."

"Who . . . wha . . . I-I'm not the Heaven Breaker," was all I could think to say.

Ren seemed to have collected himself in a remarkably short period of time. "Hi, uh . . . sir," he said. "You're looking . . . warmongery."

"Thank you," Erlang Shen said gruffly, shifting the collar of his armor. "That was exactly the look I was going for today."

He swung his three-pronged spear from hand to hand, nearly hitting a pimply teenage boy. That was the war god—grumpy and borderline threatening as always. Many times, I'd questioned why the war god would even side with the human warriors. Most likely his dislike of his uncle, the Jade Emperor, surpassed his dislike of us. I supposed that was flattering.

The warriors around me gasped. A few of the children screamed.

Erlang Shen surveyed the crowd and made a *tsk*ing noise. "Well? Don't stop praying now, humans. We need much more power than that."

"*We?*" a nearby warrior squeaked.

A shudder racked through the air, and golden light encased more of the statues. First was the long-haired boy god Nezha, wielding flaming hoops in one hand and a spear in the other. As he came to life, Nezha twirled his weapons in a great arc that caused the front row of warriors to yell and duck for cover. "Thousands of years, and you never get sick of your silly dramatic entrances, " said Nezha.

"Shouldn't you know by now to be more careful with your power around humans?" chided a female voice. Goddess of mercy Guanyin's statue came alive, wearing a serene expression on her face and a veil over her long black hair. "Boys, can't you stop bickering long enough for us to deliver our important information to the New Order warriors?" Guanyin sighed. *I guess it couldn't be easy to be the eternal babysitter for the two hotheaded gods.*

Erlang Shen, Nezha, and Guanyin: Where had they been all this time? After they'd dropped off Ren and me at the New Order during the Lunar New Year, they'd told us to lay low. We weren't even allowed to tell the New Order warriors about the other gods' true plot to vanquish the demons once and for all, at the cost of all of humanity. The gods worried that if the warriors knew about how dangerous the situation really was, they'd either be so racked with fear they'd be useless, or they'd attempt something drastic.

As far as secrets go, this was one of the harder ones I'd had to keep. Every time I passed by the Jade Emperor in the temple during prayer, I had to resist yelling, "Watch out! It's Mr. Ultimate Evil Dude!"

For these six months, Ren and I hadn't had any contact with the trio of rebel gods. Not even a single peep. They'd gone as silent as the demons had. I knew the three gods had been busy keeping the other gods from smiting all humans and stuff, but would it have been so hard to send a single "Thinking of You" postcard?

Nezha fixed his flaming eyes on Ren and me. I gasped, thinking he'd heard my thoughts and was going to turn us both into a little oil smear on the temple floor. Instead, he nodded at us. An acknowledgment that we'd fought side by side during the Lunar New Year.

"Kneel down, Faryn," Ren whispered out of the corner of his mouth, barely lifting his head. "You're spacing out."

Everyone else had knelt. Oops. Quickly, I did the same.

"Thanks," I whispered.

"You owe me a bubble tea," he responded.

"We've come back to the New Order to ask for your help, warriors," Guanyin said, answering the question that was on all our minds. "We're sorry to cut into your preparations for the Hungry Ghost Festival—"

"No, we're not," interjected Erlang Shen. He admired the tips of his three-bladed spear. "Forget the festival. What could be more fun than waging a war? Especially against that egotistical uncle of mine, the Jade Emperor."

"Waging . . . war?" gasped one of the Elders. She clutched at her pearls, quite literally. "Against—against the Jade Emperor?"

"Yes," Guanyin said solemnly. "And Xi Wangmu."

"They both have, ah, slightly evil tendencies," Nezha supplied. "Therapy didn't help."

This was news to everyone except Ren and me, and it showed in the confused and horrified expressions on the warriors' faces. I knew the gods had asked us to keep quiet about the Jade Emperor's evil plans so the warriors could peacefully concentrate on their training without mass panic, but was this really a better solution? Now half of them looked on the verge of a heart attack.

"We didn't reveal the Jade Emperor's plot earlier, because we feared it would cause panic," Guanyin explained, shaking her head.

"And what will you have us do now that we know, gods?" Xiong asked. His face was inscrutable, but the sweat shining on his brow gave away his nervousness. I hadn't seen the master of the New Order look so out of sorts since the day we'd landed here in the midst of a battle.

Nezha's face became serious. "With the Hungry Ghost Festival beginning, we don't have a moment to waste. The Jade

Emperor believes he and his deities can contain the demons as they regain their power, but he's wrong."

In a reassuring voice that reassured no one, Guanyin added, "Luckily, many of the deities have yet to choose a side. We must recruit as many as possible. If we don't stop the demons during the Hungry Ghost Festival, even the gods won't be able to withstand the evil that will wipe out the Earth."

CHAPTER

4

A short, shocked silence filled the temple. Then the warriors murmured as the news sank in. Some sounded excited. Others, frightened.

Since the olden times, the greatest of warriors undertook tasks in service of the gods. That meant protecting the people of Earth from demons when the gods were busy with their important godly tasks, like ensuring peace in the world, controlling the weather, or channel surfing through their TV shows. (Yup, gods had their own TV channels.) There was the great general Yue Fei, who never lost a battle and once even defeated one hundred thousand enemy soldiers with only five hundred men. Xuanzang, a Buddhist monk who traveled to India to bring back a set of Buddhist scriptures to China. And you can't forget the greatest of them all—the dude who invented dim sum. The list of heroes went on and on.

When Alex and I had undertaken a quest for the Jade Society during the Lunar New Year, we'd considered it an honor. Now, the thought of any warrior taking on such a dangerous and difficult task brought me no joy. Only bone-deep fear and horrible memories I'd locked away for months.

Ren's face drained of color. "This—this is—"

"Awesome," squeaked Jordan. "Fantastic. Great." He paused, and his face brightened. "Does this mean I won't have to be on laundry duty next week?"

Ashley jabbed her brother in the rib cage.

"Ow! What?"

"Don't joke about something as serious as quests, dweeb."

"I'm just trying to look on the bright side. Bright *Tide*, I mean." He nudged his sister, who stared back at him, stone-faced. "Geddit? Tide? Like the laundry detergent? 'Cause I won't be on laundry duty?"

"I'm gonna punch you," Ashley threatened.

Erlang Shen cleared his throat and closed his eyes. A familiar, peaceful expression fell across his face—the same one he'd worn when he'd revealed the riddle for our first quest in the Jade Society.

"Bad poetry incoming," I groaned.

"Bad poetry?" Ren and Jordan echoed in alarm.

> *"To seek the weapon of greatest power,*
> *five warriors must search the highest heights and*
> *lowest depths,*

and when darkness reaches its greatest hour,
an old ally will return from the brink of death.”

I had to give Erlang Shen some credit. His poetry had improved since the Lunar New Year. At least this one rhymed.

But why would Erlang Shen give us a riddle to solve instead of just telling us what to do—especially if we were short on time? Annoyance surged inside me. Even the gods who were on the warriors' side wouldn't stop making our lives difficult.

After Erlang Shen finished, the warriors began clapping and murmuring to one another. *An old ally will return from the brink of death.* My thoughts leapt immediately to my friend Moli, who'd died during our battle back on Peng Lai Island. Could that line refer to her?

Or Alex. Alex was a former ally, too. How safe was he *really* as the new Heaven Breaker and a fresh Heavenly General?

Or—Ba. He'd also come back from the brink of death. Maybe, somehow, this quest would restore Ba's memories and return him to me.

I knew it was foolish thinking, but still, hope swelled in my chest.

"Three of the five warriors will be selected from the New Order," Nezha declared, which set off more murmurs from the warriors.

"What about the other two?" Ren asked.

"They're not gonna take some Jade Society clowns, are they?" Ashley muttered not so quietly. I shot her a dirty look.

"That is none of your concern." Erlang Shen turned his three-eyed gaze to Ashley. That shut her up real quick.

A motion parted the crowd. The men, women, and children bowed their heads toward the person making his way past them—Xiong.

The old man got onto his knees, pressed the palms of his hands together, and bowed low to the gods.

"Guanyin, Nezha, Erlang Shen," said Xiong. "Thank you for gracing our Chinatown with your presence and for delivering the news of the quest."

"You're welcome," said Guanyin.

"We regard the gods with the utmost respect and welcome you to stay in the New Order for as long as you desire. To answer your call would be our greatest honor. Tonight, my young warriors will duel to determine which three are the worthiest of embarking on this quest."

"D . . . duel?" I whispered to Ren.

"Sounds, uh." He gulped. "Fun."

"The Duels are a New Order tradition going back five hundred years. The young warriors—those who have yet to come of age—must challenge one another, prove their capabilities to their elders, and earn the right to go on a quest," Xiong elaborated. "It's been fifty years since we last hosted the Duels, warriors, and this, the Ninety-Sixth Duels, shall be the grandest yet."

"Sweet. I've always wanted a fight to the death," Ashley whispered.

"You're joking," Ren said shakily. "She's joking, right? About fighting to the death?" He turned toward Jordan, sweat beading his forehead.

Jordan flashed a reassuring smile. "'Course Ashley's joking. Worst that's happened in the past were people getting hospitalized for months."

"Well, that's fine," I squeaked.

"The Ninety-Sixth Duels will be a rigorous and dangerous process," Xiong was saying to a rapt audience.

Ashley added in a pointed whisper, "Not something you'd want to try if you've only been here for half a year."

I rolled my eyes. As if I even wanted to duel people to go on another quest for the gods. I didn't have another brother to lose on this one.

"Very well," said Erlang Shen. "We'll soon see which of you young warriors are worthy to take on this quest for the gods. Don't dally. Remember—you only have until tomorrow."

Erlang Shen brought the end of his spear down against the ground, and the floor shuddered beneath us. A bright golden glow enveloped the three gods. In moments, the glow faded, and the statues of Erlang Shen, Guanyin, and Nezha became stony and still once more.

Xiong clasped his hands behind his back and drew himself to his full height.

"Stand, New Order warriors," he commanded.

Everyone obeyed, a wave of warriors straightening and clasping their hands behind their backs.

These guys were *intense*. Mao, the mistress of the Jade Society, had let her warriors train casually. She'd been more interested in reminding everyone that the demons no longer existed, and, oh yeah, that Alex and I, who'd known all along that they *did* exist, were worth less than the dirt beneath the warriors' shoes.

"It's been many, many years since we've had the honor of hosting gods in our temple and taking on a quest for them," said Xiong, "but all of you have learned in your training about the proper protocol for such an occasion."

"Shì!" shouted the warriors in unison. *Yes.*

"Tonight after dinner, you'll show up to the training arena to prove your worth and honor as warriors."

"Shì!"

Xiong nodded gravely. "Dismissed!"

The New Order warriors bowed and rushed out of the temple. Their momentum knocked me sideways, and I would've done a spectacular face-plant onto the ground if Ren didn't steady me.

"Thanks," I said.

"Ren," Xiong called. "A word, please."

"Think he's gonna chew me out for being tardy," Ren groaned. He shuffled away, his shoulders slightly hunched.

But I'd been late, too—and Xiong hadn't called me over. Weird. Many warriors ran between Ren and me, pushing and shoving me toward the door.

"Where's everyone going?" I asked as I followed Jordan and Ashley out the temple doors.

"Home, where I should have been all along," grunted a man with a huge black beard and mustache—Mr. Wan, the grouch of the New Order—as he shoved past us. "Outta my way."

The warriors cast wary looks in our direction as they filed out of the temple. Reminders that the three of us weren't as welcome as we would've liked to be. I still hadn't figured out what Ashley and Jordan had done to earn outcast status around here. The adults refused to talk about it, and the kids I'd managed to bribe with White Rabbit candy had said something vaguely about witchcraft. Then they'd burst out laughing. So basically, I lost a bunch of perfectly good candy and learned nothing.

"Where is everyone going?" I turned to Jordan this time.

Jordan's jaw was set. "Well, there are only a few hours before dinnertime. I imagine everyone's going to warm up for the Ninety-Sixth Duels tonight."

"Warm up?"

"Yeah, you know, sharpen their weapons, work on their battle cries, conquer a few small nations . . . Ah Qiao likes to impersonate a monkey." Jordan pointed toward the young boy, who was hooting and scratching his armpits. "Don't ask me why."

"You don't need to prepare, since you won't be participating in the Ninety-Sixth Duels, Faryn." Ashley smirked. "You can just go relax for a bit. Enjoy the show when Jordan and I wipe the floor with the competition."

"C'mon, Ashley." Jordan gave his little sister an exasperated look.

Ashley rolled her eyes and turned away from me but didn't say anything else. If there was only one person around the New Order who she'd listen to, it was her brother. If only Alex had been so obedient to me.

"How are you planning to prepare for the Duels?" I asked Jordan.

"Wanna come along? I'll show you."

I hesitated, mostly because the sour expression on Ashley's face told me that, no, I didn't want to come along. But even though his little sister was possibly the spawn of the nián demon, Jordan seemed cool. So far, he hadn't given me resentful looks or tried to kill me or anything. I was pretty sure that meant we were friends.

"Hey, Ash—" Jordan turned toward his sister—or rather, the empty spot where his sister had stood moments ago. I watched Ashley draw farther from us as she sprinted toward the New Order apartment complex.

"Don't follow me!" she shouted over her shoulder.

"Good luck to you, too, sis." Jordan sighed, rubbing his forehead.

"Is Ashley always so . . . ?" I trailed off, trying and failing to find a niceish synonym for "constant thorn in my side."

"Speedy?"

I cleared my throat. "Uh . . . yeah, speedy. That's the word I was looking for."

Jordan's pride for his sister glowed on his face. "Fastest runner the New Order has seen in decades. Demonically fast, some people have said. Ashley loves being first in everything."

As Jordan prattled on like the proudest parent in the world, my thoughts drifted toward Alex. I tried to ignore the pang in my chest.

I followed Jordan down the temple steps and raced out onto the cobblestone ground. Everyone was branching out, some headed down packed sidewalks and side streets, while others disappeared into nearby grocery stores. After the destruction from the demons' attack six months ago—which the news reported as a "freak storm"—many warriors had mingled with the regular humans to help rebuild Manhattan's Chinatown.

Ah Qiao the monkey impersonator found a nice tree to climb. And next to Ah Qiao's tree was . . . Ba. Our eyes met again, and he gave me that same distant, polite smile. For a moment, I considered going over to my father—but then thought better of it. What was the point? Every time I'd tried talking to Ba, he'd given me no indication that he knew I was his daughter. I'd asked around, and everyone told me he'd mysteriously shown up at the New Order one day three years ago, bedraggled and half-alive, with no memory of who he was.

I couldn't decide which was worse—being around a father who didn't remember me or having no father at all.

". . . Faryn?"

I startled, realizing I'd tuned Jordan out. Quickly, I followed him as we joined the crowd that was headed toward the entrances of the high-rise apartment.

"Sorry. What'd you say?"

Jordan gave me an annoyed look and sighed. "I was saying," he continued, "it was so cool how the gods just showed up in the temple, huh? The gods are freaking awesome. And, like, they gave us a real quest!"

"Um . . . uh-huh," I said. I stopped myself from adding, *And some gods are bloodthirsty and murderous and human hating, and we're gonna have to stop them from waging war on everything ever.*

Jordan must've sensed the lack of enthusiasm in my voice, because his smile faded. "Oh yeah. You and Ren have already been on a quest for the gods. Seeing them is, like, totally normal to you guys now."

"That's not true," I said.

"Actually, you've never given any of us a straight answer. What exactly was it like?" He lowered his voice like we were sharing a secret. "Going on a quest for the gods during the Lunar New Year?"

I didn't want to talk about this with Jordan right now—or ever, actually. Many New Order warriors had pressed me for details of the quest I'd undertaken during the Lunar New Year, but I'd kept my responses vague, for a couple of reasons. Of course, the rebel gods had told me to "lay low" at the New Order. (Apparently that didn't actually mean digging a hole in the ground and lying down in it, but that's a tale for another day. Also, why did the gods always have to be so cryptic?) I also didn't want to unpack all my family-related trauma, such as the fact that my little brother had betrayed me, with a bunch of strangers who didn't even like me.

"The quest was . . . stressful," I said vaguely. "Exhausting. Cold. Didn't pack enough Pocky. Rookie mistake."

Jordan's shiny eagerness didn't fade, despite my stiffness. "I mean, what did you and Ren *do*?"

A blast of air-conditioning greeted us as we headed inside the building. "We, um . . ." *We were on a quest, trying to find a mythical island and my father. Many demons tried to destroy us, which was slightly rude. We thought the gods would help us, but instead, most of them wanted humanity destroyed, which was even ruder. Oh yeah, and my grandfather Ye Ye and friend Moli died, and my brother, Alex, betrayed me. The food at the gods' feast was bomb, though.*

I imagined telling this to Jordan, who stared at me all wide-eyed and eager.

"Let's just say we, uh . . . we . . . crashed the Jade Emperor's banquet together," I said.

"Oh, is *that* why the dude went all cranky?" asked Jordan.

"Cranky" was the understatement of the year. "Yeah. Sure. Let's go with that."

We ducked into the stairwell and walked up to the second floor, then entered through the first set of white doors. I'd never actually been inside Jordan and Ashley's apartment before, even though Jordan had invited me many times.

"Welcome to our humble abode," said Jordan as I came to a stop in front of a black door with the number sixteen over it. He pulled a key from his pocket, inserted it into the lock, and swung the door wide open.

Ashley stood there wearing a set of pink headphones, holding a half-eaten mán tou, a steamed bun, in one hand. She bounced a red yo-yo up and down with her other hand. As soon as the door opened fully, Ashley looked up and raised an eyebrow at us both. Her eyes narrowed when they landed on me.

"Hey, sis," said Jordan happily, raising his hand in a wave. "Looks like you've already—"

Bam. The whole hall shuddered as Ashley shoved past her brother and slammed the door in our faces.

CHAPTER

5

"Sorry about the mess," Jordan said as he led me into the apartment. Ashley had already disappeared into her own room. "The New Order used to have a cleaning lady, but she got eaten by a demon during the Lunar New Year." He winced. "Kind of a messy way to go for a cleaning lady, too."

Ye Ye would've thrown a fit at the sight—and smell—of this place. There were dirty jeans and T-shirts strewn about the floor, along with random pieces of paper and empty candy-bar wrappers. I stepped on something sticky on the carpet. Chewing gum. Great.

"It's all right." I pinched my nose to keep out the stench of sweaty gym socks piled next to the small kitchen. "This isn't the worst mess I've seen."

"Really?" Jordan's shoulders sagged in relief.

"No. I was just saying that to make you feel better." Jordan frowned. I laughed. "You're too gullible, Alex."

The name slipped out so easily, as it had for my entire life, that I didn't notice I'd said anything wrong until Jordan's forehead crinkled in confusion. "Alex? Who's Alex?"

Oh. Alex wasn't here. Alex was somewhere far, far away—where I could see him only in my dreams. I hadn't told anyone at the New Order about my brother, because that would involve explaining his betrayal, not to mention the gods' devious plot against all of humanity. Not exactly dinner conversation. "He's—nobody."

"Ooookay," said Jordan. "Well, make yourself comfortable, and help yourself to the snacks."

Setting my backpack down on the floor, I sat down on the lumpy black couch and stared at the slightly grimy coffee table in front of me, which was empty except for some Chinese newspapers and American magazines. No food in sight. "Snacks?"

"Yeah." Jordan reached beneath one of the couch cushions. He pulled out a half-empty bag of shrimp chips and popped one into his mouth. "Under the couch, silly."

That was my cue to make a polite but speedy exit. Before I could, Jordan's expression grew serious as he asked, "By the way, what was it that Erlang Shen called you earlier? Heaven something?"

Just thinking about my former title made me cringe. Jordan stared at me expectantly, though. I figured I owed him an explanation.

"Yup. Heaven . . . Something," I said. "That's my nickname.

'Heaven Something.'" Jordan gave me a dubious look, but I was in too deep to backtrack. "That Erlang Shen, always the jokester. Ha-ha. Ha . . ."

Okay, I owed Jordan an *attempt* at an explanation.

"I wonder if Erlang Shen picked you out because you're different," Jordan mused.

"Different?"

"Yeah. You're half—right?"

Oh boy. Here came The Question again. "Yes." I sighed. "My father is—a warrior. My mother, she . . . wasn't."

"Same with Ashley and me," Jordan said. "Well, our mother was a warrior. We never knew our father."

"Oh." Why hadn't I grown up in the New Order, where there were parents and kids of mixed blood who could still be warriors? Why the Jade Society, where Mao had liked to remind me at every turn that Alex and I would never be warriors like the other kids?

"Heaven *Breaker*. That's what Erlang Shen called her." The couch cushion beneath me dipped as another figure plopped onto the couch. Ashley. She'd taken off her headphones and brought something else with her—her swords. Two, to be exact, both turned ever so slightly in my direction.

I scooted down to the other end of the couch as discreetly as possible.

"Heaven Breaker . . . ," Jordan murmured. "Why does that sound so familiar?"

I prayed he wouldn't put two and two together.

Meanwhile, Ashley eyed the sharp blade of one of her swords. "So, Faryn. I've been meaning to ask you something."

"Oh, is that why you're glaring at me and sprinting away all the time? I should've realized."

She ignored my quip. "Is it true what they say about the Jade Society warriors? That you guys haven't been hunting demons or even training in years? Xiong predicted it was only a matter of time before the Jade Society disbanded for good."

Even though most of the memories I harbored of the Jade Society weren't that great, indignation shot through me. Who was Ashley to act like the New Order warriors were better than us? Especially since I'd just completed a quest for the gods.

I was still trying to think of a comeback when Jordan intervened. "Hang on, Ashley. I think you're being unfair. Faryn *is* qualified."

She lowered her swords. "What are you talking about?"

"I just remembered the legend of the Heaven Breaker." Jordan's jaw hung open, as though seeing me in a whole new light. "You're the warrior of the gods, fated to take over for the great warrior Guan Yu in Heaven?"

"Yes," I blurted out. "I mean . . . no, not anymore. I mean . . . maybe?"

Ashley scrunched up her nose. Jordan stood and paced around in small circles in front of us. There was no easy way to explain the story—how Xi Wangmu had chosen me to be the Heaven Breaker, *her* soldier to control, and then Alex had taken that role from me instead.

"It's . . . complicated," I said. "Bottom line is—I'm not the Heaven Breaker now, but I know him."

"So what if you know the Heaven Breaker?" Ashley snorted. "It's not like that's going to get you into the Ninety-Sixth Duels tonight."

I didn't want to talk about the Heaven Breaker anymore. "Tell me more about the Duels," I said instead.

"What do you want to know?" Jordan asked.

"Anything. Everything."

Jordan shrugged. "We haven't hosted one in decades. No reason to. Until today, the gods haven't set foot in the New Order for years and years, much less called the warriors to answer to a quest." He exchanged a glance with his sister and then shrugged. "*We* don't really even know what's supposed to happen at the Duels."

"Yes we do," Ashley insisted. "You and I will show up with our swords, knock everyone into the next century, then win the right to go on the quest." She lunged forward and dug the tip of her sword into the wooden surface of the coffee table. "Easy."

Jordan eyed the table wearily. There were several holes shaped suspiciously like sword points on its surface. "Yup. We're gonna need new furniture soon."

A sharp knock at the door rang through the apartment.

"Open up. This is Xiong shī fu."

Jordan jolted to attention, crumbs falling off his shirt and onto the carpet. Ashley tossed aside her empty bag of shrimp chips and scrambled to her feet.

"Wh-what's Xiong shī fu doing here?" Jordan stammered.

I stared back at him cluelessly. I guess Xiong was done speaking with Ren. Hopefully he hadn't chewed out the poor kid too badly.

Jordan continued. "He's scarcely left the temple except for the occasional training session, not since . . . you know . . . with Jinyu . . ."

Jinyu. There was that name again. The name of the beloved warrior who'd sacrificed his life so that I could live. Xiong's son, his pride and joy. I really didn't want Xiong to see me here.

"I don't know what's happening," Ashley hissed, "but go get the door!"

Jordan shot off toward the door. Xiong strode into the apartment, grumbling and scolding Jordan the whole way.

When Xiong entered the room, Ashley bowed her head toward the master, so I did the same.

"To what do we owe the pleasure of your visit?" Jordan asked in an uncharacteristically deep, stiff voice.

"Why are you lowering your voice like that?" said Xiong. "You sound like a buffoon."

"S-sorry," Jordan stammered in his normal voice. Ashley snorted.

"I came to speak with Faryn," Xiong said. "Ah Qiao told me he saw you come here with Ashley and Jordan."

I snapped up my head. Xiong's unreadable black eyes met mine. Why did he want to speak with me? Was it to say something about his son, Jinyu? Also—

"Where's Ren?" I blurted out.

Xiong smiled, though he showed no teeth. "Ren went to take care of some business for me."

Oh no. I knew exactly what that meant. Poor guy was taking ten laps around Chinatown.

"Don't look so scared, child. I've come with a simple request. I have a change of clothes for you, too." Xiong brought his arms out from behind his back to reveal a white training robe. "I can't allow a guest of the New Order to go around stinking like two-week-old trash."

I guess my smell matched how I felt inside.

"Thank you," I murmured, taking the robe in my hands.

"As you know, I've just returned from the annual meeting of the warrior societies—the Yuē Huì. Mao attended." Xiong stroked a hand through the long white strands of his beard. "The Jade Society is still recovering from the demon attacks of the Lunar New Year, but they're safe."

Even though I didn't have the fondest memories of the Jade Society, I was relieved to hear that.

Xiong continued. "Now, to protect the New Order, I hope I can ask for your help, Faryn Liu."

The master of the New Order wanted *my* help? I didn't know why, but this was my chance. If I could get on Xiong's good side, I could prove myself. I could make up for the horrible first impression I'd left on everyone. Make amends for Jinyu's death. "Name it. I'll do anything."

"Outsiders are barred from participating in the Duels, but I'll make an exception just this once. You must not only participate—you must win the right to become one of the warriors who embark on the gods' quest." Xiong's eyes were glassy and emotionless, almost as empty as Jinyu's had been in his last moments. "The gods have sent me a vision. You have a very difficult choice to make, child. If you take on this quest of the Hungry Ghost Festival, you will lose someone very dear to you—*again*. But if you aren't the one to lead this quest, the warriors will fail, and every last one is sure to die."

CHAPTER

6

Someone up there must've *really* hated me.

With those words, Xiong squashed all hope I had. Of restoring my father's memory. Of finding my brother.

I should've known this quest would have something to do with me. The gods wouldn't let their old Heaven Breaker walk free so easily. I had to go, as much as I didn't want to—or others would pay the price.

An old ally will return from the brink of death, Erlang Shen's poem had said. My gut screamed at me with certainty that that line referred to *my* former ally: Alex. Or maybe Moli. It was either one of them or Uggs.

If there was even a chance that I could find and save my friend and my brother, as well as prevent many other warriors' deaths, then I had to take this quest. I *had* to enter the Ninety-Sixth Duels. And not just enter but win.

A nasty red shade rose to Ashley's face. "But, shī fu—she's not one of us. She *can't* participate in the Duels. This goes against the ancient laws of the New Order!"

"Insolent child," Xiong spat. Ashley stumbled back, and her brother steadied her. "I am the master of this society. I *am* the laws of the New Order."

A deafening silence followed his outburst. Jordan and Ashley wore the same stunned expression on their faces. Xiong wasn't his usual calm and collected self, which wasn't a good sign. I guess he sensed there was real danger on the horizon, even though the gods and I hadn't told anyone the full truth of the Jade Emperor's wrath.

"But . . . how?" I asked quietly. "How would it even be possible for me to participate in the Ninety-Sixth Duels?"

"Good question," said Xiong. "Many ancient laws and magic guard this sacred ritual. There are three ways for a New Order warrior to enter the Duels. First, the warrior is chosen by his or her family to represent the family name. There can be multiple chosen per family," Xiong said, nodding at Jordan and Ashley. "Second, the warrior is claimed by an unrelated warrior family to represent their family name. And third, the warrior takes the place of a fallen warrior."

Option one was out of the question. Even though Ba was here, he wasn't a true New Order warrior. Plus, no one knew he was my father—not even Ba himself.

Option two was a maybe. If I really buttered up an auntie

or uncle, maybe I could convince one of them to let me represent their family.

That left me with just option three. I realized what Xiong was thinking the moment the old man kneeled down before me.

"Shī fu!" Jordan and Ashley gasped in unison.

"Please, warrior," Xiong said. "On behalf of the New Order warriors, the Xiong family, and my fallen son, Jinyu"—his voice caught for just a brief second—"I would like to request that you represent us in the Ninety-Sixth Duels, that you win, and that you lead our warriors to victory."

Tears stung my eyes. "Shī fu." I knelt down in front of the old man. I didn't know what else to say.

"I'm not doing this for you, Faryn," Xiong said gruffly. "I'm doing this for the sake of the New Order warriors. And . . ." He lifted his head. His eyes shone with tears. "For the sake of the world. Fate has spoken. You are the one who must save us, Faryn."

I knew what Xiong was really asking me to do. If I fought in the Ninety-Sixth Duels and won the right to embark on the quest, I would lose someone dear to me for the second time. Xiong was asking me to protect his warriors, and the world, even at a great cost.

Just like his son, Jinyu, had.

Sweat beaded on my palms. My heart thudded. I was scared. More scared than I'd been since facing the nián.

But the thought of thousands dying was even scarier.

"I would be honored to take Jinyu's place in the Ninety-Sixth Duels," I said.

One corner of Xiong's mouth tilted upward, which was the closest he'd ever come to a smile. "Good girl. As my thanks, please accept this gift." He reached into his robe and pulled out a gleaming silver sword with a well-worn black handle. It was shorter in length than the sword I'd been using and yet looked more vicious.

"But that's . . . ," Ashley gasped.

"Jinyu's," Jordan finished in awe.

"My son would have wanted you to have his jiàn, Faryn." Xiong placed the sword in my limp palms. It was lighter than any of the swords I'd trained with at the Jade Society.

I shook my head. "I can't accept this—"

"I would feel most safe knowing it's in your capable hands," Xiong said, eyes burning into mine. "I believe Jinyu would feel the same way. Besides, you'll be hard-pressed to find a more powerful weapon than this one during the Hungry Ghost Festival."

My curiosity must have shown on my face, because Xiong explained. "At the New Order, we believe that the dead live on in not only their kin but also in their weapons." The wrinkles around his eyes softened as he gazed upon the gleaming blade, as though picturing Jinyu in its place. "My son may have left the mortal world, but his spirit lives on in his sword. It will only grow stronger as the end of the festival draws closer. Can you feel it, Faryn Liu? The strength of Jinyu's will?"

Nodding, I gripped the handle with my trembling hands. After Xiong finished speaking, a warm energy traveled from the sword into my hands, as if the weapon were greeting a new master. Maybe it was just the heat from Xiong's touch. Or maybe it was the warmth of someone else's fingers, sent from beyond this world.

I looked Xiong square in the eye. "I'll use Jinyu's sword well. I promise I won't let you or Jinyu down."

"See to it that you don't," Xiong said in a warning tone of voice.

It didn't matter if the gods foresaw glory or death in my future. I had to take on this quest. I had to save the world. I had to save Alex. And I had to restore Ba's memory, no matter what.

One hour to go until sunset. Until the Ninety-Sixth Duels.

Xiong had left to prepare for tonight. I'd changed into the white robes he'd given me. Ren hadn't returned—maybe he was still running laps. Ashley had gone back into her room to listen to her music, insisting that it was the only way for her to relax and prepare for battle. Heavy metal blasted out of her room.

Jordan danced around the piles of clothing in the apartment, shadowboxing an invisible opponent. After a while, he paused and dropped his fists at his sides. He wiped a sheen of sweat off his brow and gave me a pointed look. "You should warm up, too."

"Yeah," I said, barely listening.

"Like, right now. Especially since you've never used Jinyu's sword before."

Jordan was right. This was no time to space out. I had to kick some major New Order warrior butt. I stood up, the movement causing shrimp chips to fall from the couch onto the floor. "Spar with me?"

Jordan eyed me warily and then nodded. We circled one another around a particularly large pile of dirty clothing. Testing the weight of Jinyu's sword in my hand, I scrutinized Jordan's every movement.

Always watch the eyes, I could hear Ye Ye whispering in my head. *The eyes are where the opponent reveals all their moves.*

I struck first, hoping to catch Jordan off guard with a speedy attack to his right side. The sword was featherlight in my hand, and I went off-balance. Jordan dove out of the way. Before I could turn around, I felt the pain of a kick to my left leg.

I sliced downward with my right hand onto Jordan's leg, and he withdrew it quickly. I gritted my teeth. Guess Jordan had more moves than I'd thought. I whirled around and narrowed my eyes. He raised his fists and grinned in response.

"What're you dorks doing?" came Ashley's shrill voice.

Jordan and I both dropped our arms and turned toward her. Ashley emerged from her bedroom wearing a white robe that matched ours. She was already swinging her two swords in her hands. "Save your energy for the Duels, if you want to win." She stomped out of the apartment.

"Good luck to you, too," I grumbled.

"Ashley means well," Jordan reassured me. I stared at him blankly. "Okay, so I *think* she means well, but she can be . . . a lot."

"Understatement of the year," I muttered under my breath.

Jordan looked like he wanted to say more but instead just shook his head. "We should get down to the training grounds."

I followed him out the door and toward the stairwell. He hummed the *Warfate* video game theme song the whole way.

The New Order training grounds were located in the basement level of the apartment complex. Jordan held open the door for me, and I stepped through to find myself facing an impossibly big room. There was no way the training grounds hadn't been altered by magic. It was easily the size of a football stadium, and the ceiling hung high above our heads. It probably broke at least fifty safety codes in Manhattan. Good thing magic barred the mortal police from ever catching wind of this place.

Torches lit by flame lined the grounds, and large mats lay on the floor.

An altar for a statue of the Jade Emperor stood inside the

entrance. The golden statue glowed with the flickering flame of the incense. I resisted a shudder as I passed the Jade Emperor's shadow. Even though he'd proven he would get rid of humans if it meant restoring the gods' former might, we still had to show him loyalty or else he'd blast us on the spot.

The room filled with the steady, low, ominous beating of a drum. The older, retired warriors beat red drumsticks on huge red drums in steady unison.

Standing around the mats, wearing white robes and clasping their hands behind their backs, were the current New Order warriors.

One warrior stepped forward, and the flames from the torches lit up his face with an eerie glow. I tightened my grip around Jinyu's jiàn and squared my shoulders.

"Welcome, warriors," said Xiong, "to the Ninety-Sixth Duels, and the first of this century."

CHAPTER

7

Xiong read from a thick black rule book with weathered yellowed pages, his voice echoing against the walls.

No matter how many contenders there were for the Ninety-Sixth Duels, only three would go on the quest, as Erlang Shen had stated in his shī. We'd fight each other one-on-one in as many rounds as necessary until only three warriors were left standing. Each duel would last ten minutes or until one warrior felled the other.

"Although death isn't against the rules," Xiong said, "I urge you all to see one another as you are—as comrades—and aim to injure, not maim."

This was sounding less and less appealing by the moment.

"Every New Order warrior must be prepared to sacrifice anything for the honor of undertaking the quest. Duty above all else. So it was hundreds of years ago, and so it is now." Xiong spoke with an unmistakable note of finality. He closed the book. The sound echoed in the open space. "Now, before we begin, each young warrior will prove their lineage and worth."

Warriors stepped forward, including Jordan, Ashley, and me, forming a smaller circle on the black mats. I cast my gaze around and locked eyes with someone standing outside the small circle—Ren. For a moment, I was confused, but then I remembered the three rules for entry that Xiong had mentioned earlier. Of course, Ren didn't meet the requirements for those rules, so he wouldn't be able to take part in the Duels. I'd assumed we'd just do everything together—like how Alex and I had done everything together up until six months ago. Knowing Ren wouldn't be entering with me gave me an uneasy feeling.

Ba hung back in the shadows, away from the others. Just seeing my father looking on made me nervous.

Among the participating warriors, I counted twenty heads in total. Many looked like they were about our age, the youngest around eleven or twelve, the oldest maybe eighteen.

"Why are the adults hanging back?" I whispered to Jordan.

"Most of them are parents," he said. "Once a warrior turns eighteen, they come of age. Their duty is to family—to raise their children into an even better generation of warriors."

"That's . . . so beautiful."

Jordan shrugged. "That's what they say, but mostly, I think it's 'cause they're kinda out of shape."

That had been the case back in the Jade Society, too. I guess people aren't really up for fighting demons anymore when they're busy dropping off their kids at day care or having their midlife crises.

Several sobbing mothers pulled out handkerchiefs. On the other hand, the kids outside the circle of participants—their friends—hooted and shouted out encouragement.

Somehow, I couldn't picture the Jade Society adults—Mr. Yang, Mr. Zhao, or even Mao—letting their kids duel for the right to embark on a dangerous quest. Duty to the gods above all. The New Order really took that seriously.

The first warrior knelt down before Xiong.

"Wen," Xiong barked out.

"Zài," the warrior said. *Here.*

A blue flame burst up from the floor and engulfed the warrior's outline. Some gasped. A middle-aged woman behind the boy who could only be his mother cried out in shock. But the warrior didn't seem to be in pain and stood up to make room for the next.

One by one, the young warriors knelt down before Xiong and stated their name and family. *Zheng. Qiao. Chu. Wan.* One by one, the blue flames burst up and consumed their outlines. Ah Qiao's older brother, Ah Zhu, stepped up, and a sulky Ah Qiao stayed behind. I guessed he was too young.

Ashley and Jordan knelt down in unison when it was their turn. There were no crying parents in the space behind them.

"Wait," cried one of the Elders, just before Xiong raised his hand above the Liao siblings. The master of the New Order paused and turned his head slowly toward the Elder. "Are you sure it's safe for these two to participate in the Duels?"

"I believe them to be quite capable warriors, yes," Xiong said mildly. Yet his sharp eyes reflected some coldness that told me there was more to this conversation beneath the surface.

The Elder drew himself to his full height. I could practically feel the energy crackling between them in the air. "You know what I mean. I'm not talking about their safety. I'm talking about *everyone else's*."

Nods and worried murmuring followed his statement.

"He's right," someone called from the crowd.

Ashley's neck turned red, and Jordan hung his head. Sympathy twinged in my chest. I didn't know what everyone was talking about, but I knew exactly what it was like to be in the siblings' shoes. Alex and I had endured years of being outcasts in the Jade Society.

"We will proceed with the ceremony," Xiong boomed. "There will be no more interruptions."

This time, no one dared talk back.

When he was finished with Ashley and Jordan, Xiong fixed me with a cold stare. My heart pounded madly.

"Xiong," he said.

It was strange answering to a family name that wasn't my own, but I steadied my voice as much as possible. "Zài."

Murmurs of confusion rose from the onlookers. This

wasn't going to work. Of course it wouldn't. I wasn't a member of this society, much less of Xiong's family. What was I thinking, trying to take Jinyu's place?

But after several moments, a cooling, tickling sensation rose from my toes all the way up to the roots of my hair. More gasps. I looked down. Flames. Not blue ones, but purple flames enveloped me.

Even though we were indoors, a gentle breeze wrapped around my body. I heard a whisper, the words too faint for me to catch.

"Did you say something?" I asked Jordan, who was closest to me.

But he was too busy gawking at me with his jaw hung wide open. "You're . . . purple!"

"Thanks." I sighed. "I hadn't noticed."

I wasn't sure how this worked, now that I'd entered the Ninety-Sixth Duels in Jinyu's place. I mean, were we *sure* this was even legal if no adoption papers had been signed?

I shook the doubt from my head. All that mattered now was that I was about to duel for the right to embark on this quest. I wouldn't go down without a fight. If Xiong's word was true, then I didn't have a choice.

As Xiong lined us up on the mats across from our first opponents, my palms grew slick with sweat. The loud, low beating of large drums sounded.

"Drummers, silence!" Xiong yelled. The drummers lowered their sticks to their sides, and heavy quiet filled the room.

I faced my first opponent, a girl a little taller and older than I was, maybe thirteen or fourteen. She wore her sleek black hair in a chin-length bob and glared at me like she was picturing me skewered at the end of her sword. Her glare was so intense that her eyebrows looked like they'd been stolen off a cartoon character's face. I couldn't remember her first name, but I was pretty sure Angry Eyebrows's family name was Chu.

Jordan stood on the mat beside me, facing a considerably bigger opponent—a teenage boy resembling a bodybuilder. Ashley stared down a guy twice her size. Yet both of their opponents looked more terrified of them somehow.

My curiosity burned. What exactly had the siblings done to make everyone so wary of them?

The flames around me grew hotter. The air sizzled and crackled with an invisible power. My body buzzed with warmth and strength I hadn't felt in months—not since the Lunar New Year, when I'd channeled the power of the gods themselves to wield the mighty spear Fenghuang.

I had a feeling the gods were gazing down upon us. Watching to see which of the New Order warriors would prove themselves most worthy.

"Bow to your opponent," Xiong ordered. We obeyed. Angry Eyebrows narrowed her eyes at me as she straightened. I bared my teeth, which probably didn't look as impressive as I wanted. "Now, fight!"

Before I could blink, a sharp pain split my arm, and I crashed to the ground.

CHAPTER

8

I could count on one hand the number of times someone had brought me down in combat so quickly. And all of them had involved Ye Ye or Ba training me.

So when the New Order warrior brought me down to the mat before I could even strike, I was so stunned, so paralyzed with disbelief and pain, I couldn't move. For a moment, I thought I'd already lost.

But then I pictured Ye Ye and Ba. How they'd shout for me to get up and try again. To never, ever give up. I imagined them both beside me, urging me to stay strong.

Warmth flowed from the handle of the sword into my fingertips.

Alex, too. If my brother were here, he'd be shouting at me. *Snap out of it*, he'd say. *This isn't over. Angry Eyebrows got you. So what? You'll just have to get her back.*

Alex would never forgive me if I let anyone defeat me—anyone but him, that is. Ren wouldn't forgive me if I went down like this, either. So I couldn't give up the fight. The sword handle grew even warmer, as though encouraging me. Giving me strength.

The air above me swished as Angry Eyebrows's blade arced down toward me, but I raised Jinyu's jiàn to parry the blow. Striking while her opponent was down? This girl was *vicious*. Maybe she'd stolen the eyebrows *and* personality right off an evil cartoon character.

I leapt to my feet, senses tingling, sword clutched in my hand and raised before me. The sword fit better in my grip now, as though it had finally gotten used to its new master. Every atom of my body buzzed with energy. This was it. The feeling I lived for. The adrenaline of a fight with a strong opponent.

As if answering the call of my blood, the purple flames around me danced higher. Angry Eyebrows's blue flames grew, too.

I lunged forward, forcing Angry Eyebrows to parry my blow with her sword. Frustration flashed through her black eyes when she failed to deflect my blade like she'd wanted. I'd thrown the full force of my weight behind my attack, but that still wasn't enough to bring her down. I had to search for some kind of weakness.

Always watch your opponent's eyes, Ye Ye had told me.

I couldn't lose this battle. If I did—if this girl went on the quest instead of me—we were doomed.

"Go, Faryn!" That was Ah Qiao's voice, cheering me on. "Jiā yóu!"

I forced Angry Eyebrows backward. I watched her eyes, which reflected purple flame—and for just a moment, they darted down to her right ankle as she clenched her teeth.

That moment was more than enough. I released my weight. Angry Eyebrows dove forward, slashing her sword through the air. I ducked under her blade like a limbo champ and kicked her right leg. She screamed and lost her balance, toppling beside me on the mat.

I didn't give Angry Eyebrows the chance to recover before pinning her body to the ground with my left arm and bringing Jinyu's sword to her throat. The flames around us simply disappeared.

Angry Eyebrows scowled, but the defeat was evident in her eyes. The duel was over. I'd won.

She raised her hands above her head in surrender. "Okay, okay. You win already, jeez. Get off me!"

I sighed in relief and stood up. Angry Eyebrows's mother and father swept her away, glaring at me before leading their daughter out of the training room.

"You're much better off staying here," I whispered. Most of the other warriors had finished their first round of fights as well. Only half remained engulfed in blue flame on the mats, circling each other with fast attacks. The defeated warriors had already left, some hobbling in their friends' and parents' arms, moaning in pain.

Even though they were facing older teenagers, Ashley and Jordan were in a class of their own—Jordan especially. He won his round soon after I did and then proceeded to put himself in charge of the Ashley Cheer Squad.

"Left jab, Ashley! Make him weep for his mama!" Jordan shouted, miming the movement himself. "No, your *other* left!"

Ashley's blade twirled through the air. She held her own against her tall, burly opponent. The guy wasn't too shabby, either. I winced as he aimed a quick kick to her unguarded knee. She landed hard on her side and didn't move. The flames shrank around her small frame. The boy walked toward her with his sword held up high, his blue flames billowing about him, as though they knew he was seconds away from achieving his victory.

"Ashley!" Jordan screamed. But there was nothing he or anyone else could do. Ashley's opponent swung down.

I turned away. I didn't need to see what happened next.

"ROOOOOOOOOOOOOOOAR!"

A deep, rumbling noise ripped through the training grounds. Several warriors screamed. I held Jinyu's sword at the ready, prepared to face whatever demon was attacking the New Order.

Only it wasn't a demon. It was Ashley. Or . . . sort of Ashley.

She hovered a foot off the ground, arms and legs spread out. Her hair had lengthened until it reached past her toes, almost to the floor. Her face was longer and slimmer, making her look older—closer to sixteen or seventeen rather than her actual twelve years. The scariest part was the blue flames that danced in her eyes.

"D-demon," Mr. Wan gasped. "She's a demon!"

"The girl's been possessed," Mrs. Li yelled hysterically.

"Not again," Jordan moaned.

Before I could ask what he meant, one of the Elders ordered, "Call off the Duels now!"

"I knew we shouldn't have let those two into the ceremony!" shouted Mr. Wan.

Xiong didn't make any move to call off the Ninety-Sixth Duels. The slight part of his lips was the only indication that he was at all shocked by what was happening. Nobody moved to help Ashley's opponent, who'd fallen over, as she advanced on him.

Ashley lashed out so swiftly, my eyes could hardly follow the movement. She stood over the boy one moment and then had backed away the next. He lay unconscious on the mat. His flames disappeared, but the flames surrounding Ashley burned brighter.

"Stop, demon!" someone yelled.

I startled. I recognized that voice. Ba. My father drew his sword and pushed through the crowd toward me. My heart lifted. Even though Ba had no recollection of his daughter, was he still rushing to protect me, like he had the day we'd arrived?

Chaos ensued. As though inspired by Ba's angry yell, several of the men charged forward like angry bulls, without any rhyme or reason to their formation.

"Ba!" I shouted, but a loud, familiar roar stopped me in my tracks.

I whipped my head toward the sound just in time to see Ren—or rather, a Ren whose skin was bubbling green as his body morphed and grew.

"Another demon!" screamed Mrs. Zheng.

Turning in confused circles, the men seemed like they didn't know who to attack—demon-Ashley or dragon-Ren.

"No, Ren's harmless! He's not a demon—he's just—just— turning into a dragon!" I shouted, rushing toward Ren.

I reached out to Ren with my mind, fumbling for that telepathic communication that I'd had with him and all the dragons during the Lunar New Year. But my thoughts were met with silence. My heart pounded. I wasn't reaching Ren. I wasn't going to be able to stop his dragon form from doing something potentially dangerous. Then—

Heaven Breaker? The dragon's voice rumbled in my mind.

Yes. Relief and surprise flooded my body. I hadn't thought I'd be able to get through to him. *I mean, no. I mean—it's complicated. Just—cut that out, whatever you're doing. Please give Ren his body back!*

In a strange mid-transformation form, Ren turned toward me. His skin was mostly covered in scales, but his eyes were still his own. *And what if I don't?*

I'll—

Before I could come up with a threat that would somehow scare a dragon, a blinding flash of white light surged from Ashley's body. It flooded through the whole hall. I ducked, and the heat of the energy crackled as it shot just over my head.

When I dared to look up again, no damage had befallen the arena, except that a couple of the men were huddled in a corner sobbing. Ren had shrunk back to his normal, albeit shaken, human self. But the flames around every last warrior had extinguished—except for Ashley's, Jordan's, and mine.

Ashley had won her duel and eliminated the rest of the competition in one blow. But how? And at what price?

The mother of Ashley's unconscious opponent rushed forward and wailed. Another woman placed her fingers on his wrist and then shouted, "He's alive!"

The damage had been done, though.

"Ashley," Jordan moaned. "What'd you do?"

Xiong stepped forward. "The Ninety-Sixth Duels are over. The winners: Faryn, Ashley, and Jordan. Everyone is dismissed." Beads of sweat shone on his forehead as he surveyed the crowd. Even Xiong couldn't keep his cool in the face of what had just happened.

"But—" protested one of the men.

Xiong raised his hand for silence. "I wish to speak with the Liao siblings. And Ren. Alone."

Whispering to one another, the warriors quickly left the training room. I glanced back just before the door closed.

The look on Jordan's face reflected pure terror. Ren hung his head in shame. Ashley's reaction was to sway and then collapse onto the mat. Then the door shut.

I headed back to my room. Most of the warriors stayed out in the halls, gathering in groups and whispering.

"Always knew something was wrong with that girl," hissed an older woman to a group of other mothers. "Here's the proof."

"And that dragon boy? Knew he was no good, too," whispered her friend.

I paused, about to say something to stick up for Ren and Ashley—and then stopped. The women stared at me, as though I, too, showed signs of transforming into something nonhuman. I left without a word.

It was late evening now. My body ached from the exertion of my duel, but when I tried to sleep, my thoughts wouldn't let me rest. Instead, I got up and paced around my room.

Sure, I'd *joked* about Ashley being kind of a demoness— toward me, at least—but I hadn't expected her to actually turn out to be . . . whatever she was. Did that mean the siblings *were* demons? Was that why the warriors were wary of them? Why wouldn't they just ban them from the society?

Then there was the matter of Ren's transformation—

"Faryn?" A knock on my door and the sound of Ren's voice jolted me out of my thoughts.

I opened the door. "Speak of the devil," I said.

"Devil? Wh-where?" Ren peered around the hallway nervously. He shifted his large blue backpack over his shoulder. It was so bulky, it didn't zip all the way closed, as though he'd stuffed it full of everything he owned.

"It's just an expression." I nodded at Ren's backpack. "What's with the bag? Are you moving or something?"

I was joking, but Ren gave me a solemn nod. "Kind of. I'm . . . I've decided I'm going. To the Dragon Kings' palace, I mean."

"What?" My heart dropped to my stomach. "Why? They're—they're on the Jade Emperor's side, aren't they?"

"I'm not going to the Dragon Kings to help the Jade Emperor," Ren said firmly. "I'm going to get the training they promised. You saw what happened earlier at the Duels." Shame reddened Ren's face, and he dropped his gaze down to his toes. "It's not safe for me to be around other people."

"Of c-course it's safe," I spluttered. The idea of Ren leaving me—*just like everyone else has*—was too much. I had to convince him to stay. "You've been here six months, and that was your first time transforming. And so what? It's not like you ate an Elder or something—you didn't even eat Mr. Wan, even though he probably deserved it—"

"Faryn!" Ren jolted his gaze upward and stared at me in horror.

"What? Just telling it like it is." The man had made his dislike of us, and pretty much everything, quite clear. "You *didn't* eat anyone, right?"

"No! Of course I didn't eat anyone!"

"Then I don't see why you have to leave."

"I'm sorry." Ren's eyes shone with sorrow, which only made my heart twist harder. "I have to go, Faryn. You know I do."

I didn't want to admit it, but I knew Ren was right, even though the thought of him leaving made my insides squeeze with panic. "So you're really . . . leaving? Just like that?"

"I'll be back soon," he promised with a tentative smile. "Dragons are fast. I'll be back before you know it. Before Xiong ends his next speech, probably."

"Xiong really likes to listen to himself talk," I agreed.

Ren gave me a half wave, half salute with one hand. "I guess this is goodbye."

"You aren't gonna say goodbye to the others? Not even Ah Qiao?"

Ren shrugged, though the look on his face was pained. "It's for the best," was all he said.

There were so many things I wanted to say to Ren, but I couldn't figure out how to voice a single one. "Take care of yourself," I told him, forcing a smile. *Don't leave me behind, just like everyone else has.*

Ren reached out a hand, as if to offer a handshake—and then awkwardly placed it behind his head. "Yeah. You take care of yourself, too." He smirked. "Try not to destroy any more immortals' islands while I'm gone."

"One time! That was one time," I protested at Ren's already retreating back. "And I—*we*—hardly 'destroyed' it!"

Ren raised a hand in farewell and then left through the doorway. I waited until the sound of his footsteps disappeared down the hall.

Something told me that I wouldn't see him for a long, long time. I squashed that voice of doubt. Ren would come back. He *had* to come back, and soon.

I fell asleep to the thought of being reunited with Ren, after he'd been reunited with his mother, the pop singer Cindy You. I wasn't sure when my thoughts morphed into dreams. One moment, my mind was fixated on Ren; the next thing I knew, I was in a huge, sprawling garden, surrounded by elm trees. There was a small pond in front of me with glittering, impossibly clear water, with a wooden bridge erected over it.

Three figures stood on top of that bridge. A red dragon, a black dragon, and between them—my brother, Alex. In his right hand, he wielded the mighty golden spear Fenghuang, which had once belonged to me. It was the spear that awarded him the title of Heaven Breaker, the Jade Emperor's newly appointed general, who oversaw the entire army.

"Alex," I tried to say, but again, my voice didn't work. Nor, apparently, could Alex or the dragons see me, because they gave no indication that there was a fourth presence in the heavenly garden.

"Have you found any leads on that task I gave you?" Alex asked the dragons. His voice was magnified, as though he were standing and speaking right next to me.

The dragons both shook their great heads.

No, Heaven Breaker, the red dragon said. I guess in this vision, or dream, or whatever it was, I could hear the dragons' voices again, as I had been able to when I'd been the Heaven Breaker. Dream logic. Gotta love it.

We searched high and low, just as you asked, added the black dragon with a forlorn snort. *We did not see any sign of those whom you seek.*

My curiosity burned. Who was Alex seeking? Why were he and the dragons being so cryptic about it?

Alex whipped his head around and stared straight at me. I gasped but made no sound. He continued to stare. Even though I knew I shouldn't be here and I should *definitely* look away, I couldn't bring myself to. My brother's brown eyes had a cold and calculating look in them, but for just a second, they softened. Alex was still my brother. And I hadn't truly looked at him in months and months.

What would you like us to do for you now, Heaven Breaker? asked the dragons, bowing their heads.

"Continue searching," Alex ordered, snapping his gaze away from me. "And make sure no one else knows what I've asked you to do. Especially not"—he peered around nervously at the empty garden, then lowered his voice to barely a whisper—"the Jade Emperor. He and I . . . have very different . . . opinions."

The dragons looked at each other and then turned back to my brother. This time, I couldn't hear any of their thoughts.

After a moment, both dragons bowed low. They took off toward the sky, tails swishing through the air. In moments, they became red and black specks.

Alex gazed down into the crystal-clear pond water. I could barely see his face, but he looked, for a moment, impossibly sad. His wasn't the expression of a warrior who wielded one of the world's most powerful weapons. It was the vulnerable look of a lost young boy. A boy who needed his big sister—his family—now more than ever.

But I couldn't be there for Alex when he needed me, and knowing that hurt most of all.

The garden blurred, and the vision vanished. When I opened my eyes, I gazed up at my ceiling, with the sunlight pouring through the window of my room.

I didn't know exactly what I'd seen in this vision, but I was certain about one thing. That had felt much more real than a mere dream. And if it hadn't been just a dream, Alex was in search of something—or someone—behind the Jade Emperor's back. If the ruler of all the heavens found out what my brother was doing, Alex could be in grave danger.

CHAPTER

9

I drifted off to sleep and awoke to yelling and loud, thumping footsteps. I rolled out of bed, wiping the sleep from my eyes, and ducked through my doorway.

"Ahhhhhhhhhh!" A whizzing blur flew past me with a gust of wind. I jerked my head back out of danger's path. It was one of the children, although at that speed, I couldn't tell which one.

The source of the commotion was the younger warriors returning from tutoring. Instead of attending public school, the young warriors received private tutoring from certified instructors in the New Order. It's exactly as boring as it sounds. I had no idea how knowing the periodic table of elements was supposed to help us slay demons, but apparently, that was important. I'd rather face down ten demons than one math problem.

Mothers holding hands with their children came bustling down the hall. A few, like Mrs. Zheng and Mrs. Qiao, stopped to greet me. Most were harried-looking and just rushed past.

Before his mom could lead him away down the hall, Ah Qiao broke away from her grasp and ran up to me.

"Ah Qiao," I said, smiling. "How are you?"

"I didn't come to talk to you, ugly," Ah Qiao snapped.

"Okay. Thanks."

"Also, your hair is sticking up sideways. Did you even brush it this morning?"

"Gimme a break. I just woke up." I patted down my hair. Great. I'd sunk to new lows if young children had to point out my unkemptness.

Ah Qiao's eyes slid to either side of me and then down the hall. "Where's Ren? He's not in his room. I checked. I thought he might be with you."

Oh no. How was I supposed to explain to this kid that his hero had left the New Order and that none of us had any clue when he'd be back?

"Ren? He, um . . . uh . . . he had something very important to do. Outside the New Order. H-he'll be back soon, though."

"How soon? Before bedtime?"

"Yeah," I lied. Sheesh. Lying to a little kid's face. I was gonna go to Diyu for this. "Yeah, before bedtime."

"Did he leave me a message? Will he—?"

Ah Qiao's mother grabbed his hand and offered an

apologetic smile. I watched as she dragged him away, scolding him about being late for his lessons earlier, while Ah Qiao howled.

I sent a silent message to Ren. *Please, for all our sakes, come back soon from the Dragon Kings' palace. Preferably before bedtime, so I don't go to Diyu for lying to children.*

Instead of getting ready for tomorrow's lessons like the other kids, I had something much more important to take care of.

Later that day, I packed my backpack with *Restorative Potions* and left the high-rise apartment building. I headed straight toward the temple of the New Order. The sun already hung high in the sky, and the streets of Chinatown bustled with activity.

Alone now, I could fully unpack my thoughts on the dizzying number of events of the last twelve hours, starting with Ashley's transformation. *What in the name of Erlang Shen's long johns happened back there?*

The two marble lions guarding the temple's entrance seemed to glare at me, as if questioning why I was here this early.

"I'm not doing anything wrong," I said. "I've got important business to tend to."

I'd just spoken to two giant slabs of stone like they could hear or understand me. If anyone needed more proof that Faryn Liu was going bananas from loneliness, this was it.

I pushed open the heavy red doors. The pale-pink early morning illuminated the empty temple.

I grabbed a joss stick and hurried back into the crisp summer morning air to light the stick with the flame of the oil lamps hanging above the lions. For one heart-stopping moment, I could've sworn the stone lions' eyes were following me.

"I just want to wish my grandfather a happy start to the Hungry Ghost Festival," I hissed. "It'll only take a second, okay?"

I guess today was Faryn Talks to Random Inanimate Objects Day. Before I could start speaking to the doorknobs, I dashed back inside. I'd thought the temple was empty, but now I saw a shadowy figure kneeling before the altar in front of the Jade Emperor. The figure turned at the sound of my footsteps, and the light of the flickering fire illuminated his familiar face.

"Ba?" I blurted out without thinking.

My father gave me a strange look, and my cheeks burned. "I mean . . . good morning, Mr. Zhuang."

"Good morning, Faryn. You're up early today."

"Just, uh . . . wanted to pray to the gods before everyone else got here."

Ba chuckled. "Good girl. The gods are pleased with you, I'm sure. You did . . . very well yesterday during the Duels."

He smiled, and my heart jolted. I knew the man had no clue that I was his daughter, yet a warm glow washed over me.

Tears sprang to my eyes. I gulped hard, trying to force them back. "Th-thank you."

"Your mother and father would be pleased as well," Ba said softly. His eyes twinkled.

I averted my gaze, staring at my feet. I didn't trust myself to look at my father any longer. I was afraid that if I did, I would burst into tears.

A slight breeze whooshed past me, and a warm hand touched my shoulder. "Goodbye, Faryn. I wish you well on your journey."

Then the hand lifted. The doors creaked open once more and then shut. I was alone—for real this time.

"Goodbye," I whispered, though I knew he could no longer hear me. "Goodbye, Ba." Then I let the tears fall. They splashed onto the ground. My shoulders heaved as I sobbed.

For just a few moments, I'd gotten a taste of what it would be like to have my father back. And I knew, in my heart, that I would do anything—*anything*—for Ba to truly regain his memories. To see the spark of recognition and love in his eyes.

When the tears finally slowed, I wiped them away. "This is no time for crying, Faryn," I scolded. "Or talking to yourself."

I'd come here on a mission, and I had to see it through— quickly, before anyone else entered the temple.

By the light from the flames of the joss stick, I searched through the faces on the deities' statues until I found the one I was looking for.

Producing the Choco Pie from my pocket, I placed it beside some apples and flowers on the already full altar of Wenshu, the god of wisdom. I'd been coming to the temple almost every day trying to speak to Ye Ye, Wenshu's disciple. The last time I'd seen and spoken to my grandfather, he'd helped Alex, Ren, Moli, and me fight off the nián demon at Peng Lai Island. After that, we'd lost all contact.

I had to know that Ye Ye was safe under Wenshu, even though the god of wisdom had clearly sided against the humans. And if Ye Ye was up in Heaven with Alex, I had to know that my brother was safe, too. I also had an important message for Alex: I was going to pound him flatter than a scallion pancake the next time I saw him.

And finally—the book. I couldn't shake the feeling that that blank chapter in *Restorative Potions* held the answers I sought. Maybe Ye Ye would be able to tell me for sure.

"Please, Wenshu," I murmured, kneeling before the statue and pressing my hands together in prayer. Bending forward in a low bow, I pressed my forehead to the cool temple floor, just as Ye Ye had taught me to do back in the Jade Society. "Let me speak to Ye Ye. I know he's listening. The Hungry Ghost Festival is about to begin at sundown. Please tell him that I—his granddaughter—hope he's doing well. I miss him very much. And if he has any idea how I can restore Ba's memory, can he show me the way?"

I removed *Restorative Potions* from my backpack, opened

it to the chapter titled "Memory-Restoring Elixirs," and placed it on the ground before me before kneeling in prayer again. I waited, and waited, and waited. I waited until the flame on the incense stick almost burned out. But again, there was no response.

Just as I was about to give up, the Choco Pie I'd laid on the altar disappeared. Then a white light emitted from the pages of *Restorative Potions*, growing brighter and brighter. I gasped. Golden words appeared on the page.

Falun,

Thank you for your well wishes. I'm sorry I haven't been able to respond to your prayers before now. It's been very busy in Heaven, and Wenshu has been monitoring all his disciples and ingoing and outgoing prayers closely. We've been practicing intense meditation, so I haven't heard any news from your brother. I will send word as soon as it is safer.

In the meantime, I think you'll find this gift useful. It's a compass that represents navigation and also order and harmony. When the time comes, you'll need this compass not only to save your brother but also to restore the axis of the Earth, which the demons and gods alike have greatly disturbed in these troublesome times.

Finally, to restore your father's memory, you need to find a special elixir that can only be obtained during the Hungry Ghost Festival. To find this elixir, you will need the help and full might of all your ancestors—and that means journeying far beyond the walls of the New Order.

I'll try my best to see you during the Hungry Ghost Festival, but I can't *make any promises. Wenshu has been very strict. If I don't see you, know that I'm there with you in spirit.*

Don't forget to brush your teeth and be wary of demons,
Ye Ye

I read and reread the words and then pressed the book to my chest. As the tears slipped down my cheek, an item materialized on the altar. It was a large black compass with not one but four arrows. Each pointed in a different direction, presumably north, south, east, and west. Only I had no clue which direction was which. I shook the compass, as though that would somehow give me the answers. It didn't.

Great. Ye Ye had given me a compass that didn't work. But at least he'd given me the letter, too.

I flipped through the pages in *Restorative Potions*, but that note was the only message from Ye Ye. There were no other details, or further instructions, or some kind of cheat code for completing this quest without actually going on it. I sighed. Real life was never as easy as video games.

If I needed proof that I had to take on the quest, this was it. My gut told me I'd have to find my ancestors somewhere along the way. This wasn't just about protecting the other warriors. This was about restoring my father's memory. On my way back to the apartment, I read the note in the book a few more times, imagining Ye Ye's weathered, skilled hand penning those words.

I will send word as soon as it is safer.

I hoped against hope that that would be soon. That Wenshu would let my grandfather visit the human world during the Hungry Ghost Festival.

But something told me I wouldn't be so lucky.

Later that day, Xiong called a society-wide meeting in front of the temple. Everyone was gathered for the send-off. Some of the women had brought flowers. Xiong handed us backpacks stuffed with packaged foods like dried meat, Choco Pies, and rice crackers. We had enough food to sustain us for this quest—plus the next five, probably. The backpacks also contained prayer notes, which we could use to pray to the deities and ancestors for help if we ran into danger.

"Use these only as a last resort," Xiong warned. "We don't know which gods or spirits are on our side. Praying to the wrong one might send you to your doom." On that cheery note, he walked away, calling order to the other warriors.

Ah Qiao ran up to me. "Ren still isn't back," he said accusingly. "Master Xiong said he's gone for a long time! Why did you lie to me?"

"I'm sorry, Ah Qiao." I didn't know what Ren was up to any more than he did. For a brief moment when Ren had turned into a dragon yesterday, I'd been able to communicate with him. But now, when I reached out with my mind, I couldn't sense him anywhere.

The little boy squinted at me, like it was my fault that Ren hadn't returned. Then he sniffed and placed a clipboard with a paper and pen in front of me. "Sign this."

I obeyed without thinking, then handed the paper and pen back to him when I was finished. "What is this?"

"Your last will and testament," Ah Qiao said seriously. "It says that if you die on this quest, I get to turn your room into my video-game room."

I was not reassured by his grin and hopeful tone of voice. "Gimme that back." I reached out for his slip of paper, but he yanked it out of reach. Then he ran for his mother.

A current of fear passed through the air. Some of the warriors kept shooting the siblings frightened looks. A few of the older women, though, gave them encouraging smiles.

None of us had forgotten what had happened last night. How Ashley had won her duel with some mysterious magic. But a win was a win, after all.

"What did Xiong say to you guys last night after we all left?" I muttered to Jordan.

He shifted his weight from foot to foot and wouldn't meet my eye. "Just . . . you know," he said vaguely. "The usual. The normal stuff. The haps."

"Xiong gave you 'the haps' on a life-or-death quest? The first one in decades?" I said in disbelief. I was almost certain that Xiong had spoken with the siblings about Ashley's transformation, but I didn't want to press for details. Not yet, anyway.

"Look, we don't know any more than you do, okay, Jade Society warrior?" Ashley burst out.

"What's your problem? So what if I'm a Jade Society warrior?" I snapped. Enough was enough. I wasn't going to let Ashley keep pushing me around. Besides, the dislike was mutual. I would've given anything to have Alex, Moli, and Ren with me on this quest instead of Ashley and Jordan.

Ashley's fists clenched at her sides. "You don't know anything about how hard we've had to train for this moment. All of us at the New Order. Including Jinyu. *Especially* Jinyu. We never knew if we'd even live to see a quest." She shook her head. "You know what? Never mind. I don't know why I'm bothering to explain myself to an outsider."

Ashley stomped up the temple steps, taking them two by two, to join Xiong outside the door.

"Don't take it personally," Jordan said with an apologetic grimace. "Ashley's always been hard to get along with. She used to steal all my Pokémon action figures right out of my hands while I was playing with them and flush them down the toilet. Made me cry."

I winced. I was reminded of Luhao, who'd bullied Alex and me back at the Jade Society. "I'm sorry. Sounds like Ashley was a real childhood bully."

"Childhood?" Jordan gave me a funny look. "No, no. I'm talking about last week."

"You know I'm right, Jordan," Ashley called, startling me.

I hadn't realized she'd overheard. "Faryn *isn't* a New Order warrior. She has no idea what it means to be one of us."

I gritted my teeth. I hoped there'd be lots of hungry demons on this quest. I had an idea of what to feed them, and it rhymed with "Mashley."

"Maybe I'm not a true New Order warrior," I said, "but I *did* help save the world half a year ago. Where were you, Ashley?"

Bright-red patches rose to Ashley's cheeks. She opened her mouth to retort but then shut it again and turned away with a huff. A flash of triumph surged through me but quickly faded—especially when Jordan gave me an annoyed look.

"What? She started it," I mumbled, kicking a stone beneath my foot.

"You two." Jordan sighed.

Guilt shot through me. I didn't even have time for petty squabbles. I had to save my brother, father, *and* the world.

"Are you guys coming or not?" Ashley shouted from the top of the steps.

Jordan looked at me, and we both rolled our eyes at the same time. Together, we ran up the steps and followed behind Ashley to enter the temple of the New Order.

I looked past the statues and tables of offerings for the Hungry Ghost Festival. My attention was quickly diverted by the presence of very *real* gods and goddesses standing inside the temple.

"They got my nose all wrong." Erlang Shen glared at a statue of himself. "It's not that big. And my stomach does *not* have that much flab. I've been doing P90X for nine weeks now!" The god of war jabbed his three-pronged spear at the statue and then looked down at his own belly as if comparing the two.

Nezha hovered near his statue. "Do I really look that angry to you guys?" He stared around at the room with a worried look. "Hey, guys?"

Only Guanyin seemed satisfied with her golden statue. "My eyebrows are on fleek," the goddess of mercy said.

They turned when Jordan and I entered the temple and the doors closed behind us. Xiong and the Elders stood in front of the statues of the Jade Emperor and Xi Wangmu.

"Warriors," said Xiong. "Ashley, Jordan, and Faryn. You have proven yourselves worthy of an honor that generations of warriors have only dreamed of—to embark on a quest for the gods. Now, as we prepare to send you off, please pray to and receive this blessing from the gods."

Three Elders stepped forward. They placed smoking incense sticks into our hands. Ashley led us as she stepped in front of the table, inserting the sticks into the holders beside the food. As one, we knelt down onto the ground and prayed to the gods.

Even though my eyes were closed, I could still see the brilliant flash of light that accompanied our prayers.

"Ahhh," sighed Erlang Shen. "That feels good. That feels *powerful.*"

As we gave our prayers of thanks, I could feel the power surging into the gods, the energy crackling through the air. I was pretty sure there was enough energy filling the temple to bring down the whole town.

When Guanyin spoke, her voice sounded more distant than before, as though she were speaking from somewhere high above us. "The shī, Erlang Shen. Repeat the shī of prophecy to the warriors."

After a moment, Erlang Shen chimed in.

> "*To seek the weapon of greatest power,*
> *five warriors must search the highest heights and*
> *lowest depths,*
> *and when darkness reaches its greatest hour,*
> *an old ally will return from the brink of death.*"

I knew poetry was supposed to be vague and stuff, but that really didn't give us much to go on. Highest heights? Lowest depths? Were we talking about places or Ashley's mood swings?

And who were those other two warriors who were supposed to accompany us?

"What does that mean?" I blurted. "You sure you can't give us even a hint?" It was almost as if Erlang Shen had given us this confusing shī because he *wanted* our quest to be a miserable failure. If he and the other gods wanted us to succeed, why not be more helpful? I squinted at Erlang Shen. Or could it be . . . that the riddle was just to slow us down?

Nezha turned on me, purple flames dancing in his eyes. I froze. He seemed more serious than the Nezha from the Lunar New Year. I guess he really did mean business. "There are ancient laws that guard the issuance of quests, warrior."

"Laws you wouldn't understand," Erlang Shen added in a cold, harsh voice. "If we gods give *even a hint*, as you say, the magic of the quests will break, and there will be no hope left for us all. Humanity will be wiped out, Earth will be plunged into utter darkness—"

Okay. Next time I had a dumb question, I'd just keep my mouth shut.

"Be warned, you only have two weeks to complete the quest," said Erlang Shen. "The gates of Diyu will open at sundown, and spirits and demons will flood the Earth. As you know, the other gods will stop at no cost—even the near extinction of the human race—to rid the Earth of demons once and for all."

I could feel the others shuddering beside me.

"You may rise now, warriors," Guanyin said gently.

The sound of shoes scraping against the floor filled the temple as we stood. The three gods hovered before us, outlined in glows that were brighter than before. Outside the doors came the faint but unmistakable sound of lions roaring.

Wait. Lions?

"Your chariot awaits you," said Erlang Shen with a nod. His lips peeled back, flashing his teeth. If I didn't know better, I'd think he was *smiling*. "Go forth and fulfill this quest. The fate of the world is in your hands now."

"No pressure," added Nezha.

"We believe in you, warriors," Guanyin chimed in warmly.

Even Guanyin's reassurance didn't make me feel better. Ashley and Jordan exchanged nervous looks. Taking a deep breath, I turned around.

Xiong and another Elder opened the great red doors. The warriors stood around the temple in a circle. Xiong stepped into the center and raised something small into the air, which glinted bronze in the sunlight—a yuán, or a Chinese coin. In his other hand, he raised a remote control and clicked a button. A flash of light surrounded him, causing the warriors to gasp.

When the light faded, a huge green and gold chariot stood before us. This time, it wasn't pulled by horses but two familiar-looking white lions.

"Wicked," Jordan breathed.

"That chariot is charmed to be invisible to all but the warriors," Guanyin explained.

I looked to the left and right of the temple doors. As I'd

suspected, the two stone lions who'd guarded the temple were gone. The gods had brought them to life to pull our chariot on this quest.

I let out a deep sigh of relief.

"What is it?" asked Jordan.

"I don't have a strange and inconvenient habit of talking to inanimate objects after all," I said with a grin.

Jordan looked at me as if *I* were a stone lion come to life.

Every last member of the New Order, from the oldest of the Elders to the youngest of children, surrounded the chariot. As we descended the stairs, they began clapping, although some only brought their hands together once or twice before dropping them. My eyes zeroed in on one face in the crowd— Ba's. When he saw me, he smiled and gave a polite wave. I did my best to return the smile but found the ache in my chest made it too difficult.

"Is this what it's like to be a celebrity?" Jordan shouted.

"More like sacrificial lambs," said Ashley cheerfully. "Kidding, brother," she clarified when Jordan threw her a horrified look. Ashley just made a beeline for the chariot, ignoring the crowd.

"Warriors," said Xiong. "We are placing the hopes of the New Order on your shoulders." He pressed the chariot's remote control into my limp palm and then leaned in toward my ear.

"Remember what I said," he whispered. "You are the one to lead the quest."

I nodded, tucking the remote control into my pocket. Xiong moved away, and I caught Ashley's eye. Her face had turned bright red. I'd be lying if I said Ashley's fuming didn't bring me some satisfaction. Just a little.

"Three cheers for the warriors!" shouted Xiong, walking toward the crowd.

Firecrackers exploded above our heads, showering the sky with light. A wave of nostalgia swept over me as I thought back to the quest of the Lunar New Year, when Alex and I had looked up into a similar fireworks-filled night sky, but on the other side of the country in San Francisco.

Now I had none of my old friends by my side. The thought dampened my spirits, bringing me back to earth—although not literally.

Jordan blew kisses toward the crowd.

"Okay, stop. Now you're just being embarrassing," Ashley groaned. She dragged Jordan into the chariot after her.

"Hey, Faryn," she shouted. "You coming or what?"

"Uh . . . yeah." I paused, casting one more look around at the warriors. I thought I spotted Ren's face in the crowd. But that was just wishful thinking. Ren was far, far away. He was finding his family, his place.

I had to find my place still.

"Jià!" yelled Ashley, and the lions began moving forward. "Guess we'll see you later, Faryn!"

I jogged to catch up with the chariot and swung my legs

over the side. Jordan helped me in, and I took the spot next to him on the back bench, right in front of our backpacks of snacks. I stuffed *Restorative Potions* into one.

"What's that?" Jordan asked.

"Uh . . . just some light reading," I mumbled. I hadn't told either sibling that the warrior they knew as Zhuang was actually my father, who'd lost his memories. I'd trusted only Ren with that information.

Jordan gave me a funny look but then shrugged. Ashley stood while pulling the reins right behind the lions, of course.

I ripped open a Choco Pie package. Might as well cram as much energy into my system as I could before the life-or-death danger really kicked in.

The chariot jolted as the lions took flight.

"WAAAAA-HOOOO!" Ashley screamed. "Now *this* is what I'm talking about!"

"Oh gods," groaned Jordan. "I think I'm gonna puke."

"Not on me!" Ashley screeched. "I swear I'll throw you off this chariot!"

"Both of you, shut up," I grumbled after polishing off my Choco Pie.

"How are you *eating* at this moment?" Jordan demanded.

My ears popped as we climbed into the sky, which was streaked with pink and red. The sun had just dipped below the horizon. I glanced back to see Nezha wink at me and Guanyin flash a small, secretive smile. Erlang Shen gave me his signature glare but nodded. The gods' acknowledgment brought me a small surge of strength. Or maybe that was the sugar rush.

If the gods believed in me, then surely I could complete a second quest, even without the help of Alex, Moli, or Ren. Right?

The waving New Order warriors grew more and more distant. They became specks on the distant ground, tiny as ants, and were swallowed up by treetops.

CHAPTER

10

After the chariot leveled above the clouds, I pulled Ye Ye's compass out of my pocket. The device still pointed unhelpfully in all four directions, and I had no idea which way was north. Why couldn't Ye Ye have slipped me the instruction manual, too?

I turned the device over in my palm. There had to be something, anything hinting at how I could use it. I found nothing. Not even an inscription or a scratch.

Maybe Ye Ye had been wrong. Maybe this compass wasn't special after all.

"What is that?" asked Jordan.

I shoved it back into my pocket. "It's nothing. Just . . . something my grandfather gave me."

"Your grandfather? Where is he?"

"He's, uh . . . actually sort of . . . dead now. Well, not

exactly dead," I said quickly, as soon as the all-too-familiar look of apologetic sorrow crossed Jordan's face. "He was deified."

Why was I telling him about Ye Ye? I hadn't talked to anyone about Ye Ye, except Ren maybe once.

"That's so cool," Jordan said wistfully. "Your grandfather's a *deity*. You must get the best New Year's presents."

I thought back to the Lunar New Year. Over the course of the holiday, Ye Ye and Moli died, my brother betrayed me, and the gods declared war on all of humanity.

"Um," I said. "Yeah. The best."

Jordan stared at me as though seeing me in a whole new light. Feeling uncomfortable, I tried to divert his attention.

"Hey, why are you the one who gets to drive the chariot?" I asked Ashley. "Xiong gave *me* the remote."

"Right. So you do the navigating. I'll do the driving. You just sit back and let me handle the real work," Ashley added, raising her voice over the volume of the wind. "I'll fight all the demons and save the world *way* before the end of the Hungry Ghost Festival."

I gritted my teeth. "Ex*cuse* me? Get off your high horse, Ashley."

"This is a chariot. I am on a chariot."

"Please stop fighting," Jordan yelled. He grabbed a handful of snacks and waved them in the air. "We have Choco Pies and Pocky! Why are you both still angry?"

Ashley opened her mouth to retort, but Jordan stuffed an unwrapped Choco Pie into her mouth. "Mrrrph!"

Now I understood why Ashley was on this quest. She was our secret weapon. Put her in front of a demon for two minutes, and she'd annoy the poor thing to death.

"As much as I'm enjoying all this arguing," Jordan interrupted, "can we talk about the quest for a moment? Do we even know where we're going? Has anyone figured out Erlang Shen's riddle?"

"Figured out the riddle?" Ashley swallowed her last bite of the Choco Pie. "Of course I've figured out the riddle."

Jordan and I exchanged stunned looks. "What? You have?" we burst out in unison.

"It's obvious. I honestly don't know how Erlang Shen could have made his shī any clearer. Remember the first couple of lines? 'To seek the weapon of greatest power, five warriors must search the highest heights and lowest depths.' Where in the world can you find a place that has both the 'highest heights and lowest depths'?"

Jordan popped open a box of green-tea Pocky. He looked stumped as he chewed on a stick.

"Highest heights and lowest depths . . . sounds like a roller coaster," I tried. "Or Vegas."

Ashley snorted. "A roller coaster? And *Vegas*? Is that honestly the best you could come up with?"

"What do you think it is, if you're so smart?" I snapped.

"That riddle clearly refers to a natural place. It's the Grand Canyon."

"Oh." Jordan chewed on his Pocky thoughtfully. "Yeah. That does make sense."

"Why would the gods want us to go to the Grand Canyon?" I asked. "There's nothing there but a bunch of rocks and nature." I doubted we'd find my ancestors or memory-restoring elixirs there.

"And annoying tourists," added Jordan.

"Plus, there's the matter of the 'weapon of greatest power,'" I pointed out. A nagging voice in the back of my head—which sounded strangely similar to Alex's—told me that I should know exactly what that meant. My brother had definitely talked my ear off before about the most powerful weapon in Chinese mythology. What was it called again?

"Haven't you guys learned anything from the Elders?" Ashley huffed. "The Grand Canyon is the home of Xuanwu, the god of the north and patron god of martial artists. In the legends, Xuanwu is a powerful warrior god who used his strength to subdue a demonic snake and demonic turtle into serving him. Remember the rest of Erlang Shen's poem?"

"'And when darkness reaches its greatest hour, an old ally will return from the brink of death,'" Jordan recited.

"Right," said Ashley. "Xuanwu was definitely an 'old ally' to Erlang Shen and the other deities hundreds of years ago.

He's been in hiding for a long time. But in the darkest hour, he'll rise to the occasion."

I guess Ashley's theory did make more sense than anything Jordan and I could come up with. I had to trust that finding Xuanwu would also lead me to finding my relatives and the memory-restoring elixir. Ye Ye's compass would show us the way. Right?

We rode through blue skies with the stone lions pulling us along at a rapid pace. Normally I'd have trouble falling asleep thousands of feet in the air, zipping along at breakneck speed, but I was exhausted by the events of the past twenty-four hours. It didn't take long before I closed my eyes, and the world faded away.

I stood in a great throne room. The man sitting on the throne was the Jade Emperor himself. He wore a golden hat with dangling beads that hung to his shoulders, a sweeping gold and red robe, and a stern expression on his face.

Guards stood at every pillar, holding spears in their hands. Something serious was happening. My gaze fell upon a warrior surrounded by two guards and kneeling in front of the throne. They'd crossed their spears in front of the warrior, as though blocking any escape. The warrior's face pointed toward the ground, hidden from my sight, but I'd be able to recognize the back of his brown-haired head anywhere. Alex.

"So, Heaven Breaker. You know why I have summoned you here before me, don't you?" The Jade Emperor's cold voice boomed throughout the great hall, sending shivers down my spine. He wasn't yelling, but he might as well have been—the undercurrent of anger in his voice was more threatening than anything else.

"I . . . I do not," Alex said. I could tell by the volume of his voice that he was trying to appear confident, but his trembling body betrayed his fear.

"You do not?" thundered the Jade Emperor. "You do not recall having done *anything* that might warrant being brought here, in front of me?"

Whatever he'd done, Alex was in deep trouble. I wanted to cry out, to run over and protect my brother from the Jade Emperor's wrath, but there was nothing I could say or do in this dream. I couldn't remember ever feeling so helpless.

"I . . ." Alex shook from head to foot. "I . . ."

"Let this be a lesson," the Jade Emperor continued dangerously, "that there is *nothing* that you can hide from me, Heaven Breaker. I have eyes and ears all over Heaven, Earth, and the Underworld. I'll ask you one more time." He paused, and I closed my eyes. If the Jade Emperor was about to punish my brother, I couldn't look. "Do you recall having done anything that would warrant being brought here before me?"

"I—I . . . I've been looking for my parents," Alex blurted out. Still quaking, he seemed to shrink into himself. "I sent a couple of dragons out there to—to search for them. I know you asked me not to, but—"

"But you thought it would be a good idea to disobey me anyway?" roared the Jade Emperor. He slammed his fist against the jade throne, causing a loud *boom* to reverberate throughout the hall. Several warriors jumped. I would've jumped, too, if my body could move.

"I'm . . . sorry," Alex mumbled.

The Jade Emperor shook his head and stroked his long, thin black goatee. "I'm disappointed, Heaven Breaker. I don't see you as much of an asset at all, to be frank. If it weren't for my wife's insistence on keeping you around, I would've blasted you out of the sky long ago."

Alex gulped. I could barely stand seeing my brother look so weak in front of the Jade Emperor. I would've given anything at that moment to be able to pull him out of that throne room.

"I understand, sir," Alex mumbled.

"I already promised that I'd reveal your true parentage to you as soon as you finished carrying out the task I gave you. Why, instead, did you have to go behind my back?" snapped the Jade Emperor. "You don't need distractions right now. You need only concern yourself with the task at hand."

My curiosity burned. My anger brewed. What was this task that the Jade Emperor had given my brother—and why had he forbidden Alex from uncovering his parentage in the process? That seemed totally unfair to me.

"I understand," Alex muttered.

A silence stretched on in the hall, long enough that it became uncomfortable for even the soldiers who stood in front of the pillars. They broke their statue-still stances and fidgeted.

"This is my one and only warning to you, Heaven Breaker." The Jade Emperor leaned forward on his throne. "Cross me again, and there will be no further chances."

Alex bowed his head even lower, so that it touched the stone floor. "Yes, sir."

"Good. Now go summon all the dragons. We don't have a moment to waste, and—" The Jade Emperor stopped speaking. He slowly turned his head, and his cold black eyes met mine.

For a moment, I forgot to breathe. I had to remind myself that this was just some weird dream or vision. I was somewhere far, far away from the Jade Emperor. A faraway, safe place, where he most definitely couldn't see me.

But the horrible sinking sensation in the pit of my stomach told me otherwise.

"There's someone here," the Jade Emperor growled.

Okay. Time to nix that theory. I opened my mouth to scream, but no sound came out. My heart beat madly against my chest, as though trying to escape.

"What? Who's here?" Alex asked, whipping his head around in alarm. His eyes completely skipped over me, so it seemed like I wasn't visible to anyone else—just the Jade Emperor.

"Guards!" yelled the Jade Emperor. He pointed right at me, his goatee quivering with fury. "Capture the intruder!"

I couldn't have run away even if I wanted to. Scrambling into formation, the warriors along the pillars raised their weapons and charged straight at me. The first spear was feet—inches—from stabbing me, and then—

Ah. We've been found out, came a soothing female voice in my head.

We? Who's we? I thought. *Who are you?*

Do not fear. You are safe. I will bring you back. With every word, the Jade Emperor's palace grew fuzzier and fuzzier.

———

I jolted awake. I gasped, taking deep gulps of the fresh air. I was hardly able to take in my surroundings when something in my pocket started vibrating. I took the compass out of my pocket. It was shaking, and the four arrows had all gone haywire.

"Whoa." Jordan stared at the compass and then at me. "What the heck is that thing doing?"

"Um . . . going berserk," I said, still trying to catch my breath. I was in a chariot, thousands of feet up in the air, on a quest of the Hungry Ghost Festival. Unpacking that weird dream would have to come later. For now, I had to handle the immediate problem of the compass going haywire on me.

The compass lurched, shuddered, and then the arrows spun slower and slower until they were all pointing to our right.

Maybe the compass wasn't just some piece of junk Ye Ye had given to me. Maybe there was something to it after all. "Hey, Ashley," I said. "I think we gotta make a right turn here."

"Nope," she shouted back. "Grand Canyon is straight ahead of us."

The arrow moved slowly until it pointed behind us. The compass began shuddering again. "But—but you said I should navigate—"

"Yeah, you can navigate when you know what you're talking about—which you don't." She added under her breath, "Jinyu should've been the one leading this quest."

The compass shook and glowed in my hand, brighter than ever.

Ashley was wrong. I'd read Ye Ye's message in *Restorative Potions* so many times, I could recall what he'd written with perfect clarity.

When the time comes, you'll need this compass not only to save your brother but also to restore the axis of the Earth, which the demons and gods alike have greatly disturbed in these troublesome times.

There was no way this compass had just started shuddering for no reason. My brother was in trouble—and soon, the whole world would be, too. I had to stop Ashley before we wasted any more time.

I was no Jinyu, but I'd prove that I deserved to be on this quest as much as he had.

I stood up. The chariot rocked, and I nearly fell over. I managed to keep my balance, but I let out a high-pitched yell.

Ashley whirled around, her eyes widening with confusion when she saw me standing right behind her. "What're you—?"

The chariot rocked again to the side, even more violently this time. Ashley shrieked and fell over. I reached out to grab her, but not in time.

Ashley knocked her head against the side of the chariot. I watched in horror as she slid down to the floor, out cold.

CHAPTER

11

In hindsight, I probably could've worked a teeny bit harder to catch Ashley before she fell. The moment Ashley was out of action, the chariot became driverless, spooking the lions. They roared and plummeted toward the earth at stomach-dropping speed—taking the chariot and us with it.

Faryn, you idiot. I could practically hear Alex scolding me. "Faryn, you idiot!"

Just kidding. That was Jordan yelling at me in real time.

My feet slipped under me. My hands tumbled through the air, grasping for something—anything—solid to hold on to.

"Ashley! *No!*" Jordan bellowed.

In the chaos, I dimly registered the sight of Ashley's limp body tumbling over the side. A scream wrenched its way from my throat. My eyes darted toward our backpacks. I knew Xiong had said to use the prayer notes only as a last resort, but this was a matter of life or death.

I couldn't reach the prayer notes anyway. It was all I could do to keep myself from falling off.

A blinding flash of light burst from the front of the chariot. I slammed forward onto it, my knees colliding painfully with the floor. I gasped, my heart thudding in my chest. Somehow, miraculously, the chariot steadied.

"Um . . . this is weird . . ."

I looked up at the sound of Jordan's tremulous voice. I cried out, "You're—glowing!"

"I am aware of that!" Jordan didn't look like Jordan anymore. A white light had burst forth from his chest and spread all around the chariot, surrounding it in a glow that was almost angelic. Jordan cradled Ashley's limp form in his arms.

It took me a moment to understand. Whatever strange power Jordan had channeled was keeping us in the air. The white light grew brighter and hotter until I was forced to shut my eyes against the glow, and the heat shimmered around us at a near-unbearable level. If Jordan didn't cut it out soon, we were going to burn into shrimp crisps.

"What are you doing?" I yelled. "Make it stop!"

"I can't control it!" Jordan bellowed. At that moment, the white light vanished. The chariot remained suspended in the air. Jordan and I stared at each other in a mixture of terror and confusion. "Oh. I can control it."

"Wh . . . what kind of power *is* that?" I squeaked. "You—you—you saved us from turning into a giant grease spot on

Earth. And then you almost turned us into a giant shrimp crisp in midair. How? How'd you do it?"

"I . . . I don't know. But . . . this—this isn't the first time we've done something like this. Ashley and me, I mean."

"You're talking about what Ashley did at the Duels, right?" My mind flashed back to the way Ashley had unleashed that strange power and taken out her opponent, and pretty much everyone else, during the Ninety-Sixth Duels. "Demon," the other warriors had accused.

Did Ashley really have demon blood? Did Jordan, too?

"Yeah," said Jordan. "But even before that, there were a couple of times—when we were really little, so we only heard about this from the Elders—that Ashley and I did . . . strange things."

"What kind of strange things?"

"Oh, you know, developed some weird powers, scared off a couple of kids, and, uh, blew-out-a-wall-in-the-New-Order," Jordan mumbled, averting his gaze. "Just your average puberty stuff."

"You *what*? Blew out a wall in the New Order?"

"That was Ashley, not me! And she was two years old, okay? Being a toddler is, like, a free pass to do anything!"

"Not to blow up walls," I protested.

Instead of answering, Jordan slowly lowered Ashley from his arms to the floor of the chariot. He cleared his throat and dusted off his shirt, as though nothing out of the ordinary had happened. "Anyway," Jordan said in an unnaturally high-pitched voice. "That was fun. Back to our regularly scheduled programming. Where were we?" His gaze dropped toward the unconscious form of his sister. "Oh. Right. You let Ashley fall and get knocked out."

"Sorry," I blurted out sheepishly. "I—I panicked!"

"Ah . . . it's okay," Jordan said, although he sounded like he was convincing himself as much as he was me. "You might want to . . . stay far away when Ashley wakes up, though. She won't be happy."

"Yeah, of course."

"I mean, like, book a one-way ticket to Fiji or something. Seriously."

"Ashley doesn't scare me *that* much." As long as she wasn't yelling at everything that stood still long enough. Or blasting us with demon-like powers.

Jordan heaved a sigh. "Great. All you had to do on this whole quest was keep Ashley out of trouble. You had *one* job, Jordan. One job! How'd you mess it up so badly?" He knocked the side of his head with his fist and continued muttering to himself.

I unclenched my own fists and let my fingers relax.

Jordan took his sister's place behind the lions, taking control of the reins. "Ah, well. Ashley is upset every time she wakes up anyway. More importantly . . . what're we gonna do now that Ashley can't navigate?"

I cast one more guilty look down at Ashley. "Don't worry. I'll do it." I held up the glowing compass. The arrow pointed in the opposite direction of where we were headed. "According to Ye Ye's compass, we have to make a U-turn."

"No way," Jordan protested. He stared at the compass like it was a giant slug he'd smashed underfoot. "You said your grandfather is a deity, right? But how do we know he's trustworthy?"

"Ye Ye is a disciple studying under Wenshu," I explained, narrowing my eyes. "He was one of the bravest Jade Society warriors."

Jordan cringed.

"What?" I asked.

"You know . . . it's just . . . everyone says the Jade Society warriors don't train or even know how to fight demons anymore—"

"That's not the point. We have a quest to complete and not a whole lot of time to do it. We're already down on our manpower." I pointed down at Ashley's unconscious form.

Jordan frowned. "Yeah, but isn't that kinda your fault?"

I acted like I hadn't heard him. "So unless you have a better idea of how to get to our destination, we'd better follow this compass. Plus," I added as I recalled Alex's long-winded ramblings about ancient weapons that I used to tune out, "I know exactly where we need to go. 'The weapon of greatest power.' Isn't that—the Monkey King's staff? The Ruyi Jingu Bang?"

The Ruyi Jingu Bang, aka the Gold-Banded Cudgel. A red weapon with gold bands on either end that could grow as tall as Heaven itself or shrink to the size of a toothpick. The Ruyi Jingu Bang was said to be the most powerful weapon known to the gods. Thousands of years ago, Sun Wukong, otherwise known as the Monkey King, had stolen it from Ao Guang, the Dragon King of the East Sea.

The Ruyi Jingu Bang *was* very similar to Fenghuang, I realized. If—*when*—the time came to have a showdown with my brother, I'd need a weapon to match Fenghuang. To convince Alex to join our side once more. Especially if the dream I'd had earlier was more than just a dream, Alex was much better off far, far away from the Jade Emperor.

"Ruyi Jingu Bang?" Jordan repeated, scratching his head. "I guess . . . that might make sense."

"That's gotta be it." My voice grew louder as excitement and certainty swelled inside me. "We'll need the Ruyi Jingu Bang to defeat those heavenly goons. We might even find those two other warriors who're supposed to join us. Wherever the Monkey King—Sun Wukong—is, his Ruyi Jingu Bang can't be far. According to the myths, Sun Wukong lives on Huā Guǒ Shān." I'd seen the huge, greenery-covered mountain in picture books and textbooks. Had heard Ye Ye's stories about this mystical mountain from a young age. "I'm sure the compass will show us the way there."

As if agreeing with my words, the compass warmed in my palm.

A silence filled the chariot, which had slowed down to a snail's pace under Jordan's direction. Finally, Jordan sighed. "It's not like I have a better idea. Tell me where to go."

I moved to the front of the chariot with him. "Okay, so you'll want to make a U-turn here— Whoa! Not *that* fast!"

We rode on and soon settled into a rhythm, with me giving directions and Jordan following them without complaint. After a few hours, Ashley was still out cold on the bench. She snored with a content look on her face, although that would probably change the moment she woke up and caught sight of the purple bruise that had welled up over her right eye.

"Is my sister still asleep?" Jordan asked anxiously after a while.

"Yeah. Wake up, sleepyhead." I poked Ashley's cheek. Her head slumped over to one side, a string of spittle hanging out her snoring mouth.

"You've gotta wake her up, Faryn! What if we run into demons here?"

"We'll bait 'em with Ashley. Duh."

"You have a really twisted sense of humor!" Jordan shouted.

"Kidding," I said. "Obviously we'll bait them with you."

Jordan didn't have a chance to retort before Ashley stirred. She rubbed her eyes. They popped wide open as she took in the sights around us.

"What happened?" Ashley scrambled to her feet, and then winced and clutched her head. "Why was I asleep?"

Jordan coughed. I pretended to be too fascinated by my nail beds to have heard the question.

"Why was I asleep?" Ashley repeated, louder and more firmly.

"You fell asleep—uh, completely on your own—and we . . . didn't want to wake you," I said. "Anyway, it doesn't matter, and you should probably never think about it again!"

"Weirdo," Ashley muttered, rolling her eyes at me. "Jordan, I'm driving now."

Jordan offered no complaint, probably because he was exhausted from driving. Ashley and Jordan took turns driving the chariot. The sun rose and fell, rose and fell.

It was nighttime again, on the third day of the Hungry Ghost Festival, when the compass finally stopped glowing. By the light of the evening stars, I could see that we'd arrived at a huge, sweeping mountain covered in trees and wildlife. We were greeted by the sight of a massive waterfall that flowed white and blue and sparkled under the moonlight. It looked like it was made out of magic.

"I think we're here," I said. The guardian lions snorted and stamped their feet against the clouds, as though in agreement. "This is Huā Guǒ Shān."

Huā Guǒ Shān, one of the settings for that video game Alex was obsessed with, *Warfate*. I'd heard so much about Huā Guǒ Shān. I'd even seen it on *Journey to the West*, Alex's and my favorite cartoon show. Huā Guǒ Shān, or the Mountain of

Flowers and Fruit, was where the immortal Monkey King, Sun Wukong, reigned over his monkeys.

Except as far as I knew, that mountain was somewhere in China. I couldn't be sure, but I was *pretty* certain that we hadn't flown all the way to China. Although at this point, I was beginning to think nothing could surprise me. Maybe, like how Chinatowns had sprung up across the US thanks to Chinese immigration, Huā Guǒ Shān had been drawn to the States as well.

"We're here."

"Where exactly is *here*?" Ashley wrinkled her nose.

"It's Huā Guǒ Shān," I repeated. "We're here to see Sun Wukong—the 'old ally.'"

"This can't be right," Ashley declared. She crossed her arms over her chest and shook her head. "How can the Monkey King be the 'old ally' from Erlang Shen's shī?"

"Well, the dude is, like, a bazillion years old," Jordan said.

"It makes sense," I said. "The Ruyi Jingu Bang must be the 'weapon of greatest power.'"

"No, that *doesn't* make sense," Ashley protested. "The Monkey King, Sun Wukong, never allied with Erlang Shen in the old tales. They constantly butted heads. One time, when Sun Wukong was wreaking havoc on Heaven, the Jade Emperor even sent Erlang Shen to defeat him."

"The Jade Emperor sent *everyone* to defeat Sun Wukong," I pointed out. "Everyone and their butt-kicking grandmother.

Back then, the Monkey King wasn't friends with anyone. Remember?"

Ashley took a step toward me but stumbled when the chariot suddenly dipped. Under Jordan's guidance, the stone lions brought us to a bumpy landing on a bridge in front of the waterfall.

"Everyone get off," Jordan barked. "It's time to meet this 'old ally.'"

"What exactly are you thinking?" Ashley snapped as Jordan and I disembarked from the chariot. She stayed inside, her feet planted firmly. "I'm *not* following you guys."

"You can stay here if you want," I said sweetly, "but I wouldn't recommend it. The demons are stronger at night, you know."

"Of course I know that! As if there are any demons up here anyway!" Ashley shouted. But she didn't seem to believe her own words and rapidly turned her head from side to side, as if expecting demons to jump out at any moment.

Finally, Ashley got off the chariot. I took the remote out of my pocket, clicked the button, and watched as the chariot turned back into a small coin—which Ashley then snatched up and shoved into her pocket. Her narrowed eyes dared me to try to take the yuán from her.

I rolled my eyes and turned to the waterfall.

"What do we do now?" Jordan asked.

"Call out the Monkey King's name?" I suggested.

Jordan cupped his hands around his mouth. "Monkey King! Oh, Monkey King!"

"Stop that." Ashley slapped her brother playfully on the elbow. "As if one of the most powerful gods would answer to the sound of your stupid voice."

Jordan gave her a wounded look. "What do you suggest we do, then? Magically walk through that waterfall, like in *Warfate*?"

Although he was joking, Jordan's words stirred my memories. With startling clarity, I recalled Alex playing his favorite video game. I'd watched him play a level that involved a magic waterfall hiding a secret entrance to the Monkey King's lair. I couldn't believe my brother's dumb video games were coming in handy at a time like this. "You're right. We have to walk through the waterfall," I blurted out. "That's how Sun Wukong does it in the video game and cartoons."

Ashley scrunched up her nose. "Video games and cartoons? We're on the most important quest of the century, and you want to base our decisions off a bunch of video games and cartoons?"

"Sounds about right for the twenty-first century," Jordan said cheerfully. He stepped forward hesitantly, stretching out his fingers.

"Careful," Ashley called, eyes wide with concern. I could tell she cared a lot about her brother, as much as she tried to hide it.

"Whoa, this is so weird," Jordan gasped when his fingers met the water. "It's not wet." He moved swiftly through the waterfall. Jordan's sneakers were the last I saw of him before he disappeared.

Ashley gawked at the space where her brother had been just moments ago. "What in the—?"

Moving past Ashley, I took a deep breath, straightened, and stepped into the waterfall.

Just like Jordan had said, there was no wetness. Stepping through the waterfall felt like stepping through a cool space of air. Next thing I knew, I passed right through it and found myself inside a cave.

"Jordan?" I spun in a circle. All I could see was sparkling stalactites, rocks, and blackness.

"C'mon!" came the distant echo of Jordan's voice.

There was a light at the end of the cave. Without waiting for Ashley, I sprinted toward it. When I reached the opening, I tumbled out into the light and gasped.

Waiting for me was a scene that looked straight out of a paradise.

CHAPTER

12

I entered a clearing surrounded by thick bushes and tall green trees bearing ripe peaches. Emerald moss framed the ground, and white clouds drifted across the sky. The nature atop Huā Guǒ Shān looked completely untouched by anything impure, like demons, the Panda Express fast-food chain, or large multinational corporations. Monkeys of all shapes and sizes hung from the trees. Others stood in clusters on the ground.

In the center of the clearing stood a tall golden throne occupied by an imposing figure: half-man, half-monkey, with his arms crossed over a slightly protruding belly. He wore a leopard-print skirt paired with blue pants and black boots and a yellow long-sleeve shirt with a blue ribbon tied around his neck. There was a golden band on his head, which I knew from the old stories was what his old master had used to keep him under control.

The Monkey King couldn't have been taller than four feet, but what he lacked in height, he made up for in presence. Sun Wukong commanded our attention, and he knew it. As far as I could tell, he looked almost exactly like he did in *Warfate* and his cartoon—except for one thing. One giant, glaring, missing thing—his mighty weapon, the Ruyi Jingu Bang.

"Whoa," Ashley gasped behind me. "Am I dreaming?"

"Who dares trespass into the Water Curtain Cave inside Huā Guǒ Shān?" boomed Sun Wukong. The monkeys began screeching, those on the ground quickly climbing up into the trees. They shook the branches. I yelped as a peach hit my head.

For once, it seemed even Ashley didn't know how to respond.

I dropped to my knees. I figured showing the Monkey King some respect couldn't hurt, since he was about the most arrogant god to ever live, thinking he could take on all of Heaven by himself. He'd probably blast us for *not* showing him respect. The others quickly followed suit.

"Hey, guys? A-any ideas what to say to him?" I whispered.

"You seem to be doing f-fine," Ashley hissed, her voice trembling. "And didn't you want to be in charge? You decide."

I looked at Jordan for help, but he just nodded and mouthed, "Keep talking."

Great. Earlier they'd been all "stupid Jade Society warrior this, stupid Jade Society warrior that," and now they wanted

my help? I cleared my throat, trying to ignore the fact that I was trembling from head to toe.

I rose to my feet. "Um . . . er . . ." *Off to an impressive start, Faryn. Why don't you throw an "uh" and "mrph" and "I'm a ninny, ignore me" into the mix as well?*

As my gaze met Sun Wukong's piercing eyes, I remembered his vision was much more powerful than a mortal's or even most gods'. He could see what others couldn't, like demons disguised as humans. He'd definitely see how scared I was. Of course, that thought only made me *more* scared.

"State your purpose, strangers, or I'll feed you to my monkeys," Sun Wukong bellowed.

"P-please don't do that!" Jordan squeaked. "It w-would be a t-terrible mistake f-for you. I have—I have—acne! Terrible acne!"

Sun Wukong shocked me by grinning and smacking his hand against his knee with a barking laugh. "I'm just kidding. We're peach-atarians here."

"Um . . . peach-atarian?" Ashley said blankly.

"Don't you mean 'pescatarian'?" Jordan asked.

"No, I mean peach-atarian. We only eat peaches." Su Wukong reached up, snagged a peach off the lowest-hangir tree branch, and bit into it. "I already foresaw you three cor ing here."

"You did?" I said.

"Of course. I'm the Great Sage, Equal of Heaven. I kr

everything." Puffing out his chest, Sun Wukong finished his peach and spit the pit onto an unsuspecting monkey's head. "But I want to hear in your own words why you're trespassing on my territory."

I drew myself up to my full height. "W-we've come here to fulfill Erlang Shen's shī."

"Erlang Shen?" Sun Wukong stuck a long finger into his ear, turned it, and made a face as he flicked earwax off his nail. "What's that ugly, interfering brute want now?"

A good question that I had no clue how to answer. My memory of old stories and Ye Ye's compass had led us to the mountain, but now that I'd arrived, I worried it was all a mistake.

Still, we were supposed to search "the highest heights." Besides Heaven itself, was there anywhere located higher than Huā Guǒ Shān? We were also supposed to find "an old ally" on the "brink of death." Sun Wukong didn't look on the brink of death to me, but he had to be really, really, really old. Gods had to have *some* kind of expiration date, right?

"Dà shèng," I said respectfully, remembering Sun Wukong's chosen title, "we've come here on a quest to find you, the old ally, carrying the weapon of greatest power—the Ruyi Jingu Bang. Will you join forces with the New Order in the fight against the demons before they destroy everything— including this mountain?"

Sun Wukong laughed again. A deep, knee-smacking belly

laugh, the kind of laugh you give after someone has told a gut-splitting joke or said something incredibly stupid.

"Well, this is going well," Ashley remarked.

"*Old* ally? Do I appear 'old' to you?" Sun Wukong demanded. "I am at the height of my physical state! I have never been in better form!"

"Um . . ." Jordan tilted his head, eyeing the god's stomach.

"What makes you think I, the Great Sage, Equal of Heaven, have any interest in defending you mortals against the demons?" the Monkey King steamrollered on. "I could wipe out tons of demons while barely lifting a finger, of course. The unparalleled power of my Ruyi Jingu Bang—"

His eyes widened, and he fell silent. He suddenly seemed smaller than before.

I'd been right. The weapon that Sun Wukong always held, that he'd used to slay countless demons in the cartoons and video games, was missing.

"Where is it?" I asked. "Where's the Ruyi Jingu Bang?"

"Not . . . with . . . me . . . at the moment," Sun Wukong said through gritted teeth, as though each word physically pained him.

"You've lost the Ruyi Jingu Bang?" Jordan blurted out. "*How?*" He slapped a hand over his mouth, but the damage had been done.

"What did you say?" boomed Sun Wukong, standing up on his throne and pointing a long, hairy finger at us. He leapt off the throne, tumbled through the air, and emerged in a blur of motion right in front of us.

Up close, Sun Wukong looked even more intimidating, with razor-sharp teeth. Those black eyes were definitely trying to see if I was a demon or not. I closed my eyes and struggled to keep myself from trembling or looking like a demon, which was ridiculous because I *wasn't* a demon.

"I didn't *lose* anything," Sun Wukong continued. "One of the Demon Kings stole my Ruyi Jingu Bang. He lured me away from it by ambushing my monkeys. I would've chased that lowlife to the pits of Diyu, where he fled, but . . ." Sun Wukong cast a mournful look up at the monkeys who hung in the trees. "I needed to stay behind to protect my monkeys. The demons are stirring strongly now that it's the Hungry Ghost Festival, you see."

"Yeah," I said with a sigh. "We know."

Sun Wukong gave us a hard look. "That's why I can't help you even if I wanted to. Not only am I missing the Ruyi Jingu Bang, but I've also got to stay behind to protect Huā Guǒ Shān." He folded his arms across his chest and turned his back to us. "Now, leave."

Had Ye Ye's compass led us to the wrong place after all? Had the others trusted a "Jade Society warrior" just to have their suspicions confirmed—to know that we really were that useless?

Ashley and Jordan exchanged a quick, unreadable look—like

the ones Alex and I had exchanged so many times, before he . . .
No. I shook my head. *No thinking about Alex, remember? Concentrate on the mission.*

"Let's leave." Ashley turned and stormed back in the direction we'd come from. "This whole detour was a mistake. Like I said before, we're supposed to go to the Grand Canyon. The *real* hero, Xuanwu, is waiting for us."

"Xuanwu?" Sun Wukong echoed, sneering. "What about that lunkhead?"

"N-nothing," I interrupted. "We were just, um—"

"On our way to find the hero this world really needs—Xuanwu," Ashley interrupted.

I groaned inwardly. Why hadn't Ashley stayed unconscious? Now she was going to get all of us killed.

For a long, tense moment as we backed away from Sun Wukong, the god drew himself to his admittedly unimpressive full height. But the light that flared in his eyes was more than intimidating enough.

"I don't fight with mortals," Sun Wukong said in a dangerously calm voice, "but not every god is as benevolent and generous as I, warriors. You'll do well to remember that." He turned around once more in a dismissive motion. "If you can bring me the Ruyi Jingu Bang, I might reconsider my decision to help you."

"The Ruyi Jingu Bang?" I repeated. "But . . . you just said it's in Diyu, in the possession of a Demon King."

"It is," Sun Wukong confirmed. He cocked an eyebrow at us, his tail sweeping across the ground from side to side. "So?"

"N-nothing." But I could see in Ashley's eyes what she really meant to say. This would be a near-impossible task to complete, and Sun Wukong hadn't even guaranteed his help after we retrieved his weapon.

"Don't look so stricken, warriors. I know I'm asking for the impossible. Only the most powerful, clever, and handsome of gods could even have the strength to lift the Ruyi Jingu Bang."

I was pretty sure being clever and handsome didn't have any bearing on how strong someone could be, but I decided not to point that out.

"That would be me," Sun Wukong clarified, as though we hadn't understood his meaning. "I am the most powerful, clever, and handsome of gods. And unfortunately, there is only one of me."

"You can't just pluck one of your hairs, blow on it, and create a copy of yourself to stay behind and guard the mountain?" Jordan blurted out. "Unless that's just something made up in the cartoons."

Sun Wukong hung his head. "No, that's real. I used to be able to create an army of powerful, identical copies of myself using just the hairs on my back, but . . ." A shadow crossed the Monkey King's face. "I'm not as powerful as before. None of us gods is. So, warriors, unless you can find me a couple of gods to babysit my monkeys, I won't be joining you on your quest."

I gritted my teeth. There was no way Sun Wukong didn't know that what he was asking for was next to impossible. With powerful gods rallying against us and the few on our side stretched thin enough as it was trying to protect the humans, we didn't exactly have any powerful gods to spare.

"Forget it," Jordan whispered. "Sun Wukong is a trickster god. He can't be trusted."

"I heard that," Sun Wukong called.

I knew the Monkey King was a slippery fellow a little too fond of causing mass mayhem and panic. But on the other hand, Sun Wukong was also the most powerful of gods. I mean, he'd nearly brought down all of Heaven by himself, and he was half the size of a normal god. We needed the power of the Ruyi Jingu Bang—*and* Sun Wukong's help.

I stepped forward. "If we go to Diyu to retrieve your Ruyi Jingu Bang for you, will you join our side in the upcoming war?"

"Are you serious?" Ashley's eyes bulged as though I'd suggested we all leap off the side of the mountain. "You think *we* can bring back the Ruyi Jingu Bang? That thing weighs, like, eleventy billion pounds!"

Trying to look braver and more impressive than I was, I stood my ground.

Sun Wukong stopped in his tracks, a thunderous expression on his face. I couldn't help but shrivel back.

"Are you suggesting that I, the Great Sage, Equal of Heaven, need to rely on a handful of mere *mortals* to retrieve my Ruyi Jingu Bang?" Sun Wukong roared.

"N-no, of course not, dà shèng," Ashley said quickly. "We were just leaving."

I never liked quitting, but leaving sounded like a pretty good plan. Especially because the monkeys were shaking the trees as though they, too, could feel their master's wrath and were preparing to attack.

"I would normally smite you three for even daring to suggest that you puny warriors are more suited to the task than I," Sun Wukong continued. "However, my sworn brother, the Bull Demon King, wouldn't be too happy if I did that."

"The—the Bull Demon King?" Jordan stammered, mouth hanging slightly open.

Sun Wukong arched an eyebrow. "Of course. The Bull Demon King. Or should I say—your father?"

CHAPTER

13

Silence filled the Water Curtain Cave. Even the monkeys went still.

"Wh-what?" Ashley gasped. She exchanged a dumbstruck look with her brother before turning back to Sun Wukong. "The Bull Demon King? Our *father*?"

"Hold up." I stared at the siblings. "Am I hearing this right? You guys are the offspring of a Demon King?" The Bull Demon King. If I remembered my mythology correctly, then the Bull Demon King was the father of the Red Prince, a powerful fire demon we'd fought back in D.C.'s Chinatown. That meant the spoiled, evil little Red Prince was Ashley and Jordan's half brother. I shuddered. Could definitely see some family resemblance.

It all made sense now. I recalled what Ashley had done during the Ninety-Sixth Duels—defeating her opponent with magical abilities she'd developed out of nowhere. Jordan had displayed that mysterious white power to keep the chariot, and us, from plunging to our doom.

Ashley and her brother had to be part god—or part demon.

"No way," Jordan mumbled. "No freaking way."

Sun Wukong sighed and rubbed his head. "You mean you warriors didn't know? Why do these demons and gods always have kids with mortals and never bother to explain it to their own children? I have to speak with the Bull Demon King and bring him an autographed copy of my *Parenting 101* guidebook."

"That's just absurd!" Ashley said.

The Monkey King gave her an affronted look. "Absurd? I've become well versed in the art of parenting, girl. Living with young monkeys for thousands of years has taught me much about keeping the young and spirited under control."

"I didn't mean the part about your, um, *Parenting 101* guidebook," Ashley said hurriedly. "I—I mean, if we really were descended from the Bull Demon King, someone at the New Order would've known and told us."

There was no time to unpack the mystery of Ashley and Jordan's ancestry. The deadline for the quest drew nearer, and we hadn't checked off a single item on our Stuff We Need to Save the World laundry list.

"This is exactly why we're even more qualified to find the Ruyi Jingu Bang and bring it back to you, dà shèng," I said with as much confidence as I could fake. I was getting really good at pretending I knew what I was talking about. "The son and daughter of the mighty Bull Demon King? These two are, like, perfect for the job."

Jordan gaped at me.

Ashley hissed, "Stop talking now."

Sun Wukong's eyes flickered over the siblings, as though assessing how they stacked up in comparison to the Bull Demon King he knew. They must've passed his "Are These Kids Really the Long-Lost Descendants of a Demon King" test, because he nodded. "If you warriors *really* wish to send yourselves to an early doom, I won't stop you."

"We really don't wish that," Jordan said. I elbowed him in the ribs. "Ow!"

"Besides, you two especially might want to pay Diyu a visit." Sun Wukong's eyes were still trained on Ashley and Jordan. "Your father, and the other Demon Kings, often congregate there."

Ashley's and Jordan's cheeks had turned an ashen color, but I could tell the appeal of speaking to the Bull Demon King, their father, outweighed the fear of venturing into Diyu.

I wanted to go there, too. Ye Ye's message in *Restorative Potions* had told me I needed to find my ancestors and that they would give me an elixir to restore Ba's memories. Diyu was definitely the place for that. "Highest heights and lowest depths"—the "lowest depth" in Erlang Shen's riddle had to refer to the Underworld. Plus, there was still the mystery of those two other warriors on the quest, and it didn't look like we'd find them on this mountain. "How exactly do we get to Diyu?"

Sun Wukong pointed at the compass in my hand. "That compass will show you the way. After you arrive at the entrance, tell the first person you meet that you were sent by Sun Wukong, the Great Sage, Equal of Heaven. That'll guarantee you entrance."

"We'll return the Ruyi Jingu Bang to you," I said. "You'll see."

The Monkey King didn't respond. He returned to his throne and sat with his back to us, his body arranged into a meditation pose. I took that to mean we were dismissed.

"So," said Jordan with a dazed expression, "does someone want to explain to me what just happened?"

"We have to go to Diyu." Ashley tugged at the ends of her curly hair with her face scrunched up. "Do we even know where that is?"

"No, but I know how to find it." I raised the compass.

"Oh, no," Jordan said sourly. "It's thanks to your compass that we got into this mess in the first place. Why did it bring us *here*?"

"We're not in a mess," I insisted. "It's thanks to my compass that we unlocked part of the riddle. 'An old ally will return from the brink of death.' We'll find the Ruyi Jingu

Bang and use it to bring Sun Wukong back from the brink of death."

"Doesn't seem like he's on the brink of death," Jordan muttered. "The brink of a midlife crisis, maybe. Can gods have midlife crises? I'm not— Wait, where are you guys going?"

I hurried to catch up with Ashley, who was already heading back through the cave. The compass glowed and shuddered in my hand. The arrow spun around rapidly before settling to a stop just as I exited the waterfall.

Ashley threw the yuán onto the ground and yelled, "Faryn, the remote!"

I yanked it out of my pocket and clicked the button. The coin grew into a chariot, the two stone lions already pawing at the ground, as though itching to take flight once more.

"I know how to get to Diyu," I shouted as we all piled into the chariot. I pointed down and to our right, where the arrow was directing us.

"As if I'll listen to you," Ashley snapped.

"Don't you want to find our fathers?" I interjected.

That made Ashley fall silent. After a beat, her face scrunched up in confusion. "Wait. You said *our* fathers."

Oh. Oops. "Um . . ."

"Your father is a demon, too?" Jordan gasped.

"No! Ba's a warrior. He, um . . ." Well, there was no point hiding the truth from the siblings any longer, especially not if we could all help each other. We'd already come so far together. If we were going to successfully complete this quest, we had to trust each other. "Zhuang."

"What about Zhuang?" Ashley asked.

"He's my father. He left the Jade Society, and then he somehow lost his memories. Another reason we have to go to Diyu is—is to find my ancestors and get a memory-restoring elixir from them."

Jordan and Ashley wore twin expressions of shock on their faces. Their sibling resemblance had never been stronger.

"Whoa," said Jordan. "That's wack."

"So that's why you wanted to go on this quest. You just want to restore your father's memories," Ashley accused, her eyes flashing with anger. "This is why I said we shouldn't trust her, Jordan."

"That's not the only reason!" I protested. "Besides, don't you want to find your father, too? We can help each other save the world *and* be reunited with our fathers. We can't do either if we don't trust each other."

"What Faryn is saying makes a lot of sense, Ashley," Jordan pointed out. I shot him a relieved smile.

"You always side with her. Are you her brother or mine?" Ashley grumbled. She didn't look happy, but at least she wasn't taking a swing at me. "Fine," she said. "Do what you want. Just don't get in my way."

Without another complaint, Ashley urged the stone lions

off the bridge and down toward the earth. Jordan folded his arms across his chest and looked over the side of the vehicle, making loud sighing noises every few minutes to remind us that he wasn't happy with this plan.

My limbs ached. I knew I should get some rest, but sleep evaded me for a day and a half. Eventually, Jordan's sighs turned into snores. I tried not to be envious or do anything petty, like kick him awake. I think I showed remarkable self-restraint by letting him stay asleep.

Then my body jolted. A vision bloomed before my eyes. Different from the dreams I'd been having of Alex but no less jarring.

Faryn? Can you hear me?

Could it really be? *Ren?* I thought back. We hadn't even been apart that long, but after hearing his voice and sensing his presence, I suddenly missed him so much that my chest ached.

Ren sighed in relief. *Oh, thank the gods. I finally managed to reach you.*

How are we even able to communicate right now? I thought our connection was supposed to end after . . . you know . . . Alex became the Heaven Breaker.

There was that moment during the Duels, Ren reminded me. *I thought maybe we could connect again after that, but I haven't been able to reach you. The Dragon Kings cut off most of our communication with the outside world.*

Then how are you communicating with me right now?

There's this spot in one of the toilets that another dragon told me about, and— Wait, that's not the point. Faryn, I think I made a huge mistake. Coming here to the dragon palace, I mean.

What happened? Didn't you say the Dragon Kings would train you?

Yes—and they have.

In just three days? I thought, perplexed.

Time passes much differently at the dragon palace. I've learned so much, Faryn. More than I ever learned at crossbow lessons with Mr. Fan. Even though I couldn't see Ren, I could hear the excitement in his voice. *But it's come . . . at a price. The Dragon Kings want to recruit me into their army against the warriors.*

Recruit you?

A long pause. *Not recruit. More like . . . use. They want to use me as a tool for war.*

I shuddered. Those words sounded all too familiar. An unwelcome memory surfaced—Xi Wangmu during the Lunar New Year, telling Alex and me that because we were half–Jade Society warrior and had the blood of Turkish and Greek warriors in us, we'd been "engineered" to become stronger.

You've gotta get out of there, Ren, I urged. *I don't care what fancy new tricks the Dragon Kings have been teaching you. You can't let them use you like that.*

Ren heaved an exasperated sigh. *You think I don't know that? I've been trying to escape the palace, but I can't find a way out. They've got all us dragons locked up at night, guards sur-rounding all the exits, and I even have to be escorted to the bathroom. Do you know how humiliating it is to be escorted to the bath—?*

Ren's voice cut off in my head, as suddenly as though a switch had been flipped.

Ren? Are you still there? Are you okay?

They found me. His voice returned, full of panic and fear. *I gotta go. I'll try to reach out again—soon.*

Tell me where the palace is! I'll come find you.

No. Whatever you do, don't come. This is no place for a human warrior.

But—

The connection shut off. I awoke with a gasp. It took me a moment to gather my surroundings. I was in the chariot, under an early-evening sky, the sun setting over the horizon. Ashley was curled up asleep beside me, and Jordan had taken her place as the chariot driver.

I tried reaching out to Ren with my mind again but heard nothing. The silence in my head was deafening.

Where was Ren? Would he be okay? I hoped against hope that the Dragon Kings hadn't found and punished him—and that he'd be able to escape. I had to trust that he would. After all, this was Ren we were talking about. He'd been trained in martial arts from a young age.

Besides, it wasn't like I could drop my current mission and

go help Ren. I didn't even know how to find the Dragon Kings' palace.

I had to continue on the quest and trust that Ren would be strong and resourceful enough to make it out on his own.

"How long was I asleep?" I asked, raising my voice to be heard over the wind.

"Twelve hours," Jordan replied. "Must've been having some dream!"

I couldn't believe I'd slept for twelve hours. That meant five days and five nights had passed since we'd left the New Order. We should definitely be close to Diyu by now. My compass would be able to—

My hands were empty. I almost panicked, but then my gaze dropped down, and I saw that Ashley held my compass in her limp hand. I snatched it up, and it began to shudder and grow warm in my grip.

"Jordan—go down. We're almost there," I called out.

Our chariot hovered above the skyline of a red-pink dusk. From a distance, I recognized the Independence Hall and Museum of Art. There was no mistaking it. We were in Philadelphia.

As the chariot lowered, the buildings of Philadelphia's Chinatown came into sight, right over a great green-and-red archway. Night had fallen. The lantern-lit streets teemed with adults and children, the air filled with laughter and chatter.

"The entrance to Diyu must be somewhere around here," I shouted, staring at the compass in my hand. The arrow spun again, pointing off toward a row of shops on our right. "Keep your eyes peeled." So close. I was so close to my ancestors— and the memory-restoring elixir.

"What am I looking for?" Jordan yelled back.

Ashley stirred and sat up, blinking at me groggily. "Probably a dirty, run-down, evil-looking building. Teeming with major demon vibes."

The chariot drifted closer to the ground. We hovered above a black building with an all-too-familiar logo on it. The compass burned so hot in my palm, I almost dropped it.

"Found it! Panda Express," Jordan reported proudly.

"You think the entrance to Diyu is in a Panda Express?" Ashley raised her eyebrows.

I examined the compass. I held it up so everyone could see that it was pointing right at the restaurant building. "Hold on. You might be on to something."

"I hope this is the place," Jordan said wistfully, patting his stomach. "I'm hungry, too. We need some real food."

"Yeah, so why would we come to Panda Express?" I grumbled.

Jordan urged the stone lions down toward a landing on the street in front of the Panda Express, narrowly dodging oblivious pedestrians who were ambling on the street. I got out of the chariot and jabbed the remote to turn it back into a yuán. Then I stuffed the compass into my pocket, staring up at the tall, ugly, pagoda-shaped building.

"Man, I knew there was something awful about this restaurant chain," Ashley said as she joined me in front of the entrance. "And I'm not just talking about the orange chicken."

"I like the orange chicken," Jordan muttered.

I took a deep breath, as if that would somehow be enough to prepare me to enter Diyu. Then I pulled open the door and was instantly engulfed in a scented wave of fried, greasy, Americanized Chinese food. Yep. Made sense that the demons wanted an entrance to their world here.

Luckily, there was no one else in line. "Can I take your order?" the young cashier asked. His smile was strained, the mark of working in the fast-food industry for too long.

We were supposed to tell the first person we saw that Sun Wukong had sent us. I guess this poor college kid would have to do.

"We were sent by Sun Wukong, the Great Sage, Equal of Heaven, to journey into Diyu and retrieve the Ruyi Jingu Bang," I announced with as much authority as I could muster. A blond family eating at the nearest table looked up at me, startled. "Oh, and also I'd like to order the beef and broccoli."

"I want the Beijing beef," Ashley said quickly.

"Orange chicken for me," Jordan said.

I blushed as the college kid's jaw dropped in confusion. If the compass had led us to the wrong place, then we were going to look very stupid in about two seconds.

"Um . . . ," the cashier said, backing away, probably to do the smart thing and call the police on us. I guess we had the wrong guy after all. The cashier shook his head and mumbled, "Beef and broccoli, Beijing beef, and orange chicken. Got it."

I looked at Ashley and Jordan, who just shrugged. If nothing else, at least we'd get a greasy meal out of this place. I was dying to eat something other than Choco Pies and dried meat.

Our plates arrived quickly. My stomach growled in hunger. Even though I wasn't the biggest fan of Panda Express, I had to admit, the scent of beef and broccoli practically had me salivating. The three of us dug into our meals and possibly set a world record by finishing in about two minutes flat. When I looked up, the nearby blond family was gawking at us.

"Nothing to see here, colonizers," I snapped. They looked away quickly.

After we threw out our empty plates and napkins, we scanned the area for anything out of the ordinary, but no luck.

"Let's get out of here," Ashley suggested. "We're clearly in the wrong place. I mean, Panda Express? Everyone knows Chinese people don't come here."

A shadow loomed over our table. The cashier from earlier beckoned for us to follow him.

"This way," he said and waved us toward a room in the back.

I stared at Ashley, who was still glaring at me as if she thought I'd led us to the wrong place on purpose.

"We're not even sure we can trust that guy," she pointed out, not bothering to lower her voice.

Ashley wasn't *wrong*, but I didn't see another option. I shrugged. "If you want to search every building in this Chinatown to find Diyu, then be my guest." Then I marched after the young man, past a group of screaming children and harried-looking staff.

For a moment, I was afraid Ashley really was going to leave and take Jordan with her. But when I looked back, I found him dutifully trailing after me. Ashley brought up the rear, a guarded expression on her face. She darted her gaze from side to side nervously, as though she'd heard a report of rampaging rhinoceroses in the area.

"In here," said the cashier, waving us into a room in the back.

I entered. As my eyes adjusted to the dark, I frowned.

"There's nothing in here," protested Ashley.

The cashier stomped on the ground—one, two, three, four times. Then a huge crack formed beneath our feet in the middle of the floor.

"Safe travels," he called.

The three of us tumbled downward into the darkness.

CHAPTER

14

As I fell, a scream rang in my ears. I couldn't tell if it was my own or if it belonged to Ashley. I plummeted into the blackness, my stomach churning and threatening to leap into my throat.

I landed on soft grass after ages of falling. Beside me, Ashley was already on her feet, dusting herself off. No way was I gonna let her beat me. I stood up quickly, too.

"Ow," moaned Jordan from the ground. "Help me up?" He stretched his hand toward Ashley, who smacked it away. "Gee. Love you, too, sis."

We were in another cave. Stalactites hung high above our heads. At the exit looked to be the glimmer of a green river and bridge that went over it. I'd never been here before, but somehow, I knew exactly where we were: Diyu.

"Guys, we have to go that wa—" I started.

"This way! Follow me!" Ashley shoved past me and tore off toward the bridge.

Maybe someone should check if Ashley was secretly the god of thunder in disguise, because she was constantly stealing mine.

"This is so trippy," Jordan murmured as he took in our surroundings.

Ashley turned back and grabbed him by his sleeve, dragging him out of the cave. "Buckle up, gē. Things are about to get a whole lot trippier."

We headed toward the bridge, which was constructed out of huge gray stones and suspended in midair. It was held up by nothing I could see.

I couldn't help but shudder. The atmosphere felt full of creepy, dead things. I almost wanted to return to Panda Express. Almost. The urge to complete the quest, and be in the place where my ancestors were, propelled my feet forward.

We walked. And walked. And walked. The bridge seemed impossibly long. I couldn't see an end to the stretch of gray stones, but I knew my ancestors and the elixir lay somewhere beyond this bridge. That thought gave me the strength to keep going.

"Oh gods, whatever you do, don't look into the river," Jordan yelled in a high-pitched voice.

Of course, I looked down and instantly regretted it. The

murky green waters were filled with white skeletons. Some were whole bodies that must've been recently deceased. Some were just skulls and bones floating separately down the river. I thought I could hear the wails of long-dead souls echoing across the bridge.

"The Bridge of Helplessness," I blurted. Ye Ye had mentioned this bridge in his nice, cozy bedtime stories about the Underworld.

"Is *anything* down here alive?" Ashley asked, her voice trembling. For once, she wasn't oozing confidence. I couldn't decide if I was gleeful or terrified about what it meant for us all.

"Hurry up, slowpokes!" yelled Jordan from the other end of the bridge. I blinked. When had he gotten there? He waved his arms up and down, like he was trying to flag down a plane. "I'm gonna die of old age before you guys get over here."

"This would be the place to do it," Ashley retorted.

My eyes caught sight of figures looming out of the darkness, right behind Jordan. "Look out!" I shouted.

Jordan turned and screamed.

Even though common sense shouted for me to turn back, I ran toward him. A crowd of demons had surrounded Jordan. Some had purple fur, others scaly green skin; some were horned, and some had tall ears. The one thing they had in common was their shiny weapons, like pitchforks and spears, and their glares. Glares that said they'd like nothing better than to run us through with their weapons.

"Who are you, mortals?" snapped an ox-headed demon.

Jordan stumbled backward and almost ran into me.

Since it was clear he wasn't going to answer, I plastered a smile on my face and summoned all my remaining courage. "Sun Wukong sent us," I said, my voice miraculously steady. "The Great Sage, Equal of Heaven," I added, because I could practically hear the arrogant Monkey King scolding me for forgetting his full title.

The ox-head exchanged an indecipherable look with a horse-faced demon. Then they burst out laughing. Not exactly the reaction I'd hoped for.

"Sent here by that idiot monkey? Did you hear that, Horse-Face?" the ox-headed demon roared.

"Sure did, Ox-Head." Horse-Face chuckled. "'Great Sage, Equal of Heaven.' Pah!"

I didn't see what a pair of demons named Ox-Head and Horse-Face found so funny about Sun Wukong's name, but I decided not to point that out.

"We're on an urgent mission," I said, channeling my Oprah voice to sound more important. "Let us through, or . . . or— you'll regret it."

That only made the two demons and their friends howl with laughter.

"You sure showed them, Faryn," Ashley muttered.

"We can't let just anybody into Diyu," said Horse-Face. "Especially not a few upstart mortals. Go back to where you came from."

"Let the warriors through," commanded a female voice. "They're with me."

The demons murmured and parted a path down the middle of the group for someone to walk through. I thought for a moment that I was dreaming.

The approaching figure looked just like she had on the last day I'd seen her alive. She'd swept her long black hair up into a sleek high ponytail, and she wore faded jeans with an off-shoulder T-shirt. She still carried her sword. Even her glare was as sharp and penetrating as usual. Only difference was that her skin now gave off a slight glow, a sign that she was no longer mortal. Or maybe that she'd really upped her skin-care routine.

It hit me then—of the two warriors who were supposed to join us on the quest, one must've been her.

"Faryn Liu," Moli said, her lips twitching into a slight smile. Her eyes flickered coolly toward the other warriors. She wrinkled her nose. "And . . . some hobos."

"What? Hobos?" Ashley shrieked, looking affronted.

I couldn't believe it. Moli was here, right in front of me, looking even more vibrant than she had in life. The last time I'd seen my friend, she'd been lying on the ground after saving me from a falling chandelier at Peng Lai Island. I stared at Moli, certain that she'd disappear at any moment. "You're . . . you're . . . you're al—"

"I'm not alive," Moli interrupted. The light in her eyes appeared to dim.

"I was going to say, 'annoying,'" I lied.

Moli narrowed her eyes at me.

I added, "I—I didn't think we'd ever see each other again."

"Neither did I," Moli said. "To my relief." She smirked.

There was the Moli I remembered. I rolled my eyes, but I wasn't really upset. She was just teasing. We'd been through so much together during the Lunar New Year, after all, and Moli had even sacrificed her life to save me. I owed her my life.

Moli looked behind me. "Where's that annoying brother of yours?" She said the words casually, but the flush on her cheeks revealed her true feelings.

There was no doubt in my mind that no matter what Alex was up to in Heaven these days, he hadn't gotten over his first and longtime crush on Moli.

Or maybe he had. My brother had changed so much in the past year, I felt like I hardly knew him anymore. Maybe the new Alex had already forgotten Moli, just as easily as he'd forgotten Ba. Forgotten me.

"Alex is busy these days," I said shortly. "He's the Jade Emperor's new—"

"Heaven Breaker. I know."

I stared at Moli in disbelief. "You know?"

"I've heard all about what he's been doing up in Heaven." Moli didn't seem to want to talk about it any longer, because she turned to the demons gawking at her. She placed her hands on her hips and scowled at them. "Are you still here?"

"But, Moli," protested Ox-Head.

"That's Moli jiě jie to you," she snapped.

Ox-Head flinched and mumbled, "Yes . . . Moli jiě jie." It threw us a suspicious look. "Those ugly-looking children are mortal warriors."

"U-ugly-looking?" Jordan spluttered, looking affronted.

"They're not dead yet. King Yama wouldn't want—"

"These warriors are on a quest for some of the gods." Moli interrupted Ox-Head in a loud, authoritative voice that caused the demons to wince. "I wouldn't get in their way, lest you incur the gods' wrath."

Ox-Head and Horse-Face exchanged looks of terror. I guess the idea of angering Sun Wukong, Erlang Shen, Nezha, and Guanyin outweighed the guards' fear of King Yama, because they bowed their heads and stepped aside.

Moli tossed her hair over one shoulder and commanded, "Follow me."

She strutted away from the bridge. Hurrying after her, I tried to ignore the stares of Ox-Head, Horse-Face, and the other demons guarding the bridge. When I looked back, they followed after us, like our own personal, unwanted posse of demon guards.

"So, Jade Society warrior," Ashley hissed, grabbing my shoulder. "Who *is* that girl?"

I shrugged her off. "That's Moli. She accompanied me on my first quest during the Lunar New Year."

Jordan popped up on my other side. "Is Moli . . . ?" He gesticulated wildly through the air with his hands. "You know . . ."

"Dead?" I supplied flatly. "Yeah."

"I can hear everything you're saying," Moli shouted back. "And yes, I *am* dead." She said "dead" the way hipsters might say "vegan," like it was a lifestyle she'd proudly chosen. "All right. Stop here."

We halted in front of a huge black gate. The two doorknobs were shaped in the faces of demons. In the flickering orange-red light of the torches against the wall, the faces appeared to leer at us.

Moli banged the knocker against the door. One, two, three, four times. The gates slowly creaked open.

When no one moved, Moli threw us an exasperated look. "Well? We don't have all day."

I squared my shoulders. Then I stepped forward and followed her through the entrance deeper into the Underworld.

CHAPTER

15

The gates slammed down behind us with an echoing finality. There was no turning back now. We'd either make it out of Diyu with Sun Wukong's legendary weapon . . . or we'd stay here forever, fail the quest, and then the world would go kaput.

No pressure or anything.

We'd entered a huge room with a ceiling that seemed to open straight up into the sky, which was dark and full of stars. The chatter of ghosts filled the space. A line of recently dead people stretched on for as far as I could see.

"Where are we?" I murmured. "Where's King Yama?"

"He's at the front of the line, of course," Moli explained patiently.

"You mean we have to wait in this line to see him?" Ashley said. "What'll that take, a couple of centuries? We'll be *really* dead by the time we get up there!" She paused and squinted at Moli. "Why aren't you in line?"

"I already went through this line." Moli puffed out her chest. "King Yama offered to turn me into a deity for my self-less and heroic actions in life. I turned him down."

"You *what*?" Jordan and Ashley said at once.

"I turned him down."

"But why?" I asked. That didn't seem very Moli-like at all. The Moli I knew always acted like everyone should be falling at her feet in worship anyway. I had a hard time picturing her not jumping at the chance to be deified.

A shadow crossed Moli's face. In the dim light of the torch flames, her expression was fiercer than ever. "You've seen the state of Heaven these days. People are forgetting the lesser deities, and even the popular ones are less power-ful than before. I didn't want to become a deity just to be forgotten."

I guess Moli had a point. When we'd gone to Peng Lai Island for the Jade Emperor's Lunar New Year celebration, the minor deities had held a concert, a chūn jié wǎn huì, because they hadn't been invited to his grand feast. I'd witnessed first-hand how easily so many of the deities had been forgotten and trampled beneath the feet of the nián, the monstrous demon that had nearly brought down the whole island.

"Now I'm one of King Yama's assistants. I don't mind," Moli said with a shrug. She flashed a smile, a wicked gleam in her eye. "I boss around ghosts all day, and I even get paid vacations, sick leave, and health care."

"What the heck?" Jordan muttered. "Where do I sign up for this gig?"

A bearded man tried to cut in front of us. Without missing a beat, Moli grabbed his other arm and snarled, "You! Back of the line."

As the dead man slunk away, Moli flicked a spot of dust off her shoulder. I could picture her doing this for the rest of eternity—and even enjoying it. I mean, in just the twelve years that she'd lived at the Jade Society, she'd thoroughly enjoyed bossing the heck out of the rest of us.

"Follow me," Moli commanded, waving us toward her as she moved swiftly past the line of dead people.

"You're sure we can cut this line?" Jordan asked. He nervously eyed a group of men glaring daggers at him. The fact that they were headless and holding their heads in their hands, like they were ready to chuck them at us at any moment, made these guys even more intimidating.

"I just told you, I'm one of King Yama's assistants," Moli said in an exasperated voice. "You're with me. Of course you can cut the line."

"This girl is so . . . cool," Ashley said admiringly. "Way cooler than you, Faryn."

"Wow. Thanks."

As we followed Moli, the line seemed to stretch on forever.

Young and old, rich and poor, the dead chatted among themselves. Some called greetings to one another. They complained when we moved past but stopped when they caught sight of Moli. Paintings of bamboo covered the walls, an oddly pretty and serene backdrop to the dead who walked through the halls.

After what felt like an eternity, we finally reached the front of the line. There, looming over a huge desk that towered with books and loose pages, sat King Yama himself.

"Who dares disturb my line?" boomed the god of Diyu. Slowly, he turned his gaze down toward us.

I did my best not to freak out, but I couldn't stifle a small gasp. No offense to the god of the Underworld, but he definitely wasn't going to be called up for any modeling gigs anytime soon. King Yama's long black beard trailed from his earlobes to his desk. He wore a large gold hat bigger than his face. King Yama glowered at us, his thick, bushy black eyebrows moving closer together. The bit of skin on his face that wasn't covered in hair turned red.

"More warriors?" King Yama roared. "Why can't you meddling fools stay on Earth where you belong? Do you wish to be dead? I can easily have that arranged." He raised a huge book from the top of the tall stack on his desk. "See this? Once I find your names and stamp the word 'sǐ' over them, you can join this line for real. Until then—stay out!"

I swallowed hard and did my best to keep staring right into King Yama's beady purple eyes.

"Please, King Yama. They're with me," Moli piped up, interrupting the tense atmosphere.

Slowly, King Yama relaxed his angry stance. He lowered his book and fixed Moli with a bemused look. "With you, Moli? Why are these children with you?"

"They're on a quest for some of the gods," Moli explained.

"But why do you care?" King Yama scratched his ear, gazing at her in bafflement. "You don't care about anyone. You're one of the rudest, most self-centered, and outrageous people I've ever met. That's why I hired you."

Moli stood up taller, her cheeks turning pink with pleasure. "They're my friends," she declared. "Well, one friend, plus a couple of bums."

"In what way are we bums?" Ashley yelled. "I take back what I said about you being cool."

"I need a vacation," King Yama muttered under his breath. "Can't believe my Hawaii trip is still two centuries away." In a louder voice, he said, "Well, since Moli is one of my best employees, I'll humor you warriors. What business do you have with me, King Yama, god of the Underworld?"

I took a deep breath and straightened my shoulders. If I looked more warrior-like, maybe King Yama would take us seriously, hand us what we were looking for, and send us off on our merry way.

Even without Fenghuang and the title of Heaven Breaker with me, I was Faryn Liu, warrior who'd fought demons and gods—and lived. I'd even stood up to the Monkey King. I shouldn't be scared of some guy in serious need of seeing a barber.

"We have come to retrieve the Ruyi Jingu Bang," I said.

"The fate of the world depends on it," Jordan added. A silly smile rose to his face. "Man, I've always wanted to say that line."

"The Ruyi Jingu Bang? The weapon belonging to that monkey Sun Wukong?" King Yama threw his head back and laughed, god-speak for "heck no." "That weapon is here in Diyu, yes. I confiscated it from that idiot Demon King who brought it here, and it's now in the process of being reincarnated."

"Reincarnated? How can a stick be reincarnated?" Ashley scoffed.

King Yama glowered. "Anything can be reincarnated, especially someone or something with a strong record for committing selfless and heroic acts. The Ruyi Jingu Bang has slain 14,587 demons. In its next life, the weapon will have enough karma to become a person."

"Jeez," Jordan said. "I thought my record of five demons was pretty solid."

"Four and a half," Ashley corrected under her breath. "I had to help you with that last one, remember?"

"But we can't wait for the Ruyi Jingu Bang to be reincarnated into a person," I protested. "Sun Wukong needs it now. *We* need it now."

"Don't mention that foul monkey's name in my presence again!" growled King Yama, covering his ears with his hands. "I still haven't forgiven that upstart for coming down here, trashing the place, and erasing his name out of my book of the dead centuries ago." King Yama shuddered, as though reliving a horrible memory. "You're lucky I don't toss you into the Mountain of Flames right this moment."

I gulped. Mountain of Flames? That didn't sound promising.

The ghosts' complaints of us holding up the line grew louder. King Yama's face reddened. "All right, all right!" He pointed a stubby, dirty finger at us. "I don't know why there've been so many annoying mortal warriors visiting me today when they aren't even dead, and I don't care."

Something about King Yama's words struck me as odd. "What do you mean, 'so many'?" I asked. "There have been more?"

"Another boy, about your age. Messy hair. Very quiet and annoying. I let him in because, frankly, he's well on his way to death already."

My heart leapt in my throat. A quiet, messy-haired boy around my age. Alex? Or Ren? But what would either of them be doing all the way out here?

Whoever it was, I knew he had to be the fifth warrior mentioned in Erlang Shen's riddle.

Moli's eyes met mine. Her expression was blank. The

balloon of hope that had swelled in my chest quickly popped. If Ren were here, she would know. Wouldn't she?

"If you really wish to enter the realms of Diyu to retrieve the Ruyi Jingu Bang—though I warn you, it's a useless endeavor—I won't stop you," King Yama said. "But beware, warriors. Diyu may be emptier than usual during the Hungry Ghost Festival, but it is no less fearsome. Even I don't know what you might face in these courts."

"Can't you give us a hint?" Ashley asked.

But King Yama had turned back to his line. The message was clear. From here on out, he'd give us no help.

"This way." Moli waved us toward the left. "I'll be your guide. I know the ins and outs of Diyu, all eighteen levels."

"There are eighteen levels?" Ashley groaned.

"Yes, and they're constantly shifting. My orientation tour lasted a whole month."

Jordan's face drained of color. "Great. We're gonna be trapped here forever, guys. My great-grandkids will be trapped here!"

"Lead the way," I told Moli quickly. The faster we were out of here, the better.

Just six months ago, Moli probably would've made a snarky retort rather than listen to me. But instead, she just nodded and began walking.

Relief flooded me. I almost wanted to tell Moli that being dead had done wonders for her personality. But I figured saying, "Hey, I like you better now that you're dead!" might be a bit insensitive.

Together, the four of us headed out a side door of King Yama's chambers. The great golden doors slammed behind us, and we tumbled out into a great forest filled with trees, lit by the moonlight and stars high above.

There was only one path ahead of us now: forward.

CHAPTER

16

On the plus side," Jordan said as we trekked through the darkness of the Underworld, "it's the Hungry Ghost Festival. That means most of the evil ghosts have left Diyu to haunt Earth. So we probably won't die miserable deaths down here . . . right, guys? Guys?"

I wanted to say yes, but truth was, I didn't have a clue. Something told me that Diyu was dangerous through all the seasons and days of the year. Besides, my mind was preoccupied with what King Yama had said about other warriors—specifically, one other warrior who'd come down here.

Ren's and my shaky telepathic connection had gone silent since I'd entered the Underworld. Was he doing well? Had he managed to escape the Dragon Kings or made any progress toward finding his mother?

"Earth to Faryn?" Moli waved in front of my face. "You

heard what King Yama said just now, didn't you? You think it means . . . ?"

"That Ren is down here?" I finished. "Wouldn't you know?"

"Probably," Moli admitted, "but I'm just one spirit. I can't sense everyone who enters or leaves Diyu. Why isn't Ren with you guys, anyway? Did he get sick of looking at your face and take off?"

I frowned. "No. Ren had . . . important business to attend to with the Dragon Kings—like getting the heck away from them."

"The Dragon Kings," Moli mused. "They haven't chosen a side yet, have they?"

"I think they have," I said, gulping. "That's why Ren is trying to get away from them."

"Oh. In that case, we'd better hope King Yama was talking about Ren earlier," Moli said. Even though she was doing her best to give off her usual cool, unconcerned attitude, I could tell that she was bothered by this bit of news. Losing the Dragon Kings to the Jade Emperor would be a massive blow to our manpower.

I realized I'd fallen way behind the others, including Moli, while I was lost in thought. *Snap out of it.* I caught up to the group just in time for Moli's Great Things About Me speech.

"I'm Moli. I lived in the Jade Society with Faryn, and I taught her everything she knows. It's thanks to me that we were able to complete the quest of the Lunar New Year."

"That is false," I said loudly. But the others gazed at Moli with wide-eyed, enraptured respect. Some things never changed.

"I'm Ashley, and this is Jordan. We're from the New Order." Ashley pointed to her brother, who frowned at her. "Yes, I speak for us both. Don't talk to him unless you want to lose some brain cells." Moli's eyes flickered over to Jordan, and she arched an eyebrow and nodded.

"Hey," protested Jordan.

"Feel free to ask me any questions about the Underworld," Moli continued.

"I do have . . . one question." Ashley hesitated. "One of our . . . friends died in battle earlier this year. Xiong Jinyu. Do you know where he might be?"

"Xiong Jinyu? That name doesn't ring a bell." Moli shook her head. "If he died in battle, he could be anywhere. If it was a particularly honorable death, he may even have already ascended to Heaven."

"Oh. Okay." Ashley's shoulders slumped. Jordan patted her back. I tightened my grip around my sword—*Jinyu's* sword. I couldn't decide if I was disappointed or relieved that we probably wouldn't run into him down here. If Jinyu saw me, the girl he'd died for, holding his sword—would he be pleased or angry?

We moved past the trees and into a garden pavilion filled with flowers of all different colors. A gentle breeze blew around us. In the garden, there was a small house and a clean river that looked nothing like the one we'd crossed on the Bridge of Helplessness.

"Where are we?" Jordan marveled at the sights around us.

"Some kind of garden." Ashley bent down to pick up a white flower.

"Don't touch that," Moli snapped. Ashley froze, her finger millimeters from a petal. "Don't you remember what King Yama said? This place is dangerous, especially right now, during the Hungry Ghost Festival. You never know what might be lurking—" Moli paused. "Did you hear that?"

I shook my head. "I didn't hear anything."

"Listen," she insisted.

I strained my ears. After a moment of silence, I heard it—the rustling of leaves and then a crash as something large barreled through the garden.

Ashley screamed. Jordan let out a strangled cry and drew his sword. I drew mine, too, although my fingers shook.

Demons. A whole horde in the distance charged straight toward us. Something told me they weren't rushing to welcome us to Diyu with a big group hug.

"Guards!" Moli roared, cupping her hands around her mouth to project her voice. "Guards, where are you? Come protect me!"

"And us!" Jordan squeaked.

"I thought the hungry ghosts were all headed up to Earth,"

Ashley protested in a small, high-pitched voice. "Why are there still so many here?"

Moli shook her head. "After the demons failed to invade Earth during the Lunar New Year, many were killed and sent back down to the Underworld. What you're seeing now is a group of them, um, reformulating. All at once."

"All . . . at . . . once . . . ?" Jordan repeated in a faint voice. His face had drained of color.

"Yes, but don't panic," Moli said.

"What do you mean, 'don't panic'? There are, like, a hundred demons! Charging right at us!" Jordan yelled.

"They must've gotten loose, but the guards will catch them. And they'll listen to me. They have to." Moli stood up tall and called out in an authoritative voice, "I'm one of King Yama's assistants." Her eyes flashed. Like, literally flashed with golden light. "Back off, demons. The warriors are with me."

I guess Moli wasn't as popular in the Underworld as she thought, because the demons kept charging. There were still no guards in sight. The demons were so close that I could make out their features—there were red-skinned demons, blue-skinned demons, green-skinned demons shaped like lizards. Creatures straight out of a warrior's worst nightmares, all charging toward us.

I gulped, steadying my grip on my sword handle. Looked like we'd have to fight this one out. I'd defeated demons in the past. I could do it again, no problem. Right?

"Run!" Moli yelled.

If we were facing twenty demons, I probably would've insisted that we stand our ground and fight. Warrior's honor. Except we weren't facing twenty demons. More like two hundred. There was no way I—or any warrior, for that matter—could take that many down. With Fenghuang, maybe, but not with just a regular sword.

So I ran.

"This way!" Moli pointed off to the left, toward a huge black mountain in the distance that spurted bright red-orange lava.

"You want us to go *there*?" Ashley demanded. "Toward that volcano thingy?"

"If you don't want to turn into demon lunch, then our best bet is to head to the volcano thingy—I mean, the Mountain of Flames!"

That was enough to convince me to follow Moli. We sprinted across the moonlit grass. My heart hammered. I tried to focus on the path ahead of me, not the demons on my heels. As we leapt over rocks and dodged tree branches, I was immensely grateful for the New Order insisting on those torturous five AM jogs. They'd really raised my stamina to "fleeing at top speed from bloodthirsty demons" levels.

When we reached the end of the forest, the sounds of demons shrieking and crashing through undergrowth disappeared. I chanced a glance behind me. There were no demons in sight.

"Think we . . . lost them . . . ?" Ashley panted, wiping a sheen of sweat off her forehead.

Moli was the only one not bent over, wheezing and out of breath. "That's strange." She sounded almost disappointed. "Why did they stop chasing us?"

"I'm not complaining," Jordan said with a shudder.

As I straightened, I saw a flash of white. *Demon.* "They're still here!"

I swung my sword in an arc—but instead of slicing through demon flesh, my sword clashed against steel. Another sword.

"Faryn?" came the sound of a startled but familiar voice.

I almost dropped my sword in shock. White hair, one green eye, and one black eye. I couldn't believe it. He was actually here. "R . . . Ren?"

We'd been apart for only five days, yet it felt like several months. I'd missed him. Judging by the smile that rose to Ren's face, he felt the same.

I threw my arms around Ren. "You didn't die in the Dragon Kings' realm!"

"I did not," he agreed.

"How did you escape?"

Ren winced. "Long story. I'll tell you later. We should focus on getting out of Diyu first."

Moli cleared her throat. "All right, break it up, you love-birds. We're on a tight deadline, remember?"

Suddenly self-conscious, I stopped hugging Ren and stepped

back. Ren shuffled his feet, a red flush rising up his neck. Diyu felt too hot—and we weren't even at the Mountain of Flames yet.

"What the heck are *you* doing here?" Moli asked Ren.

"Good to see you, too."

"Yeah, yeah." Moli rolled her eyes. "Glad to see you, punk. Now, answer the question."

"It's . . . complicated." Ren sighed. "I'm just glad I managed to find you all."

"And how exactly did you find us?" I asked.

"I dunno. When I was at the Dragon Kings' palace, I saw this vision of you guys in the Underworld. Someone must've showed it to me in my dreams. Anyway, I just had a feeling in my gut that I should be here, too. Plus, I didn't know where else to go to avoid the Dragon Kings." Ren shrugged, his expression morphing into one of slight confusion. "Strange that I dreamed about you, right?"

My sword handle grew warm, as though in agreement. "Huh. Yeah. Strange."

"More importantly, Moli—you're a-alive?" Ren spluttered, no doubt taking in the fact that she was glowing. "Wait, no, you're not quite . . ."

"I'm still dead, thank you," Moli said shortly. "Very, very dead." She'd steered away from the jagged black rocks that made up the base of the Mountain of Flames. "If you two don't want to die as well, save all your lovey-dovey talk for after we're in the clear. Those demons might still be behind us!"

Ren's ears turned bright red. "Th-there's nothing lovey-dovey about this!"

My own face was flaming, but Moli was right, at least about the demons. This wasn't the spot to be catching up with old friends, even if old friends had popped up like daisies out of nowhere in the middle of the Underworld.

We needed to finish this as quickly as possible. Find the Ruyi Jingu Bang, find my ancestors and the memory-restoring elixir, get out of Diyu, and return to Sun Wukong before the end of the Hungry Ghost Festival.

"Hey," Ashley greeted Ren. "Haven't seen you since before we left the New Order. Where ya been?"

"Uh . . . here and there," Ren said evasively.

"You missed a lot of cool stuff," Jordan informed him. "We almost died a couple of times, I ate some orange chicken, and look—I grew my first bit of stubble!" He rubbed his chin and grinned at Ren.

Ren squinted. "I don't see anything."

"You gotta take a closer look than that, dude," Jordan grumbled.

"Where're we headed now?" I called to Moli over the others' chatter.

"Youdu," she shouted without turning back to look at me. "That's the capital of Diyu. It's this huge walled city where the

Ruyi Jingu Bang is being held. I've seen it. Once we get to Youdu, we need to find the Last Glance to Home Tower."

A huge walled city and a giant, ominous-sounding tower. That would be pretty hard to miss. In theory. "How do we get there?"

"Um . . . not sure. Youdu's location changes, but as long as we keep following the moon, we'll be able to find it." Moli pointed toward where the moon hung high above us, looking like it wasn't in any particular direction.

Of course. Nothing would ever be that easy for a warrior on a quest, especially not in the Underworld's mazelike setup.

We approached another mountain. This one appeared to be filled not with lava but with sharp silver objects.

"Are those knives?" Jordan gasped.

"It's the Mountain of Knives," Moli said gravely. "Sinners who have killed sentient beings with knives are trapped walking up and down it forever."

I shuddered, turning away from the sight of miserable-looking groups of men and women traipsing up and down the mountain. Beside me, Ren was turning green. For a startled moment, I thought he was turning into a dragon like he had several times during our quest of the Lunar New Year, but then I realized he was probably green-faced from the sight of the grisly mountain.

"What was it like, being at the palace?" I asked Ren.

Ren ran a hand through his white hair. "It was . . . amazing, at first. It took me only half a day by taxi to find the entrance to the underwater palace of the Dragon King of the Center Sea, and then once I did, I was able to swim and breathe underwater. It's hard to explain. I just . . . knew where to go and what to do, you know?"

I nodded like I understood, even though I couldn't even navigate Manhattan's Chinatown without Google Maps.

"So many dragons." Ren's face lit up. "Some were even like me. Half-dragon, half-warrior. We trained for eight hours every day, and we feasted on all kinds of fish at night. I almost didn't want to leave. Except . . . I got bad vibes. Not from the other dragons—from the Dragon Kings. They . . . well, at first they were divided on which side to support, but they had a meeting to make it official." His shoulders slumped. "They're going to stand by the Jade Emperor."

"Oh." I was disappointed but not surprised. The Dragon Kings answered to the Jade Emperor, after all.

"Yeah. Plus, my mother wasn't there, and I still want to find her." Ren shrugged with forced nonchalance.

"I'm sorry."

"It's okay. I didn't *really* think she'd be there," Ren said with a soft, sad smile. "Anyway, then I had that vision about you all, plus I wanted to come here . . . to get some closure about—about my mother. I'm pretty sure now that . . . that she's . . ." Ren's eyes welled up, and he turned away.

I could fill in the blanks myself. Any logical person would

conclude that, since Cindy You hadn't been seen or heard from since before the Lunar New Year, she was dead.

I put my hand on Ren's shoulder. "I'm sure we'll find your mother," I whispered. *Maybe mine, too.* My head was still swimming with heavy thoughts when I heard a high-pitched scream.

CHAPTER

17

The scream belonged to Ashley. "Look!"

We'd moved away from the base of the Mountain of Knives, but the Underworld seemed to have shifted while I'd been talking to Ren and not paying attention to my surroundings. We stopped in front of a huge, glassy building with double doors. It didn't look particularly dangerous from the outside, but I was certain there was something terrible on the inside, like fire-breathing demons or green-bean casserole.

"It's the Chamber of Mirrors," Moli said in a hushed voice. She backed away from the building.

I wasn't sure why she was so freaked out. "That doesn't sound so bad. Much better than Mountain of Flames."

"Or Mountain of Knives." Ren cringed.

"You don't understand. The Chamber of Mirrors messes with your mind." The petrified expression on Moli's face was so intense that I got the feeling she was speaking from personal experience. "It shows sinners their crimes, their regrets, their deepest fears . . ." She shuddered. "It shows them their true selves."

I had no idea what that meant. Would the Chamber of Mirrors show that pimple I'd hidden so painstakingly with concealer? I looked at Ren. He shrugged.

"Fine. We'll just avoid the Chamber of Mirrors, then," Jordan said. "Piece of moon cake." He stepped around the building. As we all followed him, I heard a low growl come from off to my left. I turned—and suppressed a scream.

Demons. At least ten had snuck up on us, and now the multicolored, snarling beasts were fast approaching with pointy, lethal-looking weapons in their hands.

Drawing my sword, I looked right. Even more demons poured in from that side. We were surrounded.

"Um . . . guys?" Jordan said. "H-how 'bout that Ch-Chamber of Mirrors?"

"Sounds good to me!" Ashley yelled, already sprinting for the doors.

The demons lunged at once with a horrific collective shriek. Ren, Moli, and I kept the wave of demons at bay as the siblings headed for the building.

I sliced the first demon clean through its midriff and kicked a second one in its chest. Out of the corner of my eye, I saw a third demon swipe at me with its sharp claws.

"Faryn!" Ren grunted.

I ducked at the last moment. My heart pattered with fear at the air swishing above my head.

As if giving me strength, warmth traveled from my sword down to my fingertips. My weapon lightened and vibrated until it felt like an extension of my body. With grace that I didn't even know I possessed, I drove the point of my sword upward into the demon's chest. It wailed, and with a puff of dust and smoke, it disappeared.

"Ew." I coughed, waving the particles away from my face.

Moli yelled, "Run, Faryn! Ren! And, uh . . . what's-your-face!"

"My name is Jordan!" shrieked Jordan.

Lunging blindly with my sword, I managed to connect with demon skin as I turned toward the sound of Jordan's voice. He was holding open the door to the Chamber of Mirrors and waving wildly at us.

I didn't check to see how many demons I'd managed to defeat or how many more were hot on our heels. Sprinting faster than I ever had before, even to the dumpling table during the Lunar New Year, I followed Moli into the Chamber of Mirrors.

Jordan ducked in behind me and slammed the door shut. And not a moment too soon. A split second later, the demons collided into the door with a barrage of thumps.

"That was . . . too close . . . ," Ren panted.

"No . . . kidding . . ." I gulped for air, waiting for my eyes to adjust to the darkness. Only now that we were out of the way of immediate danger did I realize my right arm was throbbing in pain. Gritting my teeth, I dabbed at my arm gingerly. My hand came away wet and sticky with blood. One of the demons must have gotten a good swipe at me after all.

"It's so dark in here," Ashley murmured.

"This is the Underworld. It's dark everywhere, in case you hadn't noticed," Jordan said.

I could just barely make out the outlines of my friends, as well as the glimmer of something shiny deeper within the building—the mirrors.

Moli drew in ragged breaths.

"You okay?" I asked.

"F-fine," she stammered. "Just . . . bad memories. Be careful, okay? This place can be even more dangerous than the other places we've seen."

"Whoa, guys, come here! These mirrors are *wild*," Jordan called, his voice ringing in the room. "Ashley, I see everyone from the New Order! There's Xiong, Ah Qiao, and . . ."

"What? That's impossible." Ashley whirled around and darted after her brother.

"The mirror is tricking you! Those people in it aren't real," Moli yelled. "The mirror is just showing your deepest fears and regrets."

I hesitated but then followed the siblings toward the room of mirrors. Despite Moli's warning ringing in my ear, a glimmer of hope blossomed inside my chest. If Ashley and Jordan could see the New Order, did that mean that when I looked in the mirrors, I would see the Jade Society? Or better yet, my father? Ye Ye? Alex?

I rushed to the mirrors, almost tripping in my excitement. At last, I might know the truth about Liu Bo—why he'd left Alex and me and never returned. Why he'd lost his memories. Maybe I'd learn how Ye Ye and Alex were doing up in Heaven with the threat of war still on the horizon.

I stepped in front of the closest mirror. Its dark, shiny surface gleamed, showing only my jagged reflection, my wide, curious eyes.

Then the surface shimmered and . . . changed.

What the mirror showed me wasn't Ba, or Ye Ye, or Alex. A shadowy image slowly took form out of darkness and smoke. As the details solidified, I found myself gazing upon . . . a woman.

She had curly brown hair that spilled over her shoulders and kind light-brown eyes, framed with thick lashes. There was a small, sad smile on her lips.

I'd never seen her before in real life, but I *knew* her. I knew her like I knew how to breathe.

"Faryn." The woman whispered my name as if it were the most precious gem in the world. "How you've grown."

I blinked, but that didn't stop the tears from sliding down my cheeks. The sight of a small, familiar photograph swam before my vision—the only photograph I owned of this woman. How many times had I gazed upon it, hoping for this woman to step out of the picture and back into my life? How often had I imagined the warmth of her smile and embrace?

"Mom?" I choked out.

My mother's smile grew wobbly. Tears slid down her cheeks as she nodded. "I've been watching over you every day from the Underworld, Faryn. Every day since my soul . . . departed Earth." She reached out a hand as if to touch the surface of the mirror. I did the same, extending my fingers to push against the cool surface.

But just as our fingers would have met, my mother's hand fell away. She flinched and turned behind her, as though she'd heard something. As far as I could tell, there was nothing there except darkness.

"I have to go," my mother said in a tremulous voice as she backed away.

"What? No!" Desperately, I clawed at the mirror with my fingernails. I couldn't even manage to scratch the glass, much less pull my mother back toward me. "Y-you can't leave me. Not again. Please!"

"I'm sorry. They're making me . . ." The image of my mother began shimmering. Disappearing. "Look for me, Faryn! I'm still in the Underworld. We can still . . ."

"Who's making you go? Why? Where can I find you in the Underworld? Mom!"

I banged my fists against the mirror, but it was no use. My mother's form turned back into shadow and smoke and then vanished altogether. I was so stunned and shattered by what had happened that I didn't even manage to react before another shape took hers.

This figure was even more familiar. I recognized it instantly, and my heart lurched in my throat. All thoughts of my mother vanished from my head, at least for the moment.

"Alex?"

My brother looked like he'd aged a couple of years in the months we'd been apart. Sure, I'd seen him in dreams, but not up close. Only now could I appreciate how different Alex looked. He'd gotten his messy brown hair cut shorter than I'd ever seen it. His forehead was creased with the wrinkle lines of his no-nonsense frown. He seemed taller and more mature than before—but also more tired, with dark circles under his eyes. The big sister in me couldn't help but worry. Had Alex not been sleeping well?

In his right hand, he held the glowing golden spear that had helped me slay countless demons on our first quest. Fenghuang.

I blinked rapidly to clear my eyes. I wouldn't cry in front of Alex. I wouldn't show him any weakness. I wanted him to realize that in the time that we'd gone our separate ways, I, his older sister, Faryn, had been *thriving* without him, thank you.

You haven't been, though, a voice whispered in the back of my head. *You've been absolutely miserable.*

Alex broke the silence. "You should stop this senseless quest and go home right now," he sneered. "Diyu is a maze of endless levels, filled with torture and doom at every turn. Mortal warriors like you couldn't possibly navigate it, much less track down and retrieve a mythical weapon like the Ruyi Jingu Bang."

"Oh yeah?" I countered, puffing out my chest. "Watch me."

"You will fail," Alex continued as if I hadn't spoken. The deadly certainty in his voice sent chills down my spine. "You will fail, and when you do, you won't just bring down yourself. You'll bring down everyone who came on the quest with you—Ashley, Jordan, Moli, and Ren." When he said Moli's name, my brother's eyes dimmed with sadness.

There were a million things I wanted to say to Alex. I blurted out, "You don't look good." And then I added, "Come back to our side, Alex. Heaven hasn't been treating you well. You belong here with us." *With me,* I thought but didn't say. "I . . . I had dreams. Visions, really. The Jade Emperor, he—he *threatened* you."

Alex's eyes widened with shock, but then the surprise faded away so quickly that I wasn't sure I hadn't just imagined it. Alex pointed the glowing white tip of Fenghuang at me. The glare in his eyes was accusatory. "Heaven has treated me better than the Jade Society ever did. The Jade Emperor has been nothing short of fantastic to me. You're speaking non-sense, Faryn."

"Are . . . are you sure?" Had I been wrong? Had those visions been just dreams after all? Or was Alex bluffing? Why had those dreams felt so *real* to me?

"Of course I'm sure. If anything, you should come over to our side, sister." Something like vulnerability flashed on Alex's face but was replaced with steely coldness. "You should worry about yourself, not me. This time, when you fail the quest, you'll bring down the whole world with you."

"I'm not going to fail!" Hurt and fury spiked inside me. Even though I knew there was no point in getting riled up at an image of Alex in a mirror, I couldn't help it. He looked so *real*. And the words he was saying were so hurtful.

You succeeded in your first quest, I reminded myself. *You can succeed again.*

I turned away from the mirror. But there Alex was again, reflected in a different mirror. I whirled around in a circle, my mind humming with panic. There was an Alex in every mirror. Everywhere I looked.

This was a nightmare I couldn't escape.

Alex's sneer returned, twisting his face until it didn't look like my brother's face anymore but rather a stranger's. A demon's. "Ask yourself why you're on this quest, Faryn." His voice echoed throughout the room. "Why do you care for the warriors of the New Order, or the Jade Society, or anyone else?"

"I care because I'm not heartless and selfish like you!"

"Heartless? Selfish?" Alex spat out each word like it had left a foul taste in his mouth. "I'm giving back to the world what it's given to me—nothing. Face it, Faryn. We were abandoned from birth, first by our mother, then by our father. We've never fit in anywhere, and nobody has ever really wanted us to. We don't even fit in with each other."

"Wh-what do you mean?"

"Have you forgotten? I'm not related to you by blood. We're practically strangers. And I don't need you to look out for me, ever."

I pressed my hands over my ears, as if that would drown out Alex's voice. "Take that back!"

"Nobody has ever wanted either of us," Alex continued. "You want proof? I'll show you."

The images of Alex had vanished on the mirrors. Standing there instead was Ba's doppelgänger in the New Order, Zhuang. He stared back at me with a harsh look on his face.

"B-Ba?"

"Faryn," he said in a voice devoid of any warmth.

He remembered. My father remembered me. Did that mean I no longer had to restore his memory? "Ba—"

"Call me Liu Bo," my father interrupted. "Don't call me Ba. You don't have a father. He abandoned you many years ago."

"No," I whispered, falling to my knees against the cold

stone floor. "You—my father—never abandoned me. You . . . you left to find . . . Peng Lai Island."

"Look how pathetic you are," Ba sneered. "You couldn't save your friend Moli, even though she laid down her life for you. You couldn't convince your own brother, Alex, to stay on the side of humanity. Your uselessness caused the deaths of Jinyu and many other warriors across the nation."

Each word was like a punch to the gut. I couldn't breathe. "Ba—"

"That's why you failed your mission to find me during the Lunar New Year. That's why you will never find me, Faryn Liu. I don't want to be found by you. You will never be good enough to be a warrior, much less *my* daughter."

Then Ba vanished.

Alex popped up in his place. "See? That's all the reason you need to turn back from this quest and join my side as we wipe out the rest of the warriors and humans. We were abandoned, Faryn. You heard it from our father's own mouth. What more proof do you need? We've never belonged anywhere. The other warriors never wanted us. I'm the only one who really cares about you, Faryn. Why should we care what happens to the others?"

I fell forward. I clenched my fingers into fists, willing myself not to cry.

"Why?" I whispered. "Why are you saying such cruel things?"

"Abandoned." Alex's voice grew louder and colder, sucking out all the warmth from the air inside the Chamber of Mirrors.

Abandoned, abandoned, abandoned, abandoned . . .

"No," I sobbed. "You're wrong!"

I lashed out at one of the laughing, twisted faces of Alex with my sword. The mirror shattered into pieces, showering me with sharp, jagged shards. Without pausing or registering the pain, I slashed through the next sneering Alex, then the next one, then the next one, then the next.

"I will succeed on this quest," I shouted. "And I *will* get you back on the right side—*my* side!"

When my brother's laughter finally stopped, I swayed for a moment. My head spun. Only then did I realize how long I'd been without water. My arms and legs throbbed where I'd been cut by the shards of the mirror. I was vaguely aware of shouts, and arms reaching out to steady me, before my knees gave out. Then darkness.

CHAPTER

18

When I came to, it was to see a cluster of worried faces peering down at me. I rubbed my eyes and shook my head. I'd developed a throbbing headache. To top it off, my body felt like it had been stabbed over and over by a million sharp things and then wrung through the dryer.

"Are you okay?" I registered Ren's battered face. He stared down at me, wide-eyed with concern. "You kinda . . . went berserk on those mirrors."

I blinked at my surroundings. Ren, Ashley, and Moli had pulled me away from the broken mirrors, which lay in pieces a few yards away from me. As I stared at the remnants, my memory returned.

Pain shot up and down my limbs when I tried to move.

"Yeah, you cut yourself up pretty badly," Moli said in a monotone, as though delivering the day's weather forecast. "Luckily, none of the cuts seems to be too deep."

"Feel pretty deep." I winced as my wounds throbbed.

Moli took me by surprise when her stoic expression morphed into something rare—one of concern. "Hey. You know whatever you saw in the mirror isn't actually real, right?"

"I know," I mumbled. My mind knew Moli was right, but my heart said something else entirely. Still, if a traitorous Alex was my deepest fear, and I'd just stood up to him, that had to count for something—right?

"Can you stand?" Ren asked. He extended a hand.

I took it gratefully. There wasn't a moment to waste. We still had to find the Ruyi Jingu Bang, return it to Sun Wukong, and get him to join our side before the Hungry Ghost Festival was over. I needed to find my elixir as well.

Ashley was uncharacteristically quiet. Her face had drained of color, and her eyes were wide. She trembled but smacked away Jordan's hand when he reached out to her. Apparently, I wasn't the only one who'd seen something horrendous in the Chamber of Mirrors.

At least I knew for sure that my mother was in Diyu somewhere. I had to find her and the rest of my relatives.

"Hey, guys!" shouted Jordan. "There's an exit back here!" He had cleared a path through the shards of glass that led straight to a hole in the wall, about the size of an average man. "Excellent. As handsome as I am, I was getting a little sick of seeing my face everywhere." He rushed forward into the dark.

"Can you walk on your own?" Ren asked gently.

I looked down at our hands, which I hadn't realized until this moment were still intertwined. Blushing, I dropped his hand and put a couple of steps' worth of distance between us.

Ashley gave us a strange look. Most of the color had returned to her cheeks. "C'mon, guys."

"Wait. Maybe we shouldn't go through that exit. I don't remember it being here before," Moli said, biting her nails.

"Yeah, well, you haven't exactly been the most knowledgeable guide ever, so excuse me if I want to take the first exit outta this place," Ashley retorted. She disappeared into the hole after her brother.

As far as I could see, broken mirrors surrounded us, and the entrance that we'd come through had disappeared. Shrugging at Moli, I headed after Ashley. Ren followed.

"Wait up, you idiots. You don't know the first thing about the Underworld! You need me to guide you," Moli protested.

"Yeah, right. We need you like we need those demons to attack us again," Ashley yelled back.

"Rude." Moli sniffed.

Back in the Chamber, the mirrors had given off a bit of their own light. Here, the only source was the digital watch on Jordan's wrist.

When someone grabbed my arm from behind, I screamed.

Instantly, cries of "are you okay?" echoed throughout the tunnel.

"It's just me." Moli. She lowered her voice to a whisper. "Okay. Tell me truthfully. What did you see when you looked into those mirrors?"

I'd been trying to forget all that I'd seen and heard. My mother, who was dead and still somewhere in Diyu. Ba, who had forgotten all about his family. And Alex, who'd changed so much from the brother I'd once known that he was unrecognizable.

"Nothing," I said in a tight voice. "Nobody."

"Whatever you saw in those mirrors, it isn't real. So I wouldn't put too much stake in what happened back there."

"But the mirrors show our true selves, right?" Ren piped up. "Aren't they supposed to show the truth?"

"The mirrors show a *version* of the truth," Moli corrected. "Don't forget, the Chamber of Mirrors is designed to torture sinners for eternity with their greatest regrets and fears. The mirrors aren't meant to reflect the happiest version of the truth."

"How can there be versions of the truth, though?" I asked. "The truth is the truth, plain and simple."

"Maybe on Earth. But here in Diyu, the rules are very different."

I shook my head. "You mean in Diyu, the rules make no sense."

Moli's ominous warning echoed in my head. It struck me that she had experienced much more than I had in the brief time since she'd saved me at Peng Lai Island. It was like she'd aged several years.

"What did you see in the mirror, Moli?" I whispered.

She didn't answer for a long moment. Finally, she said in a short, abrupt voice, "Just me with Bà ba."

Whatever had happened to Moli the first time she'd come to the Chamber of Mirrors clearly still weighed on her. If she wasn't asking me for details about what I'd seen, I wouldn't press her.

Jordan's voice rang throughout the tunnel. "There's a light ahead. I think we're almost out!"

"Thank the gods." Ren sighed.

I quickened my pace to a jog, putting as much distance between the Chamber of Mirrors and me as possible.

When we finally spilled onto the moonlit grounds of Diyu, relief washed over me.

"Wh-what are you doing here?" cried Jordan.

A tall, burly man built like a football player towered over Ashley and Jordan. He wore a red cape paired with a brown jacket, black pants, and black boots. He might have looked like a normal, albeit giant, man if it weren't for the horns sticking out of his head.

"The Bull Demon King," Moli gasped.

Before I could process that one of the most powerful non-god figures of Chinese mythology stood there, right before us, the Bull Demon King slammed his black spear into the ground. Something told me he hadn't showed up to thank us for beating up his annoying son, the Red Prince, during the Lunar New Year.

"Ashley," he rumbled in a low, deep voice. "Jordan."

"Hoo . . . ," Jordan wheezed. "Ha . . ."

Ashley seemed a little more collected than her brother, at least on the outside.

"You kids shouldn't be here in the Underworld," the Bull Demon King growled. He whipped his cape over his shoulder. Only then did I realize he'd brought along his ride with him—a huge qí lín with tough, leathery skin the color of jade green and horns almost as wicked and curved as the Bull Demon King's.

"Yes, you're right, um, s-sir," Jordan squeaked. "That's why we'll be—uh—leaving—now."

"Give up this quest and come home with me to the Flaming Mountain on Earth. You have no business fighting for the gods," the Bull Demon King continued.

"You aren't real," Ashley shouted at her alleged father. Instead of being happy to see him, now she seemed to only be angry—possibly frightened.

"Ashley, what're you saying?" Jordan yelped, all the color draining out of his face.

"That man—that *demon*—isn't real!" Ashley closed her eyes, as though that would make the Bull Demon King disappear. "You aren't real. You aren't real!"

I could understand where Ashley's denial stemmed from, since we'd just emerged from the Chamber of Mirrors. But I was pretty sure that the Bull Demon King standing before us was very, very real.

"Has being in the Underworld addled your brain, brat? Of course I'm real," roared the Bull Demon King. His glare could have seared through metal. He raised his hand, flexing his fingers. In a gentler voice, he continued. "I held you in my palm when you were just a baby."

This seemed to horrify rather than soothe the siblings. Before, Ashley and Jordan had been at least interested in finding their father. Now they seemed much more interested in running to the opposite end of Diyu.

"G-get away from my sister and me," Jordan said, raising his sword. It trembled violently in his hand. "You . . . Even if you *are* our father—which I won't believe until we see an official birth certificate—"

"Official what?" The Bull Demon King furrowed his brow. I guess Demon Kings didn't usually frame their kids' birth certificates.

"You can't storm in here after abandoning us for *years* and try to be our father again. It doesn't work that way," Jordan finished with a brandish of his sword.

Ashley muttered something unintelligible to herself, shaking her head and covering her ears with her hands.

I was far from Ashley's biggest fan, but pity rose within me at the sight of her so small and shriveled before her demon father.

That did it. I didn't care if the Bull Demon King was powerful and a former sworn brother to Sun Wukong. I wouldn't let him whisk away Ashley and Jordan to some place called the Flaming Mountain.

Also, I really hated his fire-throwing brat of a son, the Red Prince.

"We're going to finish this quest—all of us, including Ashley and Jordan," I said. The Bull Demon King's enormous black eyes swiveled to me. I held my sword with steady hands so that the point of the steel was aimed at the demon's head. "And you aren't going to stop us."

The Bull Demon King snorted. "You think *you*, a lowly, pitiful warrior cast out by the most powerful of gods, can stop *me*, the great Bull Demon King?"

"When he puts it that way, you do look kinda dumb, Faryn," Moli whispered.

"Who are you, my own personal un-cheerleader?" But as much as I tried to keep up the bravado, my confidence was slipping.

My mind wandered back to the Chamber of Mirrors. The image of Alex—older, twisted Alex—circled in my vision. His poisonous words echoed in my head.

"Faryn, you all right?" Ren asked.

"You see? You warriors are so pitifully fragile, you don't

even need me to do anything to you before you fall apart." The Bull Demon King cackled.

He was wrong. Even if I wasn't the Heaven Breaker any longer, even if none of the gods would help me here in the Underworld, I still had my own strength. I had all the training that Ye Ye had given me. And I had my friends to guard my back.

I shook my head violently to force Alex out of my thoughts.

"If you want to take Ashley and Jordan, you'll have to go through all of us," I threatened.

The scraping sounds of swords being unsheathed filled the air. I stood beside Moli, Ren, Ashley, and Jordan, our weapons pointed toward the Bull Demon King. The demon narrowed his eyes, as if assessing us warriors, all definitely much tinier and less impressive next to him. He chuckled, shaking his great head, and drew his hands out from behind his back, revealing two thick weapons covered with spikes.

"If we take you down, you let all of us through, including Ashley and Jordan," I said in a surprisingly steady voice. "You'll leave them alone."

The Bull Demon King nodded with a solemn look on his face. One point for the demon—he seemed to be taking me seriously. "And if I win, you'll give up this silly quest, and I'll take Ashley and Jordan home with me."

"Why do you even want to bring us home with you now when you've never taken an interest in our lives before?" Jordan demanded.

"A figment of our imagination can't take us home," Ashley spat.

The Bull Demon King drew back with a wounded look on his face. "Don't you want to come home with me? You'll never truly fit in with the mortal warriors. Half of your blood is demon blood. You'll always be stronger, faster, more powerful." His features softened. He almost looked kind. "Come home with me, my children. I'll teach you how to use your powers to their fullest potential."

A look of longing crossed Jordan's face. I could almost envision what he had to be picturing: him reigning over the Flaming Mountain alongside the Bull Demon King.

Ashley hesitated, reminding me that the siblings *had* wanted to find their father after all. Deep down, they probably wanted to say yes. I held my breath. Ashley's expression steeled. "Don't listen to him, brother. He abandoned us, remember? He doesn't want us. He wants to *use* us."

"That's enough of that, you brat!" the Bull Demon King roared, all softness gone.

I swung my blade in an arc and pointed it at the Bull Demon King. "Attack!"

Chapter

19

The first strike of my sword bounced harmlessly off one of the Bull Demon King's weapons. Ren followed up with an attack of his own, slicing at the demon's arm. The Bull Demon King dodged, but Ren swung his leg around quickly and kicked the off-balance demon right in the gut.

Ren's training at the Dragon Kings' palace had definitely paid off. His movements were so fast that he appeared to be a whir of colors and motion.

The Bull Demon King collapsed to the ground. Ren raised his sword, but before he could finish him off, the Bull Demon King leapt back to his feet and stabbed his spear at Ren.

"Ren!" I shouted without thinking, rushing forward with my sword at the ready.

With a roar, the Bull Demon King slammed his spiked weapon into Ren's sword. Ren stumbled backward and landed flat on his bottom.

Ashley and Jordan could barely beat back the spiked weapon, which the Bull Demon King brandished in his left hand. I cast a quick look at Moli and mouthed, "Together."

Moli nodded. As one, we charged toward the weapon swinging in his right hand. The Bull Demon King deflected our combined attack like it was nothing, and the force of his weapon clashing against my sword sent a jolt careening up my arm.

I was determined to hold my ground, even though I was shaking so hard that my teeth were chattering. Even my sword was vibrating.

No. Not just vibrating. My eyes widened at the sight of Jinyu's sword. It glowed golden. The handle grew warmer beneath my palms, as if to soothe and reassure me.

Hadn't Xiong told me earlier? During the Hungry Ghost Festival, my weapon—Jinyu's old weapon—would grow in power, aided by its former master's spirit. This had to be a message from them both.

The Bull Demon King lifted his weapon and slashed down toward my head. But to me, the attack occurred in slow motion.

You're smaller than he is. Use that to your advantage, came that familiar, soothing voice in my head. Maybe it was just my imagination, but it sounded louder and clearer than before.

There was no time to dwell on that thought, though. I brought my sword up at the last moment to counter the Bull Demon King's attack. My whole arm shook from the force.

The Demon King staggered backward. But that wasn't enough to deter him. He growled and launched himself at me before I could recover.

The force of the blow was too much to bear this time. With a clanging noise that reverberated in my eardrums, my sword flew out of my hands and behind me.

"Ready to give up, warrior?" sneered the Bull Demon King, his eyes glowing with satisfaction.

"Never!" Ashley shouted, hurling herself toward his middle. But the Bull Demon King deflected her as though she were a fly. Ashley stumbled backward into her brother's arms.

"Get your sword, Faryn. I'll hold him off!" Moli panted. Sweat beaded on her forehead, and her face was scrunched up with the effort of parrying the Bull Demon King's thrust. "Not like . . . I can die . . . again!"

She had a point. Without letting myself stop to think, I dashed toward where my sword had landed yards away from the fight. Not far from me, Ren was getting to his feet, wincing and shaking out his leg.

"Are you—?"

"I'm fine," Ren said abruptly. His eyes were fixed on the Bull Demon King. No, some spot beyond him that the demon didn't seem to be aware of. Ren pointed. "Faryn."

I followed Ren's gaze. "Keep pushing him back!" I yelled. The others were so focused on their fight, I had no idea if they'd heard me or not. I snatched my sword up off the ground. Sprinting back to the fight, I put all my weight behind the blade of my sword. Only a half dozen paces away from the Bull Demon King, I leapt into the air and sliced down toward his middle with my sword.

As I'd predicted, he knocked all the breath out of me when he blocked my attack easily—and took another big step back.

A little farther, I thought. *Just a little farther.*

"You don't learn, do you?" The Bull Demon King chuckled. He sounded amused, like we were nothing more than playthings to him. He reminded me of Luhao from the Jade Society, who'd sneered at me the same way. My anger burned even hotter. "You can fight me all day, and you still won't be able to win!"

I fell to the ground and braced myself against the cold stone floor with one hand. "Keep pushing!" I shouted as I launched myself back toward the Bull Demon King.

Under the combined force of all our blows, the Bull Demon King stepped backward. His feet found nothing but air.

"Nooooooo!" Waving his arms and weapons around like a really ugly windmill, the Bull Demon King tried in vain to regain his balance. He toppled and disappeared over the edge of the cliff. I saw a flash of his red cape. Then he was gone.

I darted toward the place where the Bull Demon King had fallen and peered down the edge.

"The Cauldron of Boiling Oil." Moli shuddered as she glanced downward with me. The Bull Demon King was still cursing us as he splashed around the huge, boiling black cauldron. Steam rose until it covered the Bull Demon King and I couldn't see him any longer. "He'll be out of our hair for at least a little bit."

"What's gonna happen to him?" Ren asked.

"He's in a place called the Cauldron of Boiling Oil," Ashley said matter-of-factly. She turned away, but not before I saw pain flash in her eyes. "What do you *think* will happen to him?"

An ominous silence followed her words, but then Moli interrupted.

"Actually, the Bull Demon King will be fine. He's got tough skin, and he's way more powerful than most demons or spirits. This will just be a tiny setback. In fact, he'll probably escape soon, and I have a feeling he isn't going to be happy to let us through, which is why we gotta leave—now."

Moli didn't wait for us to answer her before taking off on a path leading away from the Chamber of Mirrors. I quickly followed, with Ren, Ashley, and Jordan just behind.

"I hope we never see him again," Ashley growled as we made our way through tangled vines and ducked under low-hanging branches.

"He's our father, Ashley," Jordan said quietly.

"So what? He can boil away in that nasty cauldron until the end of time for all I care. I can't believe we're related to a *demon*. A demon who didn't even bother showing up in our lives until *now*!" Shaking her head, Ashley sped up her march through the forest.

"At least he's a superpowerful demon," Ren put in helpfully. "That's pretty neat."

"This is like Lord Voldemort telling me he's my father! Blech!" Ashley continued as though Ren hadn't spoken. Her voice grew progressively louder and more high-pitched.

"Shhhh." Moli spun around with a warning look on her face, a finger raised to her lips. "Do you want more demons to find us?"

That got the siblings to shut up.

"We're almost there," Moli said after a long stretch of walking in silence. Thankfully, we hadn't run into another demon yet.

"Are you sure about that?" Jordan asked skeptically.

I winced. *Wrong move, buddy.* I could see the regret cross Jordan's face as Moli whirled on him.

"What's that supposed to mean?" she snapped.

"Well, you haven't exactly been the most reliable guide to Diyu. Like, you didn't even know that the Bull Demon King was back there . . ."

Splotches of bright red rose on Moli's cheeks. "I'm so *sorry* I don't know everything there is to know about the entirety of the Underworld, all *eighteen* levels that have been here for millennia after only working here for a couple of *months*."

As Jordan hastily tried to backtrack, my attention was

drawn to a huge shape that rose out of the darkness of the forest. "Um . . . guys?"

"And you know what? I *rightfully* spent the first several weeks in Diyu contemplating my mortal life and everything I was supposed to be. I was supposed to go to Harvard Medical School, okay? I was supposed to be a rich, smart, beautiful doctor and marry a rich, smart, handsome doctor prince."

"What the heck is a doctor prince?" Ren murmured.

"I think it's what all good Chinese sons are supposed to become," Jordan whispered. "I dressed up as one for Career Day in fifth grade."

Meanwhile, Moli ranted on. "Now I'm stuck in the Underworld, shepherding around idiots who question *why* I haven't learned thousands of years' worth of information in a matter of months—"

"Guys!" Ren shouted, startling a furious Moli and frightened Jordan. "I think we're almost there."

Moli pushed past us. "Of course," she said smoothly. "Just as planned."

"Planned, my butt," I heard Ashley mutter.

We trekked onward, following Moli down the path. Soon, the trees and bushes disappeared. We entered a dark clearing, which led into a city surrounded by towering walls. This had to be Youdu. Its walls were much bigger than the ones built around the Jade Society. They were so tall, I had to crane my neck to try to see the tops.

"This is the last trial we have to pass before finding the Ruyi Jingu Bang," Moli said. "The Last Glance to Home Tower. The Ruyi Jingu Bang should be inside."

The tall tower loomed above the wall of the city. Only four spirit guards stood stationed directly outside the huge black doors.

"Four guards to protect the whole tower?" Ren sounded bemused.

"Well, you see, most of the dead are too busy trapped in eternal torment to try invading the Last Glance to Home Tower," Moli said flatly. "And the majority of the spirit guards took the holiday off to spend time with their families on Earth during the Hungry Ghost Festival. Like I said—we offer *great* vacation benefits."

"How're we supposed to get inside that tower?" I asked. "I'm guessing those guards won't let us just waltz in, grab the Ruyi Jingu Bang, and then peace."

Moli stared at me like I'd sprouted a third, Erlang Shen-like eye. "Of course not. Even if most of the spirit guards are off duty, the Ruyi Jingu Bang is heavily guarded by magic. We have to carefully plan how we're going to infiltrate the Last Glance to Home Tower. I'm talking power brainstorming sessions, prayers, sidewalk chalk maps—*hey!*"

"Last one to the tower is a rotten dumpling!" shouted Jordan gleefully as he tore past us down the path toward the walled city. He became a streak in the darkness as he zipped by at supersonic speed. Ashley followed suit, sprinting across the ground.

"Why do I even bother?" Moli groaned, dropping her head into her palms.

Ren and I chased after the siblings. By the time we reached them, they'd already stealthily taken down all four of the guards, leaving them sprawled out on the grass, unconscious.

"We'll definitely be going to Diyu for this." Ren sighed. "I mean, for real."

I darted after Ashley and Jordan through the hole-shaped entrance the spirits had been guarding. We were in a court-yard filled with tall, moonlit grass. The Last Glance to Home Tower stood high above us, black as the night. The pagoda levels seemed to stretch upward into the sky.

When I entered the tower, a winding staircase that seemed to go on forever greeted me. There were no signs of life—or death, I guess—anywhere inside the Last Glance to Home Tower.

"It's not normally this empty," Moli explained. "Every-thing's slower, since so many spirits have headed back to the living world for the Hungry Ghost Festival. But in our case, this works out well."

Even without a bunch of spirit guards waiting to chase us out of the Last Glance to Home Tower, this place had some seriously nifty defense mechanisms against intruders. The huge staircase was a torture device itself.

"We've been climbing for at least an hour now, haven't we?" I gasped.

"It's only been five minutes," called Jordan from somewhere above. "I'm checking my watch."

"No way. That watch has gotta be broken."

By the time we finally reached the top of the tower, my knees wobbled from the effort of climbing. "And this is where King Yama sends the *good* spirits?" I panted.

Nobody answered. I lifted my head. A golden light emanated from an object held up in the center of the room, glowing with the radiance of the sun.

We'd found it. The legendary weapon of the Monkey King. The Ruyi Jingu Bang.

CHAPTER

20

I didn't really know what I'd expected the Ruyi Jingu Bang to look like. Something that would no doubt scream, "Ultra-super-mighty weapon of the Monkey King."

When my eyes adjusted to the glow around Sun Wukong's legendary staff, I saw that it looked pretty much as my grandfather had always described it. A red body, gold-capped on either end. The Ruyi Jingu Bang could supposedly expand to the heights of Heaven itself or shrink to the size of a toothpick. But now, at the top of the Last Glance to Home Tower, the staff was about the size of an average human man.

I was drawn to the Ruyi Jingu Bang's power, like a fly to lamplight.

"Can we just . . . grab it and go?" Ren asked. "Seems a bit too easy. You guys think it's a trap?"

"The trap is the weapon itself," Moli explained.

"Huh?" Ashley wrinkled her brow.

"Honestly, don't you guys know *anything*?" Moli rolled her eyes. "According to myth, the Ruyi Jingu Bang is so heavy that pretty much only Sun Wukong has the power to pick it up. Not likely that a couple of kids could lift it."

"Just like Fenghuang is too heavy for all except the Heaven Breaker," I murmured.

"Well, someone's gotta at least try to grab that weapon, right?" Ashley pointed out. "We came all this way."

"Nose goes," Jordan shouted. There was a flurry of motion. Too late, I realized I was the only one without my finger on my nose.

I rolled my eyes and tried to give off more bravado than I felt. "Fine. I'll do it." Taking a deep breath, I strode up to the Ruyi Jingu Bang, staring right into its golden glare.

You can do this, Faryn. As the Heaven Breaker, I'd been the only one who could hold Fenghuang. Even if I wasn't the Heaven Breaker any longer, some of that power had to have stayed behind, right? I mean, I'd retained enough of it to have been able to communicate here and there with Ren.

I stretched out my fingers toward the Ruyi Jingu Bang. I touched it gingerly at first, fingertips brushing against the cool metal of the staff.

"AHHHHHHHHHH!" yelled Jordan. Startled, I whirled around. He'd flung his hands over his face. He spread his fingers wide and peeked through them. "Sorry. Thought it was going to explode."

Ashley smacked him on the head.

"Ow!"

"Stop scaring us!"

I turned back to the glowing staff. This time, I didn't hesitate before grabbing hold of the weapon with both hands. Taking a deep breath, I pulled with all my might.

It was like trying to move a metal pole that weighed as much as an elephant. No matter how much I grunted and heaved and prayed, I couldn't get the Ruyi Jingu Bang to budge, not even an inch.

"Let me try," Ashley huffed, shoving me aside.

I scowled. I could've saved her wasted effort by telling her there was no point in bothering . . . but for that shove, she could suffer a little. I stepped aside.

Ashley's hands stretched toward the Ruyi Jingu Bang.

"There's no use trying to pick that up, sweetie," said a low, raspy voice when Ashley's fingers were just millimeters away.

My hand grasped the hilt of my sword. The sound of multiple swords being drawn echoed throughout the room. I whirled around, as ready as the others were to hack the latest enemy to pieces—and froze.

Our big, bad enemy was . . . a tiny old lady. She couldn't have been taller than four feet. She wore a golden robe with a white sash. Her hands were behind her back, and she smiled serenely at us. Something about her seemed familiar, but I couldn't quite put my finger on it. A hooded figure stood beside the old lady, although their face was shrouded in darkness.

For a moment, I wondered if the woman was my grandmother. Then I shook my head. No. My ancestors hadn't shown up to help the entire time I'd been in Diyu. Why would they show up now?

I demanded, "Who are you?"

"I'm warning you, I won't hold back just because you're old," Jordan shouted.

The elderly woman raised her hand. The figure by her side—her assistant, by the looks of it—unsheathed a sword from their side and raised it toward us. Its blade was black as night.

Ashley narrowed her eyes. Jordan took a slight step back but didn't lower his sword. I stood my ground, too. No way was I gonna let Granny Underworld and Assistant Evil intimidate us.

"Let's not fight," Ren said. "We can talk this out."

The elderly woman sneered at me. "You won't be able to lift the Ruyi Jingu Bang if you don't drink the Tea of Strength." The old woman brought her hands out from behind her back, revealing a cup of hot, steaming tea.

"The . . . Tea of Strength?" I looked at Moli.

Moli lifted her gaze toward me and nodded solemnly. "It

looks like the Tea of Strength is your best bet if you want to gain the ability to pick up the Ruyi Jingu Bang, Faryn. You should drink the tea."

"The Tea of Strength will give you strength surpassing that of any mortal," the old lady explained, pushing the cup closer to me.

On the one hand, I wasn't a big fan of tea in the first place, especially not the kind that some strange old lady had brewed in Diyu. On the other hand, unless I magically sprouted the world's most massive muscles, no way could I lift the Ruyi Jingu Bang.

"You sure you don't have bubble tea on you instead?" I asked the tea lady. "At least some Capri Sun?" She just glared. Guess that was a no.

My eyes darted from the tea to the assistant's black sword to the Ruyi Jingu Bang, then back to the tea.

"Fine. I'll drink," I declared, hoping I sounded bolder than I felt.

"Faryn, are you sure?" Ren stepped closer to me. In a lower voice, he added, "What if she's trying to poison you?"

I bit my lip. That was a risk I was going to have to take. Besides, if Moli was vouching for this old woman, then she had to be okay or, at the very least, not plotting to send me to an early grave. Right?

"Well, if you *do* die, you've already made it to the last place before ascending to Heaven," Ashley said in a bright voice.

"Comforting." I sighed. I stood in front of the old woman. She was still smiling as she raised the cup of tea.

I took it from her hands and sniffed it. The aroma was . . . odd. "What kind of tea is this? Oolong? Matcha? Earl Grey?" I was babbling, but I couldn't help it. Some weird old lady was forcing me to drink tea. In the Underworld.

"It's a special tea with many different flavors," the old woman explained impatiently. "Five-Flavored Tea. Now, hurry and drink up, sweetie."

The assistant stepped forward with their sword pointed at me. I brought the cup to my lips. My mind raced. Five-Flavored Tea . . . why did that sound so familiar? Had I heard it somewhere before?

"Wait," cried Ashley. "I *know* you!"

I froze, the edge of the teacup pressing against my lip. The old woman tore her gaze away from me toward Ashley.

"You're the Lady of Forgetfulness, who makes souls drink the tea to forget the memories of their past life. You're Meng Po!" Ashley pointed her finger in accusation.

"What?" Jordan and Ren burst out at the same time.

Meng Po. The name brought one of Ye Ye's stories to the surface of my mind, of the Lady of Forgetfulness, who helped spirits move on to their next lives at the last stage of the process. Ashley was right. And I'd nearly fallen right into Meng Po's trap. I gave Ashley a grateful look, and she nodded.

Then I whirled on Moli. "You led us to Meng Po? *Why?*"

"You've got the wrong idea," Moli said, shaking her head rapidly. "Meng Po wouldn't harm mortals. She's not unfair, you know. She's a sweet old lady. Really."

Meng Po nodded and gave us a crooked-teeth smile that wasn't reassuring at all. "That's right. This tea is different. It's not my Five-Flavored Tea—although if you wish, I could brew you some of that as well. It's quite tasty, if I do say so mys—"

"No, thank you!" Jordan bellowed.

The old lady frowned. "This is the Tea of Strength. Just try it and see, sweetie," Meng Po crooned at me.

I didn't care if Moli thought Meng Po was trying to help us. I didn't trust this lady as far as I could throw her. "Not a chance."

I dropped the cup, but the old woman lunged forward to catch it before it could smash onto the ground. Miraculously, none of the tea spilled.

"You might as well drink the tea, warriors," Meng Po growled. No longer sweet and innocent, her smile looked like that of some unhinged politician. "You're not going to want to remember what's about to happen to you."

"Get back, lady!" Jordan shouted. He ran at Meng Po and stabbed his sword at her arm, but she dodged the attack with ease. Then she followed with an attack of her own, slicing her hand through the air and giving Jordan several thwacks on his back. He fell over. His weapon clattered to the floor, out of reach.

Most impressively, as much as I hated to admit it, Meng Po

still balanced the teacup in her other hand. And her assistant hadn't even lifted a finger to help.

I made eye contact with Ashley and Ren, hoping they'd be able to understand my message—that we were to charge Meng Po together. We could take one old lady and her assistant. Unfortunately, Meng Po snapped her fingers. A bunch of demon guards, armed with spears, appeared in a wisp of smoke around us.

I couldn't think of any exit plan that would get us out safely. We were severely outnumbered.

"Moli," Meng Po said in a cold, harsh voice.

Moli startled. She appeared as stricken as a schoolchild caught doing something bad. "Y-yes?"

"Tell the warriors my conditions."

"But . . . ," Moli squeaked. I'd never seen her so flustered before. Ghostly sweat beaded on her forehead, and she shook from head to toe.

Moli, who I'd thought was on our side, who I'd finally considered a real *friend*, looked on the verge of obeying Meng Po's orders.

"You . . . Did you mean to lead us to Meng Po?" I asked Moli. "Did you want us to fail? Did you want us *dead*?"

Before Moli could respond, Meng Po interrupted in a low, threatening voice. *"Tell. The. Warriors. My. Conditions."*

I stared at Meng Po's expectant gaze, following it to Moli's petrified expression. A sudden realization hit me.

Moli shook her head, but the truth of her betrayal was apparent in her tear-filled, guilty eyes. Ugly red splotches rose onto her cheeks. "I didn't—I didn't want this to happen. Faryn, you *have* to understand. Meng Po threatened—my father—"

"Oh, don't give us that," Ashley snapped. She swung her sword so that the point faced Moli, centimeters away from her nose. Ashley's face was blotchy with fury. She looked more livid than I'd ever seen her. "We should've never trusted some dead stranger—especially one wearing *high-tops*—to begin with!"

Darkness rose to Moli's cheeks. "What's wrong with my high-tops?!"

"We shouldn't have trusted you," Ren accused, although the look he gave Moli was more sad than angry.

This was my fault. Shame flooded my cheeks with heat. I had trusted Meng Po only because I'd trusted Moli and had convinced the others that she was definitely going to do her best to help us.

Well, look where trust had gotten me. Trapped by a bunch of demon guards and an evil old woman with her awful tea. Betrayed by someone I'd really thought had become a friend, since she'd sacrificed her life to save mine during the Lunar New Year.

If Alex had been here, he would've seen through this trap. He would've been more skeptical. He would've helped us make it out of here with the Ruyi Jingu Bang and our lives.

Ever since the Hungry Ghost Festival had started, all I'd managed to do was get us in a heap of trouble.

"Moli," Meng Po growled. "We had a deal. Or do you wish for harm to befall your father?"

"No!" Moli gasped. "P-please don't hurt my bà ba."

My heart was numb. I couldn't even bring myself to care about what it would mean if we drank Meng Po's tea or if we *didn't* drink her tea. "I just want to know one thing. Tell me just one thing, truthfully. Were you ever my friend?"

Tears spilled out of Moli's eyes and down her cheeks. "Crocodile tears," Ye Ye would have called them. I focused on keeping my heart cold against the sight of them. I wouldn't let Moli fool me again.

"I haven't always been a good friend, Faryn. I know that."

I snorted. Understatement of the year. Still, I'd never seen Moli look so desperate and pleading before. The sight melted my stone-cold heart just a little.

"But please believe me—I don't have any other choice. My father is being held hostage here in Diyu. He tried to lead a rebellion against the Jade Emperor earlier this year."

Even though she appeared to be upset, I couldn't help but notice a different emotion cross her face, too. Pride.

Moli's words stirred a memory in my mind that I'd almost forgotten—the dream I'd had of Alex, where he said he'd put a stop to Zhao Boyang's antics and throw him into Diyu. Fury at my brother flared in my stomach.

"If I don't help Meng Po, my bà ba will d-die," Moli squeaked.

There was no way Moli was faking those desperate tears in her eyes. The girl I'd known for twelve years would never allow herself to appear weak in front of others—unless her father was in mortal peril.

I thought of Ba. If I knew his life was in danger and the only way to save him was to put my friends at risk, would I do it?

I didn't want to know the answer to that question.

"Things weren't supposed to end up like this," Moli explained, her voice still wobbling but growing stronger. "I thought once you all reached the tower and couldn't take back the Ruyi Jingu Bang, you'd give up and go back to the human world where you belong. I didn't know Meng Po's true intentions . . ."

Moli buried her face in her hands.

"Silly child." Meng Po sneered at Moli. "How could I let warriors who have seen Diyu go back to the human world? No, they must forget." Her expression softened just a fraction. "I'm doing your friends a favor. They won't want to remember who they are or their roles in this upcoming war."

"We're not her friends," Ashley spat, glaring at Moli.

My heartbeat quickened, although it wasn't the glares of the demons that made me nervous. I would lose my memories. Everything and everyone I'd ever known and loved.

Ba. Ye Ye. Alex. Ren. All the warriors at the Jade Society and the New Order. The gods who'd helped me on my previous quest, as well as this one.

My family on Ba's side, who I still hadn't seen in the Underworld. Nai Nai, my grandmother; Gu Gu, my aunt; Jiu Jiu, my uncle.

Meng Po waved her arms. In a flash, four cups of tea emerged out of thin air to hover in front of Ashley, Jordan, Ren, and me. "Now, drink," the old woman commanded. "Don't make me force you."

The demons let out a collective growl. Meng Po's assistant raised their sword high in the air, threatening to swing it down at a moment's notice—on *me*.

I couldn't see another way out of the situation, so I did the only thing that made sense. I grabbed the teacup and smashed it to the ground, where it shattered into a thousand pieces.

CHAPTER

21

If we Chinese love one thing, it's tea. So smashing Meng Po's Five-Flavored Tea to the ground wasn't just an act of defiance against the old woman and her demon guards. To my ancestors, it probably made me the black sheep of the family. It probably made the entire Chinese diaspora disinherit me.

Oh well. "I'd rather die than drink your yucky tea!" I declared.

"How dare you. That tea is our most expensive import!" Meng Po shrieked with rage.

Ashley, Jordan, and Ren smashed their teacups into smithereens on the ground as well.

"Five-Flavored Tea sounds disgusting anyway," yelled Jordan. "Give me oolong or give me death!"

I was pretty sure Meng Po was prepared to take him up on that.

When the demon guards attacked us, I was ready. A red-skinned one stabbed its spear at me. I ducked out of the way. In the same motion, I walloped it on the head with the butt of my sword, knocking it out. The second demon charged at me so fast that I couldn't react in time. I brought my sword up to shield my face from the pointed jab of its spear. But it was far too slow and far too late.

"Get away from her," snapped Moli. She kicked the demon in its side, sending it sprawling to the ground.

"I won't forgive you just 'cause you helped me," I said coldly.

"Whatever. Just don't let down your guard," Moli replied. A demon charged right for her, and she elbowed it aside.

"Moli, we had a deal!" Meng Po snarled. "Your dear father's *life* hangs in the balance, remember?"

Moli hesitated. Then her expression hardened. She retorted, "If my father knew I let harm come to my friends just to save him, he would die of sadness anyway." Although tears shone in her eyes, Moli seemed decided.

"Moli . . . ," I said.

"Besides, if my father can lead a rebellion, then so can I!" Moli shouted.

"Fine! See to it that Zhao Boyang is put to death at once!" Meng Po barked to her minions.

"No!" Moli and I yelled in unison. I lunged forward to stop Meng Po's minions, but they'd disappeared from sight.

"C'mon!" I motioned for Moli to follow me. If we were fast enough, maybe we could catch them before they got to Mr. Zhao.

Meng Po blocked our path. Her eyes flickered bright with fury. "Oh, no. You're staying right here," she growled.

My eyes searched for any possible path of escape. Ashley was locked in heated combat with Meng Po's cloaked assistant, trading them blow for blow. Ren and Jordan held off an entire horde of demons, their swords slashing so quickly, I could hardly track the movement.

There was only one escape route—and I'd have to forge it by defeating the Lady of Forgetfulness. I swung my sword in an arc and pointed it right at the old woman. The adrenaline surging through my veins propelled me forward into motion. I didn't stop to think. I just ran at her.

"Go save your father, Moli!" I shouted without turning back. I swung wildly at Meng Po with my sword.

Although she appeared to be old and frail, Meng Po moved much faster than I'd anticipated. Using just her bare hands, she chopped down on my shoulders, then my back, knocking the breath out of me before I could react. Each blow was sharp and painful and almost brought me to my knees.

But years of bearing intense training had made me resilient. Plus, Meng Po thought she had the upper hand, which made her complacent. I was the one who had nothing to lose.

"Give up, Faryn Liu." Meng Po sneered. "You're not a warrior of the gods. I'm doing you a favor by letting you forget what a disappointment you are."

I sliced upward with my sword. Meng Po shrieked. I'd sheared off her long braid of gray hair.

"You stupid girl! Don't you understand you're holding on to the memory of ancestors who don't even *want* you? They haven't shown up to greet you once since you've been in Diyu, and it's not because they don't know you're here. They *do* know—and they don't care." Meng Po practically spit out the last few words. I winced despite myself. "Give up on your noble quest, child. Trust Meng Po ā yí. I'm doing you a favor."

The old woman's expression appeared almost gentle and might have fooled me—if her demon guards weren't intent on slicing my friends into pulled noodles all around me.

"I don't know why my family hasn't shown up," I growled, "but I know it isn't because they've abandoned me."

I hadn't been confident in my words until I spoke them aloud. In that moment, I became certain. Ye Ye, Ba, and everyone else in my family—they believed in me, had been watching over me all along.

And now I needed to believe in them. *Please protect me, ancestors*, I thought.

Meng Po's face twisted into a snarl. "You're a bigger fool than I thought, Faryn Liu." She lunged at me. I raised my weapon and ran toward her.

Ashley's scream shattered the tension. "Someone's coming!"

A gust of wind blew into the room. Demons and warriors alike scattered from the force of the blast. But I held my ground. When the wind had died down, I hardly dared to believe my eyes as I drank in the sight before me.

Spirits. Dozens of them. In shades of ghostly gray and blue, they flooded the room, bringing with them warmth that reminded me of a fireplace.

"Wh-what's going on?" Jordan stammered.

I recognized these spirits. One had Ye Ye's kind, crinkled eyes. One had Ba's wider-set eyes. One had my narrow jaw and higher nose.

These ghosts couldn't be who I thought they were. Could they?

"Sorry we're so late," said the spirit of a middle-aged woman with curly black hair. "Hongyi was pigging out in the human world." She tugged on the ear of a nearby man who looked slightly older than she was. He still gnawed on a drumstick.

"It's called the *Hungry* Ghost Festival, not the Starving Ghost Festival, Cixi," Hongyi protested. Cixi yanked on his ear again. "Ow! Let go, woman!"

The demons stirred on the ground. Meng Po pointed a finger at the newly arrived spirits. "Get them!" she screamed. A few demons got to their feet and tried to attack the ghosts, but the ghosts simply blasted them away with a wave of their hands.

"It would be a grave mistake to attack us right now," warned Cixi. "We've just eaten a grand feast prepared for us by our living descendants. Our souls will be fortified with extra energy until the end of the Hungry Ghost Festival, and even for many days afterward."

Meng Po rolled up her sleeves and shot across the floor so fast that her image blurred. Ashley and Jordan dove out of her way, and Ren coolly stepped to one side. Meng Po didn't seem to notice any of them. Her gaze was fixated on the spirits.

My ancestors.

"Look out!" I shouted.

But the spirits stood in a row like one big ghostly wall. When Meng Po flew into them, they raised their hands and sent her careening backward. Her body crashed into a nearby window and then shattered it. Down went Meng Po, right over the side of the Last Glance to Home Tower.

"Oh my gods!" shouted Jordan, throwing his hands up over his face. "Will she be okay?"

"Who cares?" Ashley cried gleefully. "Hey, Moli, are you seeing this—? Wait. Where's Moli?" She looked around with a startled expression on her face, as though realizing for the first time that Moli was nowhere to be found.

"She's gone to save her father," I explained.

"Good. At least one of us should be reunited with their father," Ashley muttered.

Ren sprinted over the unconscious demons, unintentionally

knocking out a demon that had started to get up. I followed him, careful to avoid the broken glass on the floor. Together, we looked over the edge of the tower, where Meng Po had fallen.

I squinted to try to see better in the darkness, but there was so little light that it didn't matter. The Lady of Forgetfulness had vanished.

"Don't worry, Falun. Meng Po will be all right," called Cixi.

"Drat," muttered Ashley.

Falun. My Mandarin name. It had been so long since anyone had called me Falun. So long since I'd seen Ye Ye.

I faced my ancestors. There were five of them in total, two women and three men, gazing back at me with the same interest that I imagined was on my face.

I wished someone had taught me how to react to seeing the spirits of my ancestors, my family, for the first time—and right after they'd blasted an evil old lady out of a tower. That seemed like a useful lesson to add to the training curriculum in the New Order instead of algebra. (Who uses algebra?)

"You . . . you guys are . . ." I swallowed, trying to remove some of the tightness in my throat. "You're . . . my . . ."

"Family," I urged myself to say. "Family." How hard could it be to say one word?

To my horror, something wet dripped onto my cheeks. I swiped at my tears, but it was too late. Everyone was seeing Faryn Liu, the girl who'd once been the Heaven Breaker, crying like a big baby.

"I thought you guys weren't coming," I managed to say. "I thought you . . . that you didn't . . . that you didn't consider me part of the family."

"How could that be possible?" Cixi said at the same time that Hongyi said, "Yeah, we debated that for a bit. I still vote no." She swatted him upside the head, and he howled.

Another, older woman stepped out from behind the bickering couple. Her bushy eyebrows and strong jawline reminded me of Ba.

"Nai Nai?" I said cautiously.

The old woman smiled and revealed a row of teeth, half of which were missing. "Falun."

I gaped at my grandmother, trying to pinpoint where I'd heard her voice before. And then it struck me.

"The voice I've been hearing in my head—it's *yours*." The voice that had been guiding much of my journey to and through Diyu. The voice that had been present in every one of my visions about my brother. "You . . . you showed me those dreams about Alex. You were trying to help me help him. Weren't you?"

The soft, warm smile that stretched across Nai Nai's face told me all I needed to know. My grandmother had never abandoned me. None of my ancestors had. They'd been helping me all along.

"Wait," Ren gasped. "Your voice—I recognize it, too. You showed me that vision. You showed me the way here!"

Nai Nai turned her smile onto Ren, nodding. The light in her eyes grew stronger and more serious. "Falun, you remind me of your father when he was your age," my grandmother said. "Headstrong. Reckless. To a fault sometimes."

Some of the warmth vanished from the pit of my stomach. It *would* be on-brand for my grandmother to give me a scolding the first time she met me.

"And also very brave and very honorable," added Nai Nai.

"R . . . really?"

Nai Nai extended a hand toward me and reached up to brush a lock of hair behind my ear. "Yes. You have better hair, too."

I beamed.

"I know you're worried about your father," Nai Nai continued, "but he's a strong man. Stronger than he knows he is." She reached inside the sleeve of her ghostly white robe and pulled out a small, narrow vial full of a misty purple liquid.

I gasped. In all the chaos, I'd almost forgotten one of the main reasons I'd come on this quest. "That's . . . that's the . . ."

Nai Nai nodded. "The elixir that will restore your father's memories. It is made from the essence of every member of the Liu family line."

"Our . . . essence . . . ?" I echoed, repressing a shudder. I hoped Nai Nai wasn't referring to our, like, dandruff or something.

"Yes. Unfortunately, the elixir is missing two ingredients.

One of them is your essence, Falun." My grandmother held out the vial. I edged away from it. "I'm not asking for your soul, granddaughter. Just drop a piece of your hair inside."

I yanked out a strand of hair and dropped it inside the vial. The liquid glowed bright purple when my hair hit its surface. With a flash of light, my hair disappeared, and the elixir swirled until it turned a slightly brighter shade than its original purple hue.

"Awesome," Jordan said in a hushed voice. "Try putting in a fingernail now, Faryn."

"Ew! Gross!"

"Fine, then try *my* fingernail next."

"You're disgusting!"

Nai Nai placed the vial in my palm. The glass was cool to the touch. I clasped my fingers over the vial, my hand meeting with cold air as her transparent fingers passed through mine, and my grandmother's smile dimmed. "Now the elixir is with you for safekeeping. It is up to you, Falun, to find the last remaining ingredient if you wish to restore your father's memories."

My fingers trembled as they gripped the vial. "And what is the last ingredient?"

Nai Nai didn't respond for a moment. My other relatives shifted uneasily around her, and a sense of foreboding swept through me. At long last, my grandmother lifted her head with a grim expression. "The essence of your brother."

"Alex?" Ren and I blurted out at the same time.

I'd gone far too long believing I'd never be reunited with Ba and then believing he'd never remember me. I was *this close* to having the power to restore his memories. It was almost like some cosmic joke that Alex, who'd betrayed and wanted nothing to do with me, held the key to completing the elixir. If Alex wouldn't help me, Ba would never regain his memories.

"Your ancestors and I have done our best to keep you and your brother in touch," Nai Nai explained. "It's easiest to link you both when your minds are at rest, so we've been connecting you to him in your dreams."

"Wasn't easy, either." Hongyi sniffed. "Can't believe how much of my precious spiritual power I've wasted on you dinguses."

Nai Nai cut him a look. He coughed and turned away without another word.

"We were hoping that . . . that you and Ah Li could reconcile and . . . restore your father's memories together," Nai Nai said softly.

"I don't know if a reconciliation is even possible," I admitted, "but I'm going to do my best."

"Can you find your brother, Falun? Find him and . . . bring him back to us?"

Of course I wanted that. But what if I found Alex and he didn't want anything to do with me, or Ba, or any of our family? What if he no longer cared about finding our mother or restoring Ba's memory?

"What about—my mother?" I asked. I looked around at the spirits. There was no sign of the kind-eyed, brown-haired woman. My heart sank in disappointment. In the Chamber of Mirrors, my mother—or rather, the version of her in the mirror—had said I could find her in the Underworld. But where?

"Ah." Nai Nai's forehead creased. "Let's discuss that later. More urgent matters are at hand."

I thought finding the mom I'd never known was pretty urgent. Before I could point that out, Ashley shouted, "Wait! Jinyu."

Really? She was going to guilt-trip me at a time like this? "Look, we know how much you worship the guy—"

"Ashley." Meng Po's assistant, who'd been lying on the ground, sat up. Then they did something strange. They reached up and pulled the hood off their head, revealing tangled, wild black hair, deep-set black eyes, and a prominent jaw.

I'd seen his face up close in real life only one time, but I'd seen pictures of him at the New Order many times since. There was no mistaking the identity of Meng Po's assistant.

"Jinyu," Jordan breathed.

"Hey, guys," Jinyu said, raising a hand casually, like he was just passing some old friends on the street. "It's been a while.

I'm sort of dead now." Although he said it in a flippant way, his voice cracked on the word "now," and he cast his gaze toward the ground. But a moment later, Jinyu raised his head and revealed a sunny smile, as though nothing was wrong. "Oh, and I think that old hag Meng Po was controlling my mind, which was mildly annoying. But I'm good now. Probably. What's new with you guys?"

Ashley cried out and rushed at Jinyu, arms open wide. I expected her to tackle him in the biggest, tightest hug. Instead, she pummeled the poor guy with her fists.

"Hey!" Jordan rushed forward, but Jinyu held up a hand. Jordan stopped in his tracks.

"Oh, this is entertaining. Why didn't I bring my popcorn?" Nai Nai lamented. "Or sunflower seeds?"

"You *idiot*." Ashley sobbed as she punched Jinyu with each syllable. I'd never seen the girl cry. Something about it was relieving and deeply disturbing at the same time. "You complete, utter, total doofus. You—"

"Are you done?" Jinyu groaned. "Nice to see you, too, Ashley." He flashed a smile that looked more sad than happy to me. It was as though he were gazing upon the fond memory of something long since passed.

"I can't believe you sacrificed your life to save some strange g-girl," Ashley spluttered. "Actually, wait, I *can*, you noble, stupid—" She finally stopped punching Jinyu and instead collapsed against him. He pulled her in for an awkward hug.

I stifled a laugh. Given the wary expression on his face and the way Jinyu lightly patted her, you'd think he was subduing a plague-infested hedgehog.

"Don't tell me you're gonna punch me, too," Jinyu said to Jordan.

"Tempted to," Jordan admitted. "You can treat me to a bubble tea, and we'll call it even. If there's even bubble tea in the Underworld."

Jinyu gave him an odd look. "Of course there's bubble tea in the Underworld. And it's good bubble tea, too." He laughed and shook his head, muttering, "No bubble tea. Ha. As if any soul could survive in a place like that."

"This is a very touching reunion," Hongyi interrupted. "Believe me, I'm utterly moved. But there *is* a rather urgent matter at hand to take care of. You punks still have to deal with that powerful weapon, don't you?" He tilted his head toward the Monkey King's shining golden cudgel.

"What now?" I faced my ancestors. Forget Alex and Ba's memory—first, I had to make sure we made it out of Diyu alive. "How can we bring the Ruyi Jingu Bang back with us to King Yama and then to the human world?"

Nai Nai stepped toward the glowing staff, cupping her chin with one hand and squinting at the weapon. "The Ruyi Jingu Bang is more than just a weapon," she said. "It has amassed enough good karma that it's well on its way to reincarnating as a human in its next life. If you take this weapon back to the human world, you'll interrupt a sacred process. The Ruyi Jingu Bang might not be able to reincarnate for hundreds more years."

"Nai Nai, we need the Ruyi Jingu Bang right now," I protested.

Ren stepped forward. "The world needs it if we want to try to stop a war."

My grandmother shook her head. "I'm afraid war is on its way already, warriors. One weapon—powerful though it may be—won't be able to stop that."

"What?" Ashley's sword clattered out of her hand and onto the ground. She seemed to have forgotten that she was in the middle of being mad at Jinyu, too.

"What do you mean, war is on its way already?" Jordan demanded.

"We're too late?" Ren added quietly.

Cixi stepped up beside Nai Nai. "Rumors travel quickly down here in the Underworld. Spirits grow restless with nothing better to do than wait in line or be trapped in their eternal torment all day."

Nai Nai nodded. "We believe that as soon as the Hungry Ghost Festival ends in three days, Heaven will make its first move against the humans and demons."

Ominous silence fell in the room.

"Three days? Only five days had passed when we arrived here in Diyu," I protested. "We should have nine days left!"

"Time moves differently down here, child," Nai Nai explained.

I exchanged horrified looks with Ren, Ashley, and Jordan.

"There's no way we can stop this war in time," Jordan moaned. "Can't be done. Not in three days."

"Better get a move on, then, shouldn't you, sonny?" said Hongyi. He floated upside down as he crossed his arms over his chest.

The Ruyi Jingu Bang seemed to taunt me with how close it was. I wanted to scream in frustration. How could we do the impossible?

"There is one way for you to take the Ruyi Jingu Bang with you," Nai Nai said softly.

"Name it," I said without hesitating. "I'll do anything."

My grandmother gave me a wry smile. "I had a feeling you'd say that. You're so like your father." Her eyes flickered to the staff. "Everything in Diyu operates on an equal exchange. To remove one soul from the Underworld, you must be prepared to tether another soul to it."

I didn't like the sound of that. "You mean . . . one of us has to stay behind?"

Nai Nai nodded.

"Forever?" Jordan squeaked.

"Not forever. Just until the original object is returned here. Once the exchange is complete, the person's soul will separate from their body. The soul will join us in the Underworld, while the body will continue to age as usual, until they are either rescued or . . . die."

Definitely didn't like the sound of that. "That's not happening. Nope. No way. No how."

"It's the only way," Nai Nai insisted.

"She's right," Jinyu said in a heavy voice. "The rules of the Underworld can never be bent or broken."

I glanced around at the others, standing there with variations of "nope" written across their faces. "There has to be another way," I protested.

"There isn't," snapped Cixi. "Do you think we'd lie to you if there were?"

There was no real choice here if someone had to stay behind. I just had to make sure to pass on the elixir to someone else so they could complete it and restore my father's memory.

"I'll do it," said Ren, fists clenched at his sides. "I'll stay behind."

"What? You can't," I blurted out. "*I'll* stay behind."

Ren shook his head firmly. "No. How does that make sense? Faryn, if there's one person here who *needs* to see the quest through to the end, it's you."

"Well"—Jordan coughed—"I had been kind of, like, hoping to, uh, survive, too."

"*You're* wrong." I glared at Ren. "I have the least to lose by leaving the living world." Mother gone, brother turned traitor, father memoryless. My throat tightened. Yep. It definitely made the most sense for me to stay behind in Diyu.

"I have no family left in the living world," Ren said quietly. "My mother is somewhere here in Diyu. If I stay, at least I'll be able to find her, and . . ."

He didn't need to finish his sentence. I could fill in the words in my head. *And stay with her.*

My ancestors looked from Ren to me and back to Ren, as though watching a ping-pong match.

"You're not staying behind, and that's final," I growled. If I had to fight Ren to get him to return with the others without me, I would.

"Oh, stop being so noble and annoying, both of you." Ashley stepped forward, crossed her arms over her chest, and jutted out her chin. "I'll stay behind."

CHAPTER

22

Jordan gaped at his sister as though she'd sprouted a second head. "What? Are you volunteering to do something . . . selfless? The world really *is* ending, isn't it?"

"Shut up." Ashley dug her elbow into her brother's rib cage.

Jinyu shook his head, his wild hair bouncing to and fro. "No. Absolutely not. I forbid you to stay here."

"You can't tell me what to do," Ashley growled. "You're dead."

Jinyu opened his mouth and then closed it, a wounded expression on his face.

"Sorry," Ashley added in a quiet voice.

"No, you're right. I *am* dead," Jinyu muttered. My heart squeezed painfully. Jinyu must have kept up a cheery act to hide his true anguish over his death.

"Well, *I'm* not dead, and I forbid you to stay behind, too," said Jordan. His face reflected a rare serious expression. "You can't leave me, Ashley!"

"This is an enormous responsibility, young warrior," Nai Nai said to Ashley. "You may very well be trapped down here for the rest of . . . well, eternity."

I could tell from Ashley's shaking hands that my grandmother's words had rattled her. But she lifted her chin high. "I know. I'm ready to accept this responsibility."

"Ashley, you don't have to do this," I insisted. "I—I can do it instead."

"Or me," Jordan interjected. "I'm the older one. If one of us has to stay behind, it should be me."

"Like I said, idiots, *I'll* stay behind," Ren said angrily. "I'm the one who has the least to lose."

"Since you kids are so eager to stay in the Underworld, does anyone want to swap places with *me*?" Hongyi offered. "I'd like to live again."

Nobody paid him any mind—except Cixi, who smacked him.

Something about Ashley seemed more mature, more self-assured. Much older than her twelve years. "Guys. Stop trying to be noble and all that." She rolled her eyes. "Think about it. It makes the most sense for me to stay down here."

"What do you mean?" Jordan asked.

"What do you think's gonna happen as soon as the Bull Demon King sniffs out Jordan and me? He'll come after us and try to take us back with him. At least if one of us is down here, he'll be confused for a bit. And—" Ashley paused, her face scrunching up. "If I'm down here, there's no chance that my presence will put anyone in danger."

Ashley's words conjured up a few memories. The magic she'd summoned out of nowhere during the Ninety-Sixth Duels. The spurts of power that she and Jordan would sometimes display. Unpredictable. Uncontrollable.

"What about me? If you're a danger in the human world, that means I'm a danger, too," Jordan said quietly.

Ashely gave her brother a heavy look loaded with meaning. "My powers have always been stronger and more dangerous than yours, and you know it. Besides," she added in a forced lighthearted tone, "someone's gotta keep Jinyu company, or else he'll get lonely down here."

"Hey," Jinyu protested. "I will *not* get— *Ow!*" Ashley slugged him on the arm, and he rubbed the spot where she'd punched him.

"You've still got a weak left defense," Ashley commented coolly. "I guess some things don't change, even in Diyu."

"Don't leave her here with me," Jinyu groaned. "Please." But as he said this, a small smile lit his face.

Jordan stared at his sister. He wasn't cracking jokes anymore. Something told me he wouldn't be cracking jokes for a while. "Do you really think we're a danger in the human world, Ashley? That *I'm* a danger in the human world?"

"Don't you?" Ashley threw back. She crossed her arms over her chest. She seemed to shrink into herself, a contrast to her normal confidence. "At least . . . at least your power isn't *that* dangerous."

Jordan appeared stricken by the words. He must've been thinking about how he'd used some hidden power to save our chariot from falling. Sure, Jordan had mysterious powers, too, but at least his hadn't very nearly harmed a bunch of warriors during the Duels—and apparently before that, too, when a much younger Ashley had almost blown out a wall in the New Order.

"I'm sorry, Jordan." Ashley's voice cracked. I was stunned to see more tears welling in her eyes.

"You're not sorry. You're leaving me behind, just like everyone else in our family," he said in a thick, gruff voice.

Jordan's words struck me right in my gut. They were eerily similar to the thoughts that had run through my head when Alex had left me at Peng Lai Island.

It became harder to breathe. I felt like I was living the day Alex left me all over again.

"That's why you have to come back and rescue me as soon as you can," Ashley said, eyes bright. "Promise me you will."

Jordan's face twisted, as though he were on the verge of saying no. But instead, he closed his eyes and nodded in resignation. Sticking his hands into the front pockets of his trousers, he promised, "I'll rescue you as soon as I find a way."

The siblings shared a sad, uneasy smile.

"You're sure about staying behind like this?" Jinyu asked.

"I'm sure, blockhead. Plus, this gives us plenty of time to catch up." She shot him a small, rare smile.

Jinyu's expression twisted in disgust. He shuddered. "What's that thing you're doing with your face? It's creeping me out."

Ashley stopped smiling immediately and stomped on Jinyu's foot. He howled and hobbled away from her, cursing. Once Ashley was through with the Underworld, there would be nothing left of the place, not even King Yama's boxers.

"Time is running out," Nai Nai said. "Have you decided for certain who will stay behind, warriors?"

Ashley stepped forward again. "Me. I'll stay behind. But," she added, whirling around, "I expect you guys to get me out of here soon. If you don't . . ." She cracked her knuckles and smiled sweetly. "Every Hungry Ghost Festival, I'll turn your lives upside down and make sure you never find peace."

"We'll rescue you if it's the last thing we ever do," I reassured her. There was nothing more terrifying than a threat from Ashley, not even a war between gods and demons.

Ashley huffed but then surprised me with the barest of smiles. "Thanks, Faryn. And Ren. You know—you guys aren't so bad."

"Uh, thanks?" said Ren. "You're not so bad yourself."

"You're a pretty good fighter," I admitted. "I've learned a lot just by watching you."

Ashley blinked, then flashed the smallest of smiles. "Really? You're good, too."

"And what about me? Am I chopped liver?" Jordan protested, the hurt evident in his pained expression. "Me, your own brother?"

Ashley grinned and slugged Jordan lightly on the shoulder. Her smile wobbled. "Take care of yourself, chopped liver. Don't fail the quest. You still owe me a hundred bucks and a bag of White Rabbit candies, remember?"

Jordan let out a strangled sound that was halfway between a sob and a howl. He grabbed his sister and yanked her into a hug.

"We'll come get you as soon as we can, okay?"

"Gross," was Ashley's muffled reply, though she hugged her brother back just as tightly.

Watching them say their goodbyes reminded me of Alex, and I missed my little brother all over again. I had to find and save him from himself.

At last, Ashley forced herself out of Jordan's stranglehold. She stepped back and stood up tall, but trembles racked her body.

Nai Nai grasped Ashley's hands in both of hers and led her toward the Ruyi Jingu Bang, until they were standing right beside the glow. My grandmother closed her eyes and began chanting what sounded like a sutra, her voice too low and the words too quick for me to catch.

"It's working!" Ren shouted.

The air around Ashley and Nai Nai had turned gold. The ground beneath their feet crackled with golden energy. Soon, the golden light enveloped them and grew so bright that I was forced to avert my eyes.

"Ashley," Jinyu gasped.

"Ashley!" I heard Jordan yell, a desperate scream that sounded like it had been torn from his throat.

I looked back. Where the Ruyi Jingu Bang had been, Ashley now hovered in the air, her curly hair splayed all around her head, arms and legs spread out. Her body shuddered violently and then stilled. She hung in midair, still emanating that golden light.

"What has my sister done?" Jordan dropped to his hands and knees. Ren and the spirits surrounded him, murmuring words of comfort.

"Don't worry. This is what's supposed to happen," Jinyu said in a trembling, high-pitched voice that reassured no one. "I think. Um, actually, I lied. I've never seen anything like this happen before."

"Her mortal body has frozen," Cixi murmured. She floated around Ashley, examining her like a scientist would a particularly interesting specimen. "Do not fret, warriors. In a matter of hours, Ashley's spirit will separate from her body and join us in Diyu. As long as her mortal body is tethered here, her spirit can't be harmed, and she'll be able to return to it."

Something clattered to the ground beside Ashley—a small red and gold object the size of a hairpin. For a moment, I thought it was Fenghuang.

"The Ruyi Jingu Bang," Nai Nai said softly. When I just continued standing there like a ninny, she urged, "Go on. Take it. The exchange is complete, and you now hold the power to wield the mighty weapon, Falun."

I bent over and picked up the Ruyi Jingu Bang. This time, the tiny staff felt lighter than a feather.

The legendary Ruyi Jingu Bang, the most famous and powerful weapon in all of Chinese mythology, literally sat in the palm of my hand. I wondered what Alex would say about this. He'd probably freak out, since he'd chosen it as his weapon in that dumb video game he loved, *Warfate*.

I squeezed my hand into a fist over the Ruyi Jingu Bang. I had a horrible feeling that when my brother and I met again, it wouldn't be the heartwarming reunion that I wanted.

"Remember, Falun," Nai Nai whispered, "if you want to restore your friend to the human world, you must bring the Ruyi Jingu Bang back."

I nodded. Come back to Diyu. Find the Last Glance to Home Tower. Switch Ashley out for the Ruyi Jingu Bang. Three steps. Three simple, easy steps.

Meng Po would be a headache to worry about, but that was

a problem to deal with later. First, I had to return the Ruyi Jingu Bang to Sun Wukong. And then stop a bunch of gods from waging war on all the humans.

"Good luck." Jinyu nodded at me. "My sword is with you. As long as you have it, we'll be connected. I'll be there in spirit, helping you."

The air around Jinyu shimmered with heat—at the same moment my sword handle grew warm beneath my fingertips. And then I understood. "You . . . It's you! You've been guiding me this whole time. You've been *helping* me in battle."

"We're connected through my sword, and the bond is especially strong during the Hungry Ghost Festival," Jinyu explained. "That means my strength is your strength."

"But . . . why? I thought you'd . . . hate me."

"Hate you?" Jinyu repeated, confused.

"For . . . you know. Being the reason that you . . ." I didn't finish the sentence. I didn't need to.

Jinyu shook his head, a soft, sad smile on his ghostly face. "No, Faryn. Never. What happened to me that day was my own decision. You shouldn't blame yourself for the choice I made."

Hearing Jinyu's words, I felt a huge weight lift off my chest. "Thank you," I said.

"If you want to thank me, go back out there and save the world. That'll be more than enough."

Cool. All I had to do in return was save the world. Easy peasy. "How do we get out of here?" I asked Nai Nai.

My grandmother opened up her arms and gestured toward me. "You hold the way home in your hands."

My eyebrows furrowed in confusion. I held the way home in my hands . . .

I looked down at the Ruyi Jingu Bang, and it clicked. In the legends, Sun Wukong's magical staff could do pretty much whatever he asked. Sometimes he would just twirl it in the air, sit back, and watch it slay the demons for him. If the Ruyi Jingu Bang now recognized me as its owner, too, then the answer to getting home was obvious.

Closing my eyes, I held the staff up to my mouth and commanded, "Take my friends and me back to the human world."

For a long moment, nothing happened. I felt pretty silly talking to an unresponsive stick. Maybe I wasn't cut out to use the Ruyi Jingu Bang after all. But I had to try.

"Try clicking your heels together?" Jordan suggested. "It worked for Dorothy."

"Who is Dorothy?" Nai Nai asked.

Before anyone could catch my grandmother up on the last hundred years of American pop culture, the Ruyi Jingu Bang glowed and shuddered in my palm. A light enveloped me. The last thing I saw was Nai Nai's kind, dark eyes, filled with warmth and certainty.

"We'll see you again soon, Falun," my grandmother said. "Until the Hungry Ghost Festival ends, you can use your prayer notes to summon us—and the rest of the warriors who've passed—to your aid, should you need it."

"Why can't you just come with us?" I asked.

"We aren't strong enough to stay in the human world for very long. We're still recuperating from our last trip. Good luck, Falun."

"Good luck!" Jinyu called.

There was a jerking sensation in my navel. Nai Nai, my ancestors, and the world around me vanished.

I think I screamed, but it was hard to tell. I wasn't even sure I existed anymore inside this vacuum. After free-falling for what felt like forever but was probably only seconds, I landed on two feet on the ground.

I opened my eyes and blinked against the strong, bright light from the sun. Around me, Ren and Jordan surveyed our surroundings, too.

Chatter in a mix of Mandarin and English traveled to my ears. The smells of burning incense and fried foods wafted toward my nose. Some elementary-age kids ran past me with their heads glued to their iPhones, shouting about finding a rare Pokémon.

We'd arrived back at the Panda Express in Philadelphia's Chinatown.

CHAPTER

23

I led Ren and Jordan into a back alley of Chinatown, behind Chef Wu's Kitchen and Lucky Kung Fu Tea.

"Is the coast clear?" I asked, reaching into my pocket for my yuán.

"Yeah, go ahead," said Ren.

Jordan remained silent. I had a feeling he was going to be sullen for a long time. I couldn't blame him. After Alex had decided he'd rather kick it with a bunch of warmongering gods instead of me, his amazing big sister, I'd felt as sick inside as if I'd consumed a whole bucket of Panda Express orange chicken.

But maybe there was still hope for Alex. If my ancestors' predictions were correct, I'd be reunited with my brother soon enough. Even if I couldn't persuade him to help us, I'd give him the biggest older-sister scolding of his life and, in the process, yank out some of his hair to complete the memory elixir. Piece of moon cake.

I tossed the yuán onto the ground. With a flash, the small coin turned into a gigantic chariot, complete with stone lions—right in front of a pimply teenage chef who'd just come out the back door of Chef Wu's Kitchen. Regular mortals couldn't see the chariot, but the guy must have seen *something*, because he dropped the large black garbage bag he'd been holding.

"Holy smokes!" yelled the chef.

"Nothing to see here," I shouted, scrambling over the side of the chariot and taking the reins behind the stone lions where Ashley had been before. Ren and Jordan dove in after me.

The chef ran back inside. "Yo, boss, you *gotta* see this."

I didn't hang around to hear the rest. "Up!" I urged the lions. Up they took us, higher and higher, until Philadelphia's Chinatown became the size of a toy town in the distance. We were back in the clouds. I pulled a small contraption out of my pocket—Ye Ye's compass.

The ride back to Huā Guǒ Shān, which took one day and one night, was silent. I knew we were all worried about Ashley, Jordan most of all.

There was too much to say. Somehow that meant we couldn't bring ourselves to say anything at all, except for a couple of times when I asked Ren to pass up the food. Even Pocky couldn't lift my spirits today.

"You think Ashley will get hungry down in Diyu?" Jordan's voice sounded croaky from disuse. He stared at his unopened beef jerky forlornly. "Maybe we should've left her some of this food."

"I don't think she'll get hungry," Ren said gently.

"If she does, there's bubble tea down there," I offered.

"How do you know she won't get hungry?" Jordan countered. "Have *you* ever been trapped in the Last Glance to Home Tower in place of the Ruyi Jingu Bang?" When we said nothing, Jordan crossed his arms over his chest. "Didn't think so. And what if Ashley needs to use the bathroom? I bet she'll have horrible cramps after being trapped for so long."

Ren coughed loudly enough that I took my eyes off the sky and turned around.

"I'm guessing that since Ashley will be, um, pretty frozen, all of her . . . human needs will be taken care of," I said.

I waited for Jordan's biting retort, but none came. I looked back. He was fast asleep, snoring, on a disgruntled Ren's shoulder. Ren sighed and patted Jordan's head.

The silence stretched on into the night. With Ashley gone, the chariot felt too empty. Too quiet.

When nighttime fell, it finally emerged out of the darkness—the huge, beautiful mountain. Brilliantly colored flowers bloomed with life, and birds soared above the trees. Huā Guǒ Shān, the Mountain of Flowers and Fruit.

"Down," I commanded. The stone lions landed lightly

onto the familiar bridge of the mountaintop where we'd been just days before. I let out a breath of relief as the chariot came to a stop. We'd made it back in time, and since we'd known where to go and went double speed, there were still two days left until the end of the Hungry Ghost Festival. Two days until, according to Nai Nai and the other spirits, the Jade Emperor would make his first move.

Jordan was still fast asleep, snoring on Ren's shoulder. Ren's face scrunched up in an expression that told me he'd just about lost all patience.

He leaned over into Jordan's ear. "Wake up," he shouted.

Jordan yelped and jumped in his seat, nearly tumbling out of the chariot. "Huzzah?"

"We're here," I said. "Come on. Time to greet Sun Wukong."

"You might want to wipe that drool off your mouth," Ren told Jordan.

Jordan swiped at his chin with his sleeve. After both boys disembarked from the chariot, I clicked the button on my remote. It reverted back into a coin that flew into my hands.

The last time we'd been to the Mountains of Flower and Fruit, there had still been some daylight. Now, at night, I could fully appreciate the mountain's beauty. Under the dim glow of the moonlight, the tree leaves and bushes shone with dew. The branches rustled and swayed in the gentle night breeze. Before us, the waterfall shimmered as the water rushed downward past the bridge.

I was about to step through the curtain of water when Ren put a hand on my shoulder. "What?" I asked.

He squinted up at the top of the mountain, which was illuminated by the moon. "Do you feel that?"

"Feel what?"

"Just thought I . . . Never mind. Let's go." Ren pushed past me and disappeared through the waterfall into the Water Curtain Cave.

My eyes met Jordan's. He shrugged. I followed Ren through the Water Curtain Cave. After a moment, the sound of Jordan's footsteps followed behind me.

When we emerged out of the dark cave, the monkeys were fast asleep in the trees. Some of them were cuddling. There was one pair that was wide-awake and stationed in front of Sun Wukong's throne, while the Monkey King himself sat cross-legged with his arms folded in front of his chest. I would've thought he was awake if his eyes weren't closed and if he wasn't emitting loud, rumbling snores.

"Who goes there?" hissed one of the guard monkeys. Both raised their spears at us.

I stepped forward with my hands up to show we didn't mean any harm. "We've come back to see your king, Sun Wukong. We've brought the Ruyi Jingu Bang."

Sun Wukong's ear twitched. His eyes flew open. "Weren't there more of you warriors before? I seem to remember a small, annoying girl."

"My sister's name is Ashley," growled Jordan.

Ren cleared his throat and muttered under his breath, "Play nice with the monkey."

If he heard either of them, Sun Wukong gave no indication. Lazily, he stretched out a hand. "Let's see my Ruyi Jingu Bang, then. If it indeed *is* the real Ruyi Jingu Bang and not a fake. You foolish mortals couldn't tell the difference."

Now I understood why all of Heaven had tried to take out this guy hundreds of years ago. Dude was just plain obnoxious.

Aware that the monkeys were studying us with great interest, I walked quickly toward Sun Wukong and knelt before him. Ren and Jordan did the same, though I could almost see the reluctance in their stiff movements.

I reached into my pocket and pulled out the tiny, toothpick-like weapon. I held it flat on my palm before him. "The Ruyi Jingu Bang."

Sun Wukong's fur brushed and tickled my palm as he picked up the tiny staff. I held my breath, my gaze fixed on the grass beneath my arms and legs. This was the moment of truth. I was pretty sure we hadn't been fooled by the entire Underworld, but if this wasn't the real Ruyi Jingu Bang, Sun Wukong was going to send us right back to Diyu—and this time for good.

"Biàn," Sun Wukong commanded. *Change.*

With a popping noise, the Ruyi Jingu Bang lengthened into a spear in Sun Wukong's hand. He examined it thoroughly, even tucking one end under his armpit to scratch it. This went on for a while.

The staff must have passed his test, because Sun Wukong stuck the Ruyi Jingu Bang into the ground and gave us an approving look. "It seems you've done well, warriors. This is indeed my Ruyi Jingu Bang."

I breathed out a sigh of relief and stood up on slightly shaky legs. "Thank you, dà shèng."

Sun Wukong gazed upon the Ruyi Jingu Bang with reverence. "I have to thank you for retrieving this weapon for me. To be honest, I wasn't sure if I'd ever see it again."

"So you'll be able to join us in the fight against the Jade Emperor, then? We have to move now," Ren said all in a rush. "We've heard rumors that the Jade Emperor plans to strike against the humans and demons as soon as the Hungry Ghost Festival ends. That only gives us a little less than forty-eight hours, and—"

"Hold on, kid." Sun Wukong squinted at Ren. "Who said anything about joining you in this fight?"

My heart almost dropped into my stomach. "You did," I pointed out. "You said you'd aid us if we could bring back your Ruyi Jingu Bang, remember?"

Sun Wukong threw his head back and laughed. The other monkeys joined in.

"And people say *my* jokes are bad. I don't see anything funny about this at all," Jordan shouted.

Sun Wukong wiped a tear from his eye. He explained in

the slow, careful voice one might use with a toddler. "It's funny because I lied."

"That's even less funny!" Jordan protested.

"You—you can't lie," I blurted out in a panic.

Sun Wukong's eyes danced with amusement. "Oh? Why can't I lie, warrior? Don't you know who I *am*? I'm the biggest trickster in all of Chinese mythology. The Monkey King, the Great Sage, Equal of Heaven, who almost brought Heaven to its knees hundreds of years ago."

I looked toward Ren and Jordan for help. Jordan glowered at Sun Wukong as though he'd like nothing better than to beat him up with the Ruyi Jingu Bang. Ren shook his head from side to side, as if all his greatest fears had come true.

"You won't get away with this," Jordan snapped. His fists trembled at his sides. "My sister's down in Diyu still! She stayed behind, risking her life, so we could bring you your stupid stick. And this is how you repay us?"

Sun Wukong picked his staff back up and then brought it down again in a dramatic, thunderous motion that shook the ground. "You go too far, warrior," he growled.

I knew the smart thing was to tell Jordan to shut up before the Monkey King unleashed his wrath. But I was so angry with Sun Wukong that I didn't care how badly Jordan—we— insulted him. Someone had to put him in his place.

"Jordan's right. You're just a coward," I accused. "You don't want to fight the Jade Emperor because you're scared you'll lose. Just like you lost the first time you tried to fight Heaven!"

"Oh boy," Ren murmured.

My insult struck home. A dark shadow crossed Sun Wukong's face, and his whole body began to shake and glow. This was it. He was going to blast us to smithereens.

But the explosion I was waiting for didn't come.

"Monkeys!" Sun Wukong commanded, clapping his hands together.

There was a rushing sound of running feet, and a group of monkeys assembled behind us. They slammed their spears together onto the ground in one smooth, coordinated movement.

"Here!" they shouted.

Sun Wukong didn't even glance at us when he barked, "Please escort our guests off the Mountain of Flowers and Fruit. They've done me a favor, and now it's time for them to go."

Small arms wrapped around me. The monkeys began dragging us away from Sun Wukong's throne, despite how hard I struggled against them. "Please, dà shèng. We need your help." I hated myself for begging, but I didn't see any other choice. "You're the greatest, most powerful hero of Chinese mythology. And I just remembered—my brother even dressed up as you for Halloween once! Doesn't that mean *anything* to you?"

"You're the old ally we've been searching for. You have to help us," Ren pleaded.

"I'm flattered, but I'm no ally," Sun Wukong growled. "I have no alliances. And I don't *have* to do anything. I do as I please, and I don't fight in wars that don't benefit me. The sooner you silly humans stop believing those old tales about me, the better. Now—begone!"

"Coward!" Jordan screamed as the monkeys hauled us down the path. "Filthy, stinking coward!"

Sun Wukong grew smaller and smaller in the distance. The monkeys pulled us into the cave, and he was swallowed up by the darkness.

CHAPTER

24

The monkeys dumped us outside the Water Curtain Cave, on the other side of the magical waterfall.

"And don't come back to bother our dà shèng again," spat one of the monkeys. They all raised their tails at us and left, leaving a heavy silence in their wake.

Jordan was the one who broke it. "Well, that went well."

"Couldn't have gone better," Ren deadpanned.

I ran my fingers over the blades of grass beneath me, pulling out tufts in frustration. Before, the remaining two days of the Hungry Ghost Festival had felt like plenty of time. Now, they felt like no time at all. How were we supposed to complete this quest?

"So . . . what do we do now?" Ren asked.

"Why are you guys looking at me?" I said.

"You're the one with the compass and chariot," Ren pointed

out. "And Erlang Shen, Guanyin, and Nezha still see *you* as the Heaven Breaker. You've gotten us out of tough situations before." His eyes shone with pride when they met mine.

I blushed. "I . . ."

"Plus, my sister hated—*hates*—your guts," Jordan added. "It's rare that Ashley hates anyone that much. That means you're probably someone to respect."

"Uh, thanks." I averted my gaze. I wished they wouldn't look at me like I was supposed to pull a brilliant solution from thin air. I was completely out of brilliant solutions. Or even horrible solutions.

Think, Faryn. Two days until the end of the Hungry Ghost Festival. How could we stop the Jade Emperor before then?

Wait a minute. What had Nai Nai told me? Until the end of the Hungry Ghost Festival, I could summon the spirits of my ancestors to leave Diyu.

I yanked my backpack off my shoulders and unzipped it. After digging past the last of my granola bars and beef jerky, I pulled out the thin bundle of prayer notes. I handed a note to each of us.

"Y-you're praying at a time like this?" Jordan spluttered.

"We're praying *because* it's a time like this," I said shortly. Xiong had told us to use the prayer notes only as a last resort. Well, this was the occasion for a last resort if I'd ever seen one.

Ren caught on first. "You want us to rally our ancestors."

His flat, skeptical tone told me he wasn't exactly in love with my plan.

I nodded.

"You think our ancestors will be enough to convince Sun Wukong to join our side?" Ren asked.

"I don't even know if I want that dude on our side," Jordan grumbled. "Are we sure Massive Monkey Migraine is the 'old ally' we're looking for?"

"He's the one, Jordan," I insisted. He had to be. Otherwise, we were completely screwed. "Do any of you have a better plan? Or feel like going back to the New Order having failed the quest?"

That shut them up. I was right, and we all knew it. Our best bet was summoning our ancestors and asking for their help.

I pressed the prayer note between my palms. The others followed suit. I closed my eyes and raised my hands in front of my face. *This is Faryn Liu. Please, ancestors, if you can hear me, we need your help convincing Sun Wukong, the Monkey King, to join our side.*

A warm energy enveloped me, the kind of comforting embrace I imagined a mother might give. I opened my eyes.

"Hey." Jordan pointed up toward the sky with a dazed look on his face. "The stars are brighter than usual tonight."

I followed his gaze. Jordan was right. Lit up by countless stars, the sky was more brilliant than it had been before.

"No," Ren said softly. "Those aren't stars."

I narrowed my eyes. "Those are . . ." My voice trailed off as the glimmering, swirling lights formed into more solid shapes. The shapes of people. Our ancestors.

A breeze billowed over the grass, whipping my hair around my face. Bright-red dots hung in the sky. As the dots drew closer, I realized they were actually lanterns—which our ancestors gripped in their hands.

"Wow," Ren breathed. "This is . . ."

"Magic," I finished.

Old and young, tall and short, thin and thick, the bright spirits of our ancestors floated in the sky above us. So many that they could've populated a small village. Their shadows blocked out the moonlight. They surrounded us in a circle of gray-blue light.

"We could've had a whole army of spirits at our disposal this whole time?" Jordan asked in disbelief.

I couldn't quite believe the sight before me. Even after meeting my ancestors in Diyu, I wasn't sure until now if they truly considered me, who was only half-warrior, part of their family. My eyes filled with tears. I wiped them away as discreetly as possible.

A familiar elderly woman broke away from the circle of spirits descending above our heads.

"Nai Nai," I said. "You came. You all came."

"We meet again sooner than I thought we would, warriors,"

my grandmother responded. "We've received many prayers during this Hungry Ghost Festival. Many more than usual. I have never felt this strong."

"Faryn!" Out of nowhere, a ghostly pair of arms reached out toward me as though to grab me in a tight hug, but they instead just passed through me, leaving a cold chill.

I shivered and looked up into a familiar, though slightly confused, face. "Moli!"

"Oh. Forgot I can't do that anymore," she said with a sigh. She awkwardly folded her arms across her chest. "I totally wasn't trying to give you a hug or anything anyway."

"Uh . . . yeah, no worries," I said. My eyes fell upon the jovial-looking man standing on a cloud beside Moli. He seemed very much alive. I hadn't seen him in six months, but I'd still recognize the twinkly eyed, kind, slightly chubby man anywhere. "Zhao shū shu! You—you're alive!"

"I'm alive." Moli's father beamed. "Thanks to my wonderful daughter." Mr. Zhao gazed at Moli as though she were the most precious thing in the world to him—which I knew she was.

"I was pretty great. I rescued Bà ba, restrained all those pesky demons, and put Meng Po in her place." Moli tossed her hair over one shoulder. "You should've seen me."

"Won't King Yama be mad about you disturbing the peace?" I asked.

"Nah," Moli said smugly. "King Yama actually gave me a

promotion. Said he was glad I put an end to the ruckus all the spirits were stirring up. I'm now his personal assistant, and the best part is I get to boss around Meng Po."

"Oh . . . okay. Congrats?" said Ren, scratching his head.

Moli grinned. "Thank you."

Nai Nai coughed and gave us a stern look. "Your request sounded quite urgent, Falun. What do you need?"

"A monkey tamer," Jordan muttered.

"Sun Wukong went back on his promise," I explained. "We gave him the Ruyi Jingu Bang, and he refused to join our side in the war."

The spirits exchanged knowing looks.

"That isn't surprising," my grandmother said heavily. "The Monkey King is known for being—"

"A trickster figure," I finished. "Isn't there something you all can do about this?"

The solemn expressions on my ancestors' faces didn't reassure me.

"We spirits?" Nai Nai shook her head. "I'm afraid Sun Wukong is beyond our control. Frankly, he's beyond anyone's control."

Great. "Then what are we supposed to do?"

"You, child?" A woman stepped forward, her long, silvery hair blowing in the breeze. I recognized her almost immediately. Cindy You. Her eyes found Ren, and a warm, sad smile rose to her lips.

"Mama," he said.

My heart slammed in my chest. Oh no. If she had been summoned here among the rest of the spirits, then there was only one explanation. Ren's mother walked among ghosts in the Underworld now.

"Ren," Cindy said. Her eyes swam with ghostly tears. "My son. My boy. I'm so sorry I couldn't be with you growing up. But I've always been watching you from afar."

"Ren . . . ," I whispered.

His eyes, when he turned them to me, shone with wetness. But he didn't cry. "It's okay. I'm not sad. I think I . . . I already knew."

I heard Ren's unspoken words. *I can't cry over a woman I didn't even know.* I reached for his hand and squeezed it. My own mother was still nowhere to be found. All the chaos overwhelmed my emotions. I'd have to worry about finding my mother later.

Cindy watched us, her sharp black eyes still shining with tears. "To answer your question, Faryn Liu, you warriors should prepare to fight." She tilted her head up toward the sky. A huge, dark shadow of a cloud had just shifted over the moon. "If our hunch is correct, Sun Wukong will need *your* help very soon."

"Our help?" Ren echoed. "Why would he need our help?"

A drumming noise sounded beyond the tall trees of the Mountain of Flowers and Fruit.

I gasped. It wasn't just a dark cloud that had passed over the moon, as I'd thought. Figures stood on top of that huge black cloud. Powerful-looking soldiers who were dressed for battle. Several banged huge red war drums. And hovering in the air above the soldiers were . . . dragons. The magnificent creatures' scales shone black instead of the colorful hues that I was used to seeing, as though someone had taken a calligraphy brush and painted right over their scales.

A current of palpable fear traveled through the spirits, chilling me to the bone.

"What is it?" I whispered. "What's going on?"

"Our information was wrong," Nai Nai said in a shaky voice. I'd never heard my grandmother sound so fearful. "The Jade Emperor wasn't planning to launch an attack in two days. He's starting it now."

My heart thudded wildly. I reached into my backpack and pulled out my sword. Ren's and Jordan's panicked gazes told me we were thinking the same thing. We were completely, totally unprepared for this war.

"Don't fear, Falun." Nai Nai placed a ghostly hand on my shoulder, leaving a chill. "You have us by your side. Your family is behind you."

I glanced around at the spirits behind Nai Nai. A lump welled in my throat, and I couldn't speak. But I think my grandmother understood what I wanted to say.

Shakily, I raised my sword in front of me. Then I tossed

my yuán onto the ground before us. "Get in," I told Ren and Jordan.

"Wait, we're really doing this? We're fighting those guys?" Jordan gawked at the dark cloud of Heavenly soldiers as it drew closer.

"Are you a warrior or not?" I demanded.

Jordan hesitated. Then he nodded, albeit reluctantly. I guess the idea of not living up to the title of warrior bothered him more than facing down a bunch of Heaven's soldiers. He got into the chariot after Ren. I urged the stone lions forward, through the waterfall, and into the Water Curtain Cave. The spirits followed behind us.

"A chariot." Moli sighed, giving our ride a sad, wistful look. Just six months ago, Moli had driven our chariot during the quest of the Lunar New Year.

We emerged at the other end to find Sun Wukong leading the smaller monkeys in what appeared to be a martial arts training formation. They stopped what they were doing at the sight of us.

"I thought I made it clear that you warriors aren't welcome here," Sun Wukong growled. "You dare not only to come back but also to bring the dead with you?"

Nai Nai stepped forward. "If you won't listen to the living, perhaps you'll heed the warning of the dead."

"Pah. The dead don't scare me. Leave—before I send you back to the Underworld the hard way." The Monkey King raised his arms above his head. Ruyi Jingu Bang appeared in his hands, glowing bright.

Many spirits drew back, but my grandmother stood her ground. "Your mountain is about to be under attack," she announced.

Several monkeys gasped and tittered at the news.

Sun Wukong, however, didn't even flinch. "I know."

"You *knew*?" I blurted out. "How could you have known this would happen and not do anything about it?"

Sun Wukong turned his glare onto me. His eyes blazed with fire. "Centuries ago, I was strong enough that I almost took down everyone in Heaven on my own. My monkeys and I together will defend our home just fine. We do not need your help."

I clenched my teeth. The size of Sun Wukong's ego was seriously ridiculous. Bigger than this whole mountain. If he was so confident that he could hold the Mountain of Flowers and Fruit on his own, then I wouldn't waste breath trying to convince him otherwise. We had a quest to finish. Not to mention, there was still the matter of rescuing Ashley from the Underworld.

I could feel the pressure of everyone's eyes on me, both the living and the dead. "Fine," I spit out. "Good luck defending your mountain."

Without sparing another glance toward the monkeys or their king, I directed the stone lions to turn around toward the cave exit.

"Wait, Faryn. We're leaving? Just like that?" Ren asked.

"We can't just let Sun Wukong boss us around!" Moli protested. Her father tried to soothe her, but she floated away from him. "I didn't claw my way through the Underworld to be thwarted by some *monkey*!"

"I heard that!" bellowed the Monkey King. "You're lucky you're already dead, kid!"

"Falun, think carefully," Nai Nai urged.

The voices of the spirits grew louder as they argued among themselves. I ignored them and continued forward. I didn't know where I was headed or what I planned to do, but finding a place to regroup before dealing with the Jade Emperor's army would be a good start.

"Look out!" Jordan cried. "Above us!"

A figure dropped into the middle of our path. I forced the chariot to a stop. The stone lions roared in protest, nearly throwing the chariot sideways.

The figure stood up. He brushed himself off, from the top of his black helmet to the bottom of his black combat boots. Then he took off his helmet and shook out his brown hair, which he'd swept over to one side.

I froze. I knew that narrow face and slim frame like the back of my hand. And the golden, white-tipped spear clutched in his right hand, I would recognize anywhere.

Alex straightened and gave me a cold smile.

"Hello, sister."

CHAPTER

25

Sister.

How many days, weeks, months had it been since anyone had called me that?

Tears burned in my eyes, but I forced them back. I couldn't be weak now that Alex and I were finally face-to-face. There were no mirrors this time. No more nightmares or visions.

Alex was Alex. And he stood in front of me, in flesh and blood. Alex as the Heaven Breaker and leader of the Jade Emperor's army, wielding Fenghuang.

I couldn't show my brother all my weaknesses that had been brought out in his absence. I had to prove I was stronger than Alex. I had to make him regret choosing the Jade Emperor over doing what we both knew was right. And I had to convince him to help me complete Ba's memory elixir and then join my side.

The tense silence was shattered by Jordan's bemused voice. "Am I missing something? Did that punk with the weird hair just call you *sister*?"

"Alex," Ren growled in greeting.

"Dragon boy," Alex sneered.

"A-Alex!" Moli interrupted.

My brother froze. His body clenched up. I watched his eyes grow wider and rounder in recognition.

"Alex," Moli said shakily, "it's me. Remember me? It's Moli."

"Seriously, what's going on? You three know this guy?" Jordan asked.

Slowly, as though every movement cost him a great effort, Alex faced Moli. I read the pain etched across his features as he gazed upon the girl he had a massive crush on. He raised a hand in a half-hearted wave. "Oh . . . hey, Moli. You . . . came back as a spirit?"

"Yeah, I came back to haunt *you*, traitor." Moli looked ready to smack Alex.

"This is weird," Jordan whispered. "Does anyone else get the feeling that this is weird?"

"Shut up, Jordan," I hissed. He must've—correctly—interpreted the warning tone in my voice, because he clammed up.

Alex started, "Moli, I-I'm sorry about—"

"Don't talk to me." Moli whirled around on her heels,

folding her arms across her chest—but I didn't miss the ghostly tears glittering in her eyes. "I have nothing to say to you. And don't you *dare* apologize. Not to me, at least. I'm doing well. Very well. The person you owe an apology to is your sister."

Alex flinched, a wounded expression on his face. I guess one thing would never change—Moli's hold on my brother. His eyes slid toward me. "My . . . sister?"

I wanted nothing more than to embrace Alex, but I knew I couldn't—not yet. I had to appear strong, at least on the outside. Even if I was slowly crumbling to pieces on the inside.

"Don't call me *sister*. You don't deserve to call me sister," I declared in a remarkably steady voice. "Not until you do what's right—and join our side."

The ghost of a smile rose to Alex's lips. In the darkness of the night, it looked more terrifying than anything else. "Not a chance."

He raised Fenghuang. I ignored the pang in my chest at the sight of my brother wielding the weapon that had once belonged to me.

"Alex!" Moli called, but he ignored her. I guess when Alex's mind was really made up, even Moli couldn't sway him.

Ren and Jordan unsheathed their swords at the same moment, but I held out my arm to stop them. I had to give this one last shot. Alex was still my brother, after all.

The rest of the world disappeared. There was no Ren, no

Moli, no Jordan, no spirits. Nothing. Just Alex and me. My brother and me. Like always.

"Wait. We don't have to fight, Alex. I . . . I found Ba," I blurted out.

Alex lowered his weapon and gaped at me. The animosity in his expression disappeared, replaced by vulnerability. It reminded me of the little brother I'd spent years protecting from bullies in the Jade Society.

"Ba?" Alex's voice trembled.

"He's alive, but he's lost his memories," I explained. "The only way to restore them is for you to put some of your essence—just a piece of hair—into this elixir."

Alex stared at the container. Then his features steeled. "You're just trying to trick me."

"What? No! You've got to listen—"

"I don't have to do anything you say. I don't have to listen to anyone who's in the Jade Emperor's way."

"Please, Alex," I begged. "You have to help Ba—and me. You have to do the right thing."

"Oh, the *right* thing?" Alex barked out a harsh laugh. "As if *you* can talk to me about right and wrong."

"What do you mean?"

"You were the one who chose everyone else over me, Faryn," Alex spat, his eyes shining with fury. "You sided against the Jade Emperor—against me—for a bunch of humans who never cared about us."

"I didn't choose anyone else over you," I said quietly. "I chose what my heart told me to do."

"Spare me the dramatics." Alex rolled his eyes. His grip tightened around Fenghuang, and the weapon glowed brighter. "What matters is that in the end, you didn't choose family."

"You're wrong, Alex. In the end, family is precisely what I chose." I spread my arms out, gesturing toward the spirits who hovered around us. The spirits of my ancestors.

Sheer surprise replaced Alex's sneer as he seemed to take in the spirits' presence for the first time. His eyes swept over the figures.

"Ah Li." Nai Nai's firm voice echoed in the tense air.

Alex's gaze snapped to our grandmother. Shock slackened his jaw. The anger in his expression faded. "You . . ."

Our grandmother shot him an impatient look, as though he were a schoolboy who'd underperformed on a test. "You know who I am, don't you?"

After a beat, Alex murmured, "Nai Nai."

"Do you recognize these people around me?" Nai Nai gestured toward our other ancestors. Cixi, Hongyi, and a few others who bowed their heads. "They're all your family. We're your family, Alex."

"Not by blood," he said bitterly. "The only family I want to see is my blood family."

"There are bonds stronger even than blood," Nai Nai said sternly. "If you don't believe me, ask your sister."

My brother's eyes darted to mine. For a moment, his gaze softened. I gave him a small smile, but then he turned away.

"We're always on your side," our grandmother continued.

An emotion flashed across Alex's face, too fast for me to catch. Then that hardness returned to his expression once more. "What use is it if you're on my side? You're all dead."

Nai Nai stiffened. Cixi stormed forward. "Liu Ah Li!" she barked, but then my grandmother threw out an arm to stop her.

"You have to make a decision now, Ah Li. We've all chosen. We're siding with your sister—and humanity."

Gratitude swelled inside me, replaced by sadness when I glimpsed the crestfallen look on Alex's face. But I had to remain firm. I'd made my choice. I had to stick to it. "You know on which side your family is choosing to fight. Will you choose your family, or will you choose war?"

My brother hesitated. Hope bloomed inside me. Maybe the Alex I'd always known wasn't gone after all. Maybe we could save him.

Then Alex shook his head, and the shred of hope shriveled. "No. The Jade Emperor promised me he'll introduce me to my *real* family once I'm through with all of you. I've wasted enough time talking to you idiots. Faryn." He turned to me, and I recognized the vulnerability of the old Alex in his expression. "I'm giving you one last chance, because you *are* my family, and family is supposed to stick together." The accusation and hurt in his voice caused tears to well in my eyes. "Will you join the Jade Emperor in rebuilding a better world?"

"Alex, I—I— You know I can't." I forced confidence into my voice. "I *won't.*"

"So be it." My brother's words rang with finality. "Soldiers!" he shouted, raising Fenghuang. A bolt of white energy shot out of the top, crackling like thunder in the sky, illuminating the night. "Take this mountain, and capture every last creature living on it!"

The war drums' beating grew louder. Monkeys screeched as they held their weapons toward the sky. But they were leaderless. Sun Wukong had vanished from his throne.

"Eyes up here, kid!"

We all looked up. The Monkey King floated on a cloud high above, the Ruyi Jingu Bang giving off enough power that it alone held back most of Alex's army.

"F-Faryn?" Ren said shakily.

I turned toward Ren and gasped at the sight of his body shaking and trembling. Oh no. Fenghuang had the power to control all dragons. Now that Alex had called upon the weapon's power, the dragon inside Ren was struggling to come out.

C'mon, fight this, Ren, I thought. He hadn't gone into specifics, but I knew that during his time with the Dragon Kings, Ren had undergone intense mental training to become one with his dragon. I hoped it had been enough to know when to shake off the dragon's influence.

"Faryn, look out!" shouted Jordan.

I turned around to see and hear an object rush at my head. My reflexes, sharpened through years of training, kicked into action just in time. I yanked my sword up to block Fenghuang.

But the effect was so minimal that I might as well have not done anything at all. The force of the golden spear slamming into my sword sent me flying backward. I landed on my back on the grass, and a sharp pain shot up my tailbone. There was no time to check if I'd broken or twisted something. The next moment, a shadow fell over my head as someone—*something*—loomed overhead, no doubt to deal the finishing blow.

Adrenaline pumped through my veins. I wouldn't let it end like this. I didn't care how powerful Alex and his army were. I wouldn't go down without putting up a fight.

With a roar, I drove the point of my sword upward. It clashed against the steel blade of another sword.

"Wait—it's me, Faryn! It's Ren! I'm trying to *help* you!"

I blinked. It *was* Ren. I'd almost stabbed Ren.

"Get up," he commanded, holding a hand out toward me.

"You're . . . yourself," I said stupidly. I grabbed Ren's hand and propelled myself off the ground. "Not . . . a dragon."

Ren's breathing was irregular, and sweat mixed with dirt beaded on his forehead, but he gave me a shaky grin. "Training's paid off, huh?"

From where we stood, I could see everything that was going on. A ghostly swarm of our ancestors surrounded Alex and several members of his army. Even with the aid of Fenghuang, which glowed in bursts of golden light, my brother couldn't overcome the sheer numbers of angry spirits overwhelming him. They swelled against him, wave after wave. Although Alex beat them back, more kept coming.

I couldn't help but feel a burst of pride for my family. Few of them carried actual weapons, but their combined power was enough to hold back the army.

"Take that, you awful nephew!" shouted one ancestor, who whacked Alex with her hairbrush. "Bringing dishonor and shame to the family. You won't be getting any blessings from *me* this year!"

I said an inward prayer of thanks to everyone, young and old, who'd prayed to their ancestors and given them food during the Hungry Ghost Festival. They'd probably prevented us from being barbecued by Alex and Fenghuang just now.

But my euphoria was fleeting. A sound like a cannon going off exploded through the clearing. When I looked up, my jaw dropped in horror.

Heaven's immortal warriors had broken through the powerful light of the Ruyi Jingu Bang. Sun Wukong was little more than a streak of red and yellow and brown, fighting back a dozen warriors with his staff. But many more soldiers and dragons flooded past the monkeys into the clearing.

In the chaos, Jordan had somehow instated himself as the temporary leader of the monkeys. They charged into battle with him at the front of the lines, engaging Heavenly warriors in combat.

"Any ideas for holding off this attack?" Ren asked.

No matter how I looked at it, the situation didn't seem good for us. Even if our spirits and monkeys outnumbered Alex's forces, the Heavenly soldiers had trained for battle among the best. Plus, they were immortal, which made them pretty hard to defeat.

There was no way around it. If we wanted to win this battle, we'd have to fight fire with fire.

Dragons with dragons.

"Ren, you're going to have to take your dragon form." I eyed the two black dragons that circled the mountain from high above, as though biding their time for the perfect chance to attack.

Ren paled. "I can't. You know I can't."

"You have to."

"But I—I haven't mastered control yet. I didn't finish my training with the Dragon Kings. If I lose myself again—"

"Ren." With my free hand, I grabbed his arm and yanked him toward me so that our faces were only inches apart. He was forced to look me in the eyes. "When I was the Heaven Breaker, you trusted me, didn't you? You trusted me not to make you or your dragon do anything against your values."

He nodded, gulping so that his Adam's apple bobbed.

"I'm not talking to you as the Heaven Breaker but as your friend. We've trained together for months now. If you trust me, then remember me when you transform—and remember yourself."

Again, Ren nodded.

I held his gaze for one second that lasted a century. "Now—transform!"

Ren hesitated for the space of a heartbeat. Then his eyes flashed once more. His whole body shuddered, racked with tremors. I backed away as his body morphed and began growing. Skin became scales, and fingers and toes turned into claws. Within moments, the transformation was complete. Before me stood the familiar blue-green dragon.

I'd been terrified that something would go wrong. Maybe Ren wouldn't recognize me. Maybe he'd succumb to the powers of the Heaven Breaker instead. But his huge yellow eyes snapped to mine, and he nodded. It was all the invitation I needed to sprint toward Ren and leap onto his scaly back.

"Go up! Toward Sun Wukong!" I shouted, flinging my arms around Ren's neck.

Ren spread his wings and took flight. We soared up past the spirits, still locked in combat. We passed one auntie beating back a Heavenly warrior with her slipper.

"Take that, you evil hún dàn!" she squawked.

Ren climbed higher into the air. The wind whooshed past

my face, whipping my hair around my head. A Heavenly soldier wielding a red spear sped toward us on a cloud. I batted him away by parrying his attack. I thrust upward with my sword, knocking his weapon out of his hands. Unfortunately, the warrior wasn't alone. At least a dozen Heavenly soldiers rushed toward us in his wake.

Ren gave a low, ominous growl. The sound seemed to come from his core, and it shook his scaly body from head to tail.

Got one more trick up my sleeve, Ren said. A column of water burst forth out of his mouth, blasting the Heavenly warriors. They didn't have a chance to scatter before the full force of the water hit them. Down they went, tumbling through the sky.

Wow. I gasped once the water stopped coming out of Ren's mouth. *The Dragon Kings taught you that, too?*

Oh, I've always been able to do that. The Dragon Kings just taught me how to control and aim. Unfortunately for them.

I grinned. Now that the Heavenly warriors were out of our way, Sun Wukong came into sight. Only now I realized the flashes of color that I'd thought were afterimages of his speed were actually clones of Sun Wukong. There were three of them, and all three were holding their own against the many Heavenly warriors. But with each passing moment, Heaven's soldiers slowly pushed the Sun Wukongs back to the ground.

One of the black dragons dove toward the Sun Wukong in

the middle, whose attention was focused on the warriors he was battling.

"Look out!" I shouted.

The middle Sun Wukong dove out of the way just in time and swung his Ruyi Jingu Bang in an arc. The weapon landed a painful blow against the dragon's head. Roaring and shaking, the dragon fell back.

The three clones reverted back into the original Monkey King. He spun the Ruyi Jingu Bang in a circle and let it go. The staff whizzed around Sun Wukong of its own accord, knocking weapons out of the warriors' hands and causing them to scatter.

"I thought I told you to leave!" boomed Sun Wukong, glaring at us as he kicked a Heavenly warrior in the gut.

· "You might not want to accept our help, but you need it," I retorted. "Face it, dà shèng. This isn't like before. You can't take down all of Heaven by yourself."

"I certainly don't need help from a bunch of mortal warriors," he spat.

I willed myself not to lose my patience. "Really? Because it sure looks like the mortal warriors and spirits are the ones saving your mountain."

Sun Wukong's expression scrunched up in anger. Before he could respond, the second black dragon shot toward him.

"Ren, go!" I shouted.

Beneath me, Ren's body lurched, nearly tossing me off.

I grabbed hold of his neck with both hands, just barely keeping a grip on my sword.

Ren let out a mighty roar as his body slammed into the black dragon. I gritted my teeth against the impact. Then both dragons were roaring, claws tearing at each other as they tumbled through the air. I squeezed my eyes shut, hugging Ren's neck even more tightly. Forget trying to fight. It was all I could do to avoid getting thrown off.

When I dared to open my eyes, Ren had managed to knock the black dragon into a nearby tree. The dragon bellowed and clawed at the tangle of leaves and branches, trying to get himself out.

"I could've handled that dragon on my own!" Sun Wukong sliced with his staff, taking out two more warriors.

"You don't have to do this alone," I yelled back. "Work with us. We can help each other!"

Sun Wukong didn't respond, possibly because he had to duck as a warrior launched his spear at his head. Another warrior swung his curved sword at me, but I blocked with my sword at the last moment. Ren batted him away with his tail.

"You . . . mortal, you can wield the Ruyi Jingu Bang, can't you?" Sun Wukong asked reluctantly. "Since you were the one who brought it to me earlier."

I didn't let my expression reveal my surprise at the question. "Yes," I shouted over the wind and chaos. At least, I hoped I could still wield the mighty weapon.

"Here, then! You can't expect to help me using just that pathetic sword of yours."

I watched as Sun Wukong split the Ruyi Jingu Bang in two. He tossed one of the staffs to me, and I nearly fumbled the catch in my shock. I sheathed my sword.

Sun Wukong's eyes were grave when they met mine. Even if he didn't look it, I guess the Monkey King felt more cornered than I'd thought. That was the only reason he'd willingly let me use his weapon.

I raised the staff in my hand. A wave of energy crackled from the body of the weapon into my palm. Just like the first time I'd held Fenghuang, I felt powerful.

"Not so fast, kiddo!" bellowed a deep, oddly familiar voice.

A huge force slammed into me. My body twisted from the impact, and I barely held on to Ren's back. I caught sight of my assailant's weapon—a gleaming three-pronged spear.

Erlang Shen.

Relief flooded through me. I lowered my weapon and grumbled, "In the future, if you ever need to get my attention, please tap me on the shoulder instead of almost killing me—"

"You warriors are getting easier and easier to trick, you know that?" Erlang Shen interrupted. "Gods too. So naive."

"What are you talking about?" I paused. Something was wrong. The two gods I'd grown used to seeing beside Erlang Shen weren't at his shoulder. "Wait. Where are Guanyin and Nezha?"

"Ahhhh. You won't be hearing from those two for a while."

"Huh?"

Quick as a flash, the warrior god whipped around his spear and slammed it into my gut.

Pain shot up and down my body. And then I was tumbling through the air, falling toward the ground.

CHAPTER

26

That might have ended tragically if someone didn't fly by and snatch me out of the air. With a thud and "oof!" I landed on a cloud, wobbling on my knees. I looked up toward my savior—Sun Wukong.

"Get up and fight," barked the Monkey King. "There's not a moment to waste!"

"But—but Erlang Shen, he—he betrayed—"

"Erlang Shen betrayed no one. He has always been the Jade Emperor's right-hand servant and spy," the Monkey King explained. "Have you opened your eyes now, warrior?"

The truth was almost too awful to bear. "So he . . . Erlang Shen . . . was never on our side?" I thought back and remembered how I'd found it odd that Erlang Shen was giving us another riddle to solve—as though he *wanted* to stall for time. Maybe he had. He'd been shady all along, and I'd ignored the signs.

"Of course he wasn't on your side. And you're all fools for thinking otherwise. Now, stop sniveling and get up. If you want to teach Erlang Shen a lesson, we'll have to work together. I owe him a good pounding," growled the Monkey King.

Sun Wukong was right. We were in the middle of a battle. This was no time to let the truth of Erlang Shen's allegiances shake me.

I took in my surroundings, counting the opponents who circled us. I stopped after ten, because it was too depressing. High above, Ren was locked in battle with both the black dragons.

"So what's the plan?" I asked. Sun Wukong and I circled on our cloud, back-to-back, weapons facing the Heavenly warriors. "Any specific formations you want to try out on Erlang Shen? Fancy techniques?"

"Destroy him! And everything else in our path!" roared the Monkey King.

Okay, that was pretty easy to understand.

We made a beeline toward Erlang Shen, who scattered spirits like they were made from paper. Five soldiers charged me from all sides. I swung the Ruyi Jingu Bang in a wide arc, pushing them back.

I hadn't fought with the Monkey King's weapon yet, but I'd fought many times with Fenghuang. The Ruyi Jingu Bang shouldn't be too different. As Sun Wukong and I battled back-to-back, I soon found that I was both right and wrong about that. The magical staff was about the same size as Fenghuang, but that was where the similarities ended.

When I was the Heaven Breaker, my actions had pretty much been controlled by Xi Wangmu, the Queen Mother of the West. Wielding the Ruyi Jingu Bang was something I did completely on my own.

"Erlang Shen!" Sun Wukong yelled once we got within fighting range of the warrior god.

Erlang Shen brushed a pair of monkeys off his shoulders, as easily as though they were feathers. He sneered down at us, his eyes glowing bright with the fire of battle.

"Monkey," he roared. "You've let yourself go since we last fought, I see. Eating too many peaches?"

"Eat *this!*" Sun Wukong opened his mouth and hurled out a column of flame. Erlang Shen dodged it and launched himself forward.

The two gods met in a clash of golden light and noise that seemed to shake the entire world. I rushed to the Monkey King's aid, but a purple-skinned warrior leapt out of nowhere, brandishing two lethal-looking knives.

I blocked both of his attacks, first from the knife in his right hand and then his left. I delivered a finishing blow by knocking him over the head with the Ruyi Jingu Bang. The warrior fell backward and crashed into the warriors behind him, knocking them over like a roll of very angry dominoes.

The Ruyi Jingu Bang already felt more familiar to me than

Jinyu's sword. Maybe it was because of the sacrifice we—especially Ashley—had made to get it back from the Underworld. Maybe it was the magic of the Hungry Ghost Festival giving power to all the dead, including this weapon.

Every time I lifted the Ruyi Jingu Bang, I could picture Ashley's face in my head, egging me on to keep fighting.

"C'mon! Is that the best you've got?" Erlang Shen blasted Sun Wukong with purple flames.

"Are you trying to roast me or tickle me with that pathetic fire?" The Monkey King rolled out of the way and unfortunately tumbled into a crowd of the Jade Emperor's army. They surrounded him with their weapons pointed right at him.

Erlang Shen let out a deep, satisfied belly laugh. "It's the end for you, Sun Wukong!"

"Not if I can help it!"

A streak of color shot through the sky, so fast it was almost like it had shot out of a cannon. The figure collided into Erlang Shen, sending the warrior god back with a roar.

I gasped at the sight of the familiar god who'd arrived on the scene: Nezha. He traced fiery circles with his hoop in one hand, his red spear grasped in the other.

"Erlang Shen," he bellowed. "You traitor. Did you really think you could trap Guanyin and me in that cave for long?"

Erlang Shen circled back to Nezha on his cloud, already recovered from the boy god's attack. "No. I didn't need you to be trapped for that long, though. I've been looking forward to taking you down in battle."

With a cry, Nezha launched himself toward Erlang Shen. I felt a gentle hand on my shoulder. I looked up into the warm glow of Guanyin. The goddess of mercy wore a cold, almost thunderous expression on her normally kind face.

"You've been well, warrior?" she asked.

I nodded. "I—I have. But Erlang . . . he . . . ?"

The sadness that crinkled Guanyin's face told me all I needed to know. "Don't fear. We may have lost one powerful ally, but many other deities might yet be swayed to join us. Now, I must help Nezha." She patted me softly on the shoulder. "This is one battle I'm afraid he likely won't win—not without my help."

Guanyin soared toward where Nezha and Erlang Shen were locked in battle, taking her warmth with her. As the full realization of the warrior god's betrayal hit me, fury bubbled up from the pit of my stomach.

Erlang Shen hadn't just abandoned Guanyin and Nezha. He'd abandoned the warriors and humans. And if there was one thing I couldn't stand, it was that dreadfully hopeless, lonely feeling of abandonment.

He wasn't going to get away with it. Not if I could help it.

CHAPTER

27

Power surged through my veins as I hurtled toward the warrior god.

"No, Faryn! Go back!" shouted Guanyin. I ignored her warnings.

Erlang Shen laughed maniacally as I drew close. He turned his feverish, wicked eyes on me. The normal Faryn would have panicked. But somehow, I knew what to do.

"Zhǎng!" I commanded the Ruyi Jingu Bang. *Grow.* The staff became heavier in my hands, thickening and lengthening in my palm. I spun the weapon around my head the way I'd seen Sun Wukong do earlier and hurled the spinning staff at Erlang Shen. He dove out of the way. The staff instead slammed into the crowd of warriors surrounding Sun Wukong, toppling them out of the sky. The spinning Ruyi Jingu Bang followed them until it knocked every last one of the warriors down to the earth.

I turned my gaze back toward Erlang Shen, only to see that he was locked in combat with both Nezha and Guanyin. The boy god was surrounded by a blaze of fire as he rapidly wove in and out with his weapons, attacking Erlang Shen on all sides. Guanyin hung back. She'd drawn out her white vase and flung a droplet of clear liquid toward Erlang Shen. It sprouted into a huge vine that snaked over his body, rendering him temporarily immobile.

As my fury ebbed into anger, I realized the gods didn't need my help handling Erlang Shen at all. And with Alex still engaged in battle, I had other business to take care of.

Sun Wukong floated down toward me on a cloud. He stared at me with a strange mixture of admiration and mistrust. "Where did you learn how to use my weapon, mortal?"

"I . . . was watching you earlier."

He squinted. "You learn fast."

I shrugged. Even I couldn't explain why the Ruyi Jingu Bang felt so easy for me to wield. Maybe the magic of the Hungry Ghost Festival had extended a little bit to me, too.

"I didn't need your help, by the way," Sun Wukong growled. "I made those morons think they'd gotten me, but I had the upper hand the whole time."

"Oh . . . right. I knew that."

"As if I, the Great Sage, Equal of Heaven, would require the aid of a mere mortal—"

"*Faryn! And Monkey!*"

"That's Monkey *King* to you!" Sun Wukong whipped around indignantly.

Alex had broken free of the spirits. After I dropped my gaze below, it was easy to see why. Most of the dead were now fixated on backing up the monkeys and engaging the Heavenly warriors in combat. Both black dragons had fallen to the earth, and they seemed to have been knocked out cold. Ren, still in his dragon form, picked off some of the last remaining warriors, one by one.

My brother glared up at us. As he drew closer, I appreciated just how eerily similar Alex was to the version of himself I'd seen back in the Chamber of Mirrors. He was definitely taller, his muscles more defined than before. There was a steeliness in his expression that hadn't always been there, and his eyes made him seem much older than his true age.

"Give it up and come to our side, Alex." I tried to keep my voice stern but big sisterly, even though my non-big-sisterly instincts were telling me to strangle him. "Think logically. Your warriors are down. You can't win this battle."

Alex's expression scrunched up, as though he were actually giving thought to my words. Yes. At long last, I was getting through to him.

"Please, Alex. Please do the right thing," I coaxed softly. I held out the memory elixir in the palm of my hand. "Just one piece of your hair will finish the elixir and restore Ba's memories."

"Ba's memories . . ." Alex raised a hand up to his hair—but then paused. "Why would my hair have the power to restore Ba's memories if I'm not even related to him?"

"You're Liu Bo's son," I said simply. "And you are my brother, blood-related or not."

Alex's cold expression crumbled. I held my breath. *Please, Alex. Please do this for Ba. For our family. For me.*

I almost sighed in relief when my brother pulled a piece of hair from his head, reached out, and dropped it into the elixir. The liquid fizzed white and shook the whole vial, but I held on to it tightly. When the liquid settled, it had turned a brilliant red color.

"It worked," Alex marveled. His eyes filled with wonder—and tears. "I . . . didn't really believe it would work."

My own eyes were suddenly a lot wetter than before. Tucking the elixir into my backpack, I stepped closer to Alex and held out my arms for a hug. "Of course it worked. Like I said—you're my brother. My dì di."

Alex inched forward and hesitantly opened his arms, as though about to accept my hug.

Sun Wukong barked out a laugh that startled us both.

"Atta boy. Now you know not to behave in such a foolhardy manner around the gods. You have a millennium to go before you can stand on equal footing with the likes of me, pathetic warrior." Sun Wukong sniffed. "Best that you give up your foolish thoughts now, before you hurt yourself."

Alex's eyes snapped from Sun Wukong to me, and his shoulders stiffened. He dropped his arms.

"Wait, Alex—" I blurted out.

"You're wrong. You're both wrong. I will never give up," Alex growled. "The Jade Emperor asked me to punish you both—and I plan to obey. I *have* to obey," he added in a quieter voice, almost to himself, "if I ever want to meet my true parents."

No. I'd come so close to convincing Alex to rejoin our side.

But a twisted, conflicted part of me understood Alex's reasoning. He wanted to find his family. Just like I did. How could I fault my brother for that?

Now all I could do was defend myself against Alex's inevitable attack. I clenched my hands around the Ruyi Jingu Bang, ready to strike as soon as my brother did.

In normal hand-to-hand combat, I could probably beat Alex eight out of ten times. The rules were different when it came to our weapons, though. Plus, there was the tiny matter of Alex having an entire army of dragons at his disposal. I had . . . monkeys. Didn't take a genius to imagine how *that* battle would turn out.

"The Jade Emperor isn't here, Alex," I pointed out in a last-ditch effort to get him to change his mind. My brother had to listen to me. When we were little, Alex always listened to me. "You can make your own decisions."

"Don't treat me like a baby, Faryn. I *am* making my own decisions. And who said the Jade Emperor isn't here?"

A sudden chill ran down my back. Unless I was imagining it, the sky darkened.

"The Jade Emperor and Xi Wangmu are always, always watching, Faryn." Alex's words sounded robotic and rehearsed. "You need to be careful about what you say."

I wanted to retort that the Jade Emperor and Xi Wangmu should join the battle themselves if they really wanted to make their point, but the small, logical part of my brain told me that was a bad idea.

My fingers tightened around my weapon. "I'm sorry it has to be this way, Alex." I refused to let myself appear weak in this moment. I wanted my brother to see me exactly how he'd always seen me when we were younger—as the strong, protective older sister, who'd fight off anyone to protect those I loved.

Only now, it meant fighting against those I loved.

Alex's cold expression morphed into one of pure anger. He raised the gleaming golden spear into the air, high above his head. "I'm sorry it has to be this way too, jiě jie."

Older sister. Hearing the honorific at this moment stung me with worse pain than any weapon could have delivered. The air between us crackled with electricity—maybe lightning from the darkening, stormy clouds; maybe magic from Fenghuang; maybe both.

The black dragons soared through the air. Those dragons had been my allies just six months ago.

Dragons, I thought, more out of desperation than anything else. *Remember me? It's your old Heaven Breaker pal. It's Faryn. Yeah, the wiser, better-looking Heaven Breaker.*

At first, only silence answered. My concentration broke when a green-skinned Heavenly warrior charged at me with his spear. I blocked his blow with the Ruyi Jingu Bang, sending him soaring away through the clouds.

Old Heaven Breaker? came a deep rumble in my head. The two nearest dragons stopped in midair. They turned their massive heads toward me, and their bright-yellow eyes met mine.

Yes, I urged. Relief flooded through me. *Please help your old master.*

But the Heaven Breaker . . . he would not like this. The dragon on the left turned back toward where the other dragons were fighting the rebel gods and monkeys.

If you care about this world and want to protect it from destruction, you'll help me instead. Now, by all the power that remains in me, I command that you help me, your true master!

Somehow, my shouting worked. Both dragons flew over at once and bowed low toward me.

Trying not to let my giddy relief ruin my composure, I added, *Fight off the Heavenly warriors. Aim to injure, not kill. Understood?*

Understood.

The dragons took off in unison. I turned my attention back to the battle at hand. Alex fought off several monkeys, but they were more of a nuisance to him than a real threat. Any moment now, he'd turn back to me—and I'd have to face my brother and the mighty Fenghuang once and for all.

But technically there were two of us against one. And for all his faults, Sun Wukong *was* one of the most powerful figures who'd ever lived. He was fighting alongside me, not Alex. I had nothing to fear.

Without waiting for Sun Wukong to make a move, I launched myself toward Alex. He didn't hesitate before lunging toward me. A bolt of lightning jolted down from the sky and traveled into the tip of Fenghuang. Spear slammed into staff. The resulting clash sent jolts up my arm. I clenched my teeth and glared into Alex's eyes, which crackled with the light reflecting from our weapons. It took every last drop of my strength to push back up against Alex, to keep him from knocking me out of the sky and down to the ground.

"You—can't—win—Alex." I hoped he'd listen. That he'd remember how we'd always fought on each other's side. That he'd want to keep fighting on each other's side.

His eyes narrowed, a light dancing inside them. Taunting me. "Go back and tell Ba—I've—already—won!"

Sun Wukong slammed Alex in the side with his Ruyi Jingu

Bang. The combined force of both our attacks was more than enough to take Alex down. With a cry of pain, my brother fell off his cloud, plunging downward.

"Alex!" I screamed. Without thinking, I dove to catch him before he hit the ground, but a force dragged me back.

"Let the foolish boy fall," Sun Wukong sneered. "He deserves it for trying to invade my mountain. Oh, don't start crying. Your brother, Andrew—"

"Alex!"

"Amanda, whatever, he won't die. He can't. He's the Jade Emperor's Heavenly General—he's immortal now."

"Still!" I protested. Did it hurt immortal beings when they fell out of the sky? Had Alex at least remembered to wear his kneepads to battle? I had no clue.

Jerking away from the Monkey King, I turned again to face the spot where Alex had fallen—only to realize that far below, a new nightmare had unfolded.

A huge fissure had opened in the ground, and the spirits were being sucked inside it. I watched in horror as Cixi and Hongyi whizzed into the dark crack in the earth, taken in by an unseen force. Cindy You followed, frantically waving goodbye to us. Then Moli, eyes wide with shock, shouted, "G-goodb—!" but the rest of her farewell was torn away by the wind.

"Cindy! Moli!" I cried, but they were already gone.

Nai Nai was the last to go. Her eyes met mine, and she opened her mouth. I barely heard her over the howling wind. "Faryn, your mother—betrothed to a Demon King—Underworld—!"

"My mother? *Betrothed?* What does that mean?"

I lunged forward to grab Nai Nai, but it was too late. With her arms still stretched out toward me, my grandmother disappeared down into the fissure as well.

"Nai Nai!" I screamed. "Wait!" I urged the cloud beneath my feet to travel down to her, but Sun Wukong held me back.

"No! If you go down there, you'll be sucked in, too," he shouted.

"What's happening? Where are they all going?"

"Back to Diyu, of course. This must be King Yama's doing. Bet he didn't like the fact that those spirits came to my mountain to aid me. He's had a grudge against me for centuries, the old coot. All I did was nearly destroy the Underworld once. Jeez."

I let out a slow, shaky breath. Even if King Yama had taken my ancestors back to Diyu, I could still see them again. Somehow. I *had* to see them again. Plus, if I understood Nai Nai's words correctly, my mother was still in Diyu, betrothed to a Demon King. It sounded like she was in deep, deep trouble—and I had to rescue her. I hadn't even gotten to say goodbye.

"More importantly—my monkeys!" Sun Wukong yelled, his voice trembling with fury.

Before I could turn to see what he was talking about, the

cloud dipped beneath my feet. A scream clawed its way out of my throat. My stomach swooped until it just about dropped through my body. We came to a jarring halt that churned the contents of my stomach again in front of the Heavenly warriors, who'd bound the monkeys with their rope. Ren, back in his human form, had also been tied up, along with Jordan. They struggled and kicked against their rope.

"Guys!" I jabbed the Ruyi Jingu Bang at their captors, who dove aside. Before I could free my friends, more Heavenly warriors stepped up to replace their comrades. They slashed their spears at me. I staggered back to avoid the point of their weapons.

Sun Wukong's fury turned his eyes a flaming, brilliant red. His body began shaking violently. With a whoosh and a flash of light, yellow flames enveloped his fur.

"Let my monkeys go!" he commanded. The Ruyi Jingu Bang shifted to thrice its normal size in Sun Wukong's hand. He swung it in an arc, knocking away several warriors.

A large, bronze-armored man with green skin warned, "You should be more concerned for yourself, Monkey King. And your monkeys."

"What?" snapped Sun Wukong.

The Heavenly warrior nodded toward the sky. "Look up."

Sun Wukong and I followed his gaze. I gasped.

The Monkey King shouted, "No!" and launched himself skyward, disappearing in a flash.

Alex. My brother had climbed to the very top of the Mountain of Flowers and Fruit, where the mossy surface of the mountain was illuminated by the light of the moon. He raised Fenghuang above his head.

"What's he doing?" Jordan cried.

I had a horrible feeling I knew what Alex would do, the moment before he followed through with it.

Sun Wukong reappeared right next to Alex—just as my brother slammed the glowing white tip of Fenghuang onto the mountain. A bolt of lightning struck down from the sky. Rain poured out of the clouds overhead, steady at first, then faster and harder. With a boom, a ring of pulsating white energy shot out of the spear and enveloped the whole mountain.

Monkeys and people alike screamed. Alex's army dove for cover in the sky, riding their clouds far away, abandoning their prisoners. Sun Wukong dove toward his monkeys.

I tossed the yuán onto the ground. It turned into a chariot. Without pausing for breath, I yanked Jordan and Ren to their feet. "Go!" I shouted. They didn't need me telling them twice. Hands and feet still bound, they dove into the chariot. I followed a heartbeat later, commanding the stone lions to get as high and far away from the crippling blast as possible.

White-hot energy sizzled above me, slicing off some of my hair. I screamed at how close the heat was, but we made it just in time. The stone lions climbed higher and higher into the air, closer to safety.

After we'd put a safe distance between us and the mountain, I chanced a look back. I stifled a groan.

"Oh my gods," gasped Jordan.

"That's not good," Ren added.

Below us, the Mountain of Flowers and Fruit, home to the Monkey King and so many legends, was crumbling. Huge chunks of rock broke away from the surface. I was so transfixed by the chaos below that I almost missed someone whizzing by us. By the time I looked up and realized who it was, it was too late.

"Alex!" I called. "Wait!"

If he heard me, my brother gave no indication. I thought I heard Alex laughing. But maybe it was just the wind.

Alex was there one moment, Fenghuang held high in his hands. Then, with a spark of light, my brother simply vanished.

CHAPTER

28

I don't know how long I stood there on a cloud, struggling to comprehend the events of the past hour or so. Erlang Shen had betrayed us. Alex had almost returned to my side—and then changed his mind.

Xiong had warned me before I left that I'd lose someone dear to me yet again. Now I knew what he'd meant. I was sure, even if only for a second, that I'd had Alex back—and then he left me once more.

After what might have been moments or hours, I felt a familiar warmth near me. Guanyin. I knew even before looking up into the goddess's kind black eyes.

"You did well, warrior." She cast her gaze around at the battered monkeys and warriors, plus two black dragons. "You all did well."

"Where's Erlang Shen?" I asked.

"Gone back to Heaven with the rest of 'em." Nezha popped up behind Guanyin. The scowl on his boyish face revealed his deep disgust. He twirled his flaming hoop through the air and caused a few nearby monkeys to edge away nervously. "We'll have to pay him back another time. Soon."

"For now, we must leave you all to regroup," Guanyin said. She and Nezha exchanged a brief but heavy look.

"We'll meet again soon. Don't worry," Nezha reassured me. I blushed. I guess my inner panic must have shown up on my face.

With that, the gods ascended on their clouds. In moments they were gone, as quickly as they'd come.

I turned to Ren. "Ren. My mother—I know how to find her. My nai nai said my mother is down in Diyu, betrothed to a Demon King."

Ren's jaw dropped. "Betrothed to *what*?"

"We have to rescue her."

Ren nodded. "And Ashley."

"So . . . should we do an icebreaker?" Jordan interrupted.

Ren and I stared at him in confusion. "Icebreaker? Like the mint?" Ren asked.

"No, I mean the icebreaker that, like, breaks the ice between strangers? To avoid awkward situations like . . . this." Jordan gestured behind us.

Sun Wukong and his swarm of monkeys sat on a gigantic cloud, behind our chariot. Several of the monkeys were nursing injuries, but on the whole, they seemed to have made it out of the battle all right. Mr. Zhao sat next to the monkeys. He appeared quite unharmed, although he wasn't smiling like he usually was. Hovering near the monkeys, looking completely out of place, were the two dragons I'd somehow managed to convince to join our side.

"I don't think any number of icebreakers will break this awkwardness," I said.

Jordan considered this a moment, frowning. "That's fair."

After Sun Wukong had realized that the Mountain of Flowers and Fruit was now an unsalvageable wreck, he'd reacted with much greater calmness than I'd have expected, given his reputation. I guess hundreds of years hiding away in a peaceful mountain had mellowed him out after all. He'd just seemed . . . tired. And sad. He hadn't even given chase to the Heavenly warriors and instead focused his attention on attending to his wounded monkeys. We must've looked like a really big, ugly parade float.

"You're sure this . . . warrior mountain will be suitable for my monkeys?" Sun Wukong called.

"The New Order is a warrior *society*, not a mountain," Jordan corrected. "We've hosted other warrior societies there in the past for tournaments. So there's definitely enough space."

"Tournaments?" Ren and I both said.

"Oh, yeah. Used to be really big in the past. Then people got busy, and demon hunting became less important, and tournaments are super expensive in the first place . . ." Jordan's voice trailed off. "Anyway, there's room at the New Order for all of us. Just tell those monkeys to stay the heck away from my video games."

It was early morning now. The sky was painted a brilliant orange and pink. I followed Ye Ye's compass, which pointed toward the horizon. We'd been traveling about an hour now, but we still had at least another couple of hours to go before reaching Manhattan's Chinatown.

"So," Jordan said after a long moment of silence. "Who exactly was that punk with bad hair? You called him *brother*, Faryn."

Much as I didn't want to talk or even think about Alex, I could tell this was a conversation we were going to have at some point or another. I *did* owe Jordan an explanation, anyway.

"Listen, as far as little siblings go, you've got it easy with Ashley," I told Jordan. "At least she hasn't tried to kill you yet."

I gave Jordan the rundown of everything that had happened between the Lunar New Year and now. Ren added any details or facts that I'd forgotten.

"Whoa," Jordan said when I was finished giving him the my-brother-turned-into-devil-spawn spiel. "Suddenly I'm missing Ashley a lot . . ."

"Little brothers are the worst," I grumbled. "One moment

they're breaking your dolls. Next moment they're plotting world domination and destroying you."

"But Alex failed, right?" Ren gave us a tentative, hopeful smile. "His goal was to destroy all of us, including Sun Wukong. All he managed to do was destroy the mountain. That's a win for us, right?"

I didn't want to burst Ren's bubble, but it was hard to say. "Dunno. I guess we'll have to find out when we report back to the New Order."

"Right." Jordan nodded. "We'll report back to the Elders and then go on a new quest to the Underworld."

"Another quest?" Ren groaned. "We just finished one and almost died, and you want to go on *another* one?"

Jordan's face turned beet red. "My sister's still down there!"

"Yeah, but you know the terms of the deal," I told him as gently as I could. "We won't get Ashley back until we're finished with the Ruyi Jingu Bang. Do you really think you'll be able to get that any time soon?" Jordan said nothing, just crossed his arms over his chest with a sulking expression on his face. "Trust me. I want to go get Ashley, too, but we'll probably have to sit tight for a bit."

Jordan turned his head away from Ren and me. I couldn't blame him. If I were in his shoes and Alex had been trapped in Diyu, I would've done anything in my power to get to him. Betrayal or no betrayal.

"How much longer until we're there?" Sun Wukong yelled.

I checked my compass. The sun had climbed higher into the sky, so it was probably about ten or eleven in the morning now.

"Uh . . . half an hour," I guessed.

"We could've already been at your warrior mountain if you'd let me take us there in a somersault," the Monkey King groused. "It's not too late, you know. You could just let me—"

"No," I said firmly. I knew all about Sun Wukong's powers, including his ability to travel 34,000 miles in a single somersault. I also had a hunch that if he tried to bring everyone via godly somersault to the New Order, something would go horribly wrong, and at least somebody might lose a limb or two.

Sun Wukong settled down with a grumble, and I concentrated on the road ahead of me. Ren and Jordan fell silent. The sound of Jordan's soft snores behind me soon told me why.

"Falun."

I whipped around in surprise. I'd almost forgotten Mr. Zhao was with us, too. Moli's father stood. Still unsmiling, he wore a stern expression on his face—one I'd never seen on him before. "The New Order warriors are already preparing for war, aren't they?"

"I . . ." Now that I thought about it, I wasn't totally sure what they were doing.

"We need to alert them immediately. Very soon, we will be

entering all-out war with the gods. They must not make the same mistake that the Jade Society did. They *must* heed our warnings."

"They will," I reassured Moli's father.

Forty-five minutes later, Manhattan's Chinatown came into view. The place appeared just as it had been when we'd left it. Red lanterns and decorations for the Hungry Ghost Festival hung in the shop windows and streets. Everywhere, people milled about in the markets.

I led the stone lions to a landing in an empty alley.

"We're here," I shouted up at Sun Wukong. He and his monkeys hovered above in their cloud, peering down at us uncertainly.

"Hmph. This is a huge downgrade from the Mountain of Flowers and Fruit," Sun Wukong said churlishly. His cloud landed on the ground and then disappeared, leaving a group of monkeys in the middle of the Chinatown alleyway.

The chariot turned back into a coin, which I tucked into my pocket. As I led us out onto the streets, it occurred to me how odd we must look: a trio of dirty, worn-down warriors leading a troop of monkeys, two massive black dragons, and one very angry-looking Monkey King.

Sun Wukong waved his Ruyi Jingu Bang through the air. Nothing happened.

"What was that supposed to do?" Ren asked.

"Turned us invisible," the Monkey King explained curtly.

Just as he finished speaking, a middle-aged businessman bumped into him. "Hey, watch it!" Sun Wukong snapped. The man reeled back, gaping at what he must've thought was thin air yelling at him.

"Oh my gods! The peaches are alive!" screamed a nearby shop owner, abandoning his fruit stand. Sun Wukong's monkeys had helped themselves to the barrel of peaches, which would've looked to any outsiders like the peaches were floating in midair. Also, one of the black dragons had accidentally knocked over an entire stall.

Invisibility or no, we'd have to move through here quickly.

"Where can I speak to the king?" Sun Wukong demanded.

"There's no king here." Jordan snickered. "But there is Elder Xiong."

"Then take me to this Elder Xiong!"

I made a beeline across the square, straight for the New Order temple. I had a feeling Elder Xiong would be in there, as he usually was at this time of the day. Once we'd all reached the temple, Sun Wukong waved his Ruyi Jingu Bang again, turning us visible.

Jordan pried open the great black doors and peered inside. "Elder Xiong?"

Several people were inside, praying. The two nearest to the entrance were Elder Xiong and Ba—Zhuang. They glanced up at the sound, eyes widening when they saw me there, along

309

with probably the strangest crowd they'd seen in ages. Xiong stood up, and I knelt down on the floor in front of them. Beside me, Ren and Jordan did the same, followed by Mr. Zhao.

"Faryn, Jordan, and Ren." Xiong acknowledged us with a nod. "You've returned, I see." He narrowed his eyes. "And . . . Ashley?"

A heartbeat of tense silence. I opened my mouth, struggling to find an answer. I knew my words would be met with disappointment no matter what I said.

Jordan beat me to it. "Still down in the Underworld."

"What happened? Why is she down there?"

"Ashley volunteered to exchange her own freedom so we could take a powerful weapon. But we can't leave her there. We must rescue my sister, Xiong shī fu."

"That indeed we must," agreed the Elder. He turned next to Mr. Zhao, who gave him a respectful nod. "Brave Jade Society warrior, please stand. I've heard much about your role in rallying the Jade Society warriors against the plot of some of the gods. Thank you, Zhao Boyang."

Moli's father had always given me the impression of being a clumsy man, but now he stood tall and proud, back straight, chin up. I watched in awe as the Elders inclined their heads respectfully toward Mr. Zhao.

"The Elders are bowing," gasped a familiar voice. Ah Qiao. "They never bow to anyone!"

"Shhhhh." His mother.

Slowly, everyone around me sank to their knees. I did the same.

"Please stand." Moli's father laughed nervously. His cheeks were so flushed with heat, we could've fried an egg roll on them. "Please. I—I didn't do much. Really. I just did what had to be done."

"You may rise," Xiong called out after another moment. In unison, the warriors rose.

A ghost of Mr. Zhao's old, jovial smile passed across his lips, but it was gone in a moment. He had changed since the quest of the Lunar New Year, after Moli's death. I wondered if he'd changed *because* of Moli's death.

"We have much to discuss," Xiong said gravely. "The warrior societies *must* stand in strong unity against the demons, or else we will all perish."

"I agree," Mr. Zhao said with an air of equal seriousness. "Our warrior societies must reconcile any and all differences if we are to protect humanity."

Xiong swept his gaze across us with a tiny smile. "But first, you warriors must rest."

"Rest?" Jordan cried out. "How do you expect me to rest when—?"

Xiong gave Jordan such a cutting look that he stopped speaking at once. "Please, brave warriors, tell us all about your quest."

I nodded toward the monkeys behind me. "Elder Xiong, we believe we've found the 'old ally' from the shī. This is Sun Wukong," I said, feeling kind of dumb. I was pretty sure the Monkey King's identity was obvious. How many monkey kings were there, after all?

Xiong glanced past us toward Sun Wukong, who just sniffed and crossed his arms over his chest.

"*You're* the king?" Sun Wukong asked. "Jeez. No wonder these kids are in a mess."

Xiong didn't seem fazed by the rudeness. On the contrary, he bowed his head to show respect. "I wouldn't go quite as far as to call myself *king*, but I am the leader of the New Order. And you must be the legendary Monkey King, Sun Wukong, dà shèng."

Sun Wukong's chest puffed out. "The one and only."

"What brings you to the New Order, Monkey King?"

"My monkeys and I . . ." Sun Wukong hesitated and pinched up his expression, as though asking for help were causing him physical pain—which it probably was. "We don't have a home right now. We're hoping you could give us somewhere to stay."

"The two dragons need a place to stay, too," I added quickly. "Thanks."

"Dragons?" yelped one of the Elders in alarm.

"And?" I prompted, ignoring the murmurs of confusion and giving Sun Wukong a we-had-a-deal look.

He rolled his eyes and gritted his teeth. "And in return, we'll help the warriors win this war against most of Heaven."

Xiong nodded and stroked his beard. "Very well. We'll make sure that Sun Wukong, dà shèng, and his monkeys will be treated as honored guests during their stay at the New Order."

This seemed to appease Sun Wukong, because he actually shut up.

I took advantage of the momentary silence to step forward. "I—I need to speak to my father. The warrior Zhuang. It's urgent."

Xiong turned his gaze toward me. But rather than the confusion or surprise I'd anticipated, I saw understanding. "You have something to give him, don't you?"

I nodded. I reached toward my backpack, where I carried the elixir. Xiong's eyes followed the movement, a small, knowing smile stretching across his face.

"Zhuang," called the master of the New Order.

My father turned around and stood up slowly with his eyes closed. When they opened, they met everyone's eyes one by one—everyone's except mine. I tried not to let that get to me.

I stood there, unsure what to do next. Xiong placed his hand on my back and gave me a gentle push forward. Aware of the many pairs of eyes on me, I took one step forward, then another and another.

Ba's eyes finally met mine when I stood right in front of him.

Raising the vial toward my father, I said, "Please drink this."

"What is it?"

"Um . . ." Well, I couldn't tell my father it was a memory-restoring elixir. That'd probably make him run for the hills. "It's, uh, a tonic for your . . . muscles." In a moment of inspiration, I added, "The gods gave this to me as a gift for completing their quest."

Ba stepped away, eyes wide. "Then you should use it, Faryn."

"I already had some," I lied. "Trust me, you'll feel better once you've taken this tonic."

Ba gave me a small, appreciative smile. "Thank you, child." He took the vial from my hands, raised it to his lips, and tilted it back. The purple liquid poured out of the vial, and with three big gulps, it all disappeared down Ba's throat.

"Ah." My father sighed once he'd swallowed the last gulp. He shook his head and gave us a thoughtful look. My heart hammered in my chest. The silence seemed to grow louder with each passing moment. "Powerful tonic. I do feel stronger, and—"

Ba gasped and lurched down to the ground.

"Ba!" I cried without thinking at the same time others shouted, "What's happening?"

I bent down and placed a hand on my father's back. His body was racked with shivers. But after a few moments, the shivers passed.

"Ba?" I said uncertainly.

My father straightened. My arm slid off his back and returned to my side. I found myself face-to-face with Ba, and for the first time in years and years, we were looking at each other—really looking.

"F-Falun?" Ba whispered.

My throat closed up. I nodded. Something wet splashed down my nose and cheeks. Tears.

Then Ba leaned forward and wrapped me in the biggest, tightest hug I'd ever received in my life. I could barely breathe, but I didn't even mind.

"I'm . . . back," my father said in a choked voice. "I'm—I'm late. So very late, nǚ ér." *Daughter.*

"Ba," I gasped.

We hugged, the warmth of the embrace saying all the words that we couldn't speak. After a while, someone cleared their throat. I blinked back tears and looked up. Several warriors had pulled out tissues and were wiping away their own tears. Even Xiong's eyes were redder and brighter than usual.

Reluctantly, I pulled away from Ba's embrace. My father helped me to my feet, and we stood side by side as the master of the New Order gathered everyone's attention on himself once more.

"Now that the warriors have returned successfully from their quest, I have good news and bad news," Xiong announced in a firm voice. "The bad news is, as you may have noticed, Nezha, Guanyin, and Erlang Shen are no longer with us."

Anger flared anew in my chest at the mention of Erlang Shen's name.

"Erlang Shen joined the Jade Emperor's army," I said. "No—he was always part of it. He was a traitor all along."

I expected this news to shock Xiong and the others, but they exchanged heavy expressions that told me they already knew. Even Ba didn't seem surprised.

"Yes, I'm afraid we didn't discover the true nature of his intentions until it was too late," Xiong said. "One of our warriors stumbled across the traitorous god as he was confiding in one of his allies in secret. Erlang Shen fled the New Order, but he'd already collected enough information from us to do quite some damage, I'm afraid." Xiong shook his head. "As for Nezha and Guanyin, they left to do reconnaissance and convince some other gods to join our side."

While we'd been gone, it seemed as though the New Order had been through a lot, too.

"And the good news?" Ren asked.

"All hope is not lost," Xiong said, a grim smile on his face. "We received a crane from Nezha and Guanyin earlier today. One of the most powerful goddesses, Nüwa, will join our fight."

Cheers rose from the monkeys. We had the mother goddess of the Earth on our side. Maybe there was hope after all.

As the warriors chatted among themselves, my father turned to me with a smile stretching across his face. I couldn't help but smile back. My heart hadn't felt so light in years.

"Nǚ ér," he said slowly, as though relishing each syllable. "Daughter. Falun. Won't you give your father another hug?"

I threw my arms around the warrior I thought I'd lost forever. My father. Ba. Maybe if I hugged him long and hard enough, it would make up for all the hugs we'd missed over the years.

For the moment, nothing else mattered—not the war, not Alex's stubbornness, not Erlang Shen's betrayal. Nothing mattered but the fact that here, at long last, in Ba's arms, I was safe. I was home.

My father pulled back and held me at arm's length, examining me from head to foot with a tearful expression in his eyes. "I'm so proud of you, Falun. We have quite some catching up to do, don't we?"

"Yes. Yes we do." I blurted out, "Nai Nai said my mother—or her spirit—is trapped in Diyu. With a Demon King."

Ba's eyes widened, and horror dawned on his face. "That won't do. The first thing we'll do after this is pray to Ye Ye for help," my father said. "Now, then. About your brother. He . . . he's turned over to the other side, hasn't he?"

"Yes, but . . . not completely."

Alex had helped me complete the memory elixir for Ba's sake, after all. He wasn't beyond saving. He only wanted to find his own blood-related family and do what he thought was right.

Alex was still the brother I'd grown up with for twelve

years. Just as Jordan and Ashley had always fought for each other, I now had to fight for Alex. Even if he tried to kill me in the process. Or I tried to kill him. After all, what are siblings for?

Besides, I didn't have to do any of this on my own. I had Ba's help this time.

"How are we going to save Alex and my mother? And the world?" I hoped my father still had all the answers, like he did when I was younger.

Ba smiled at me—a warm, intelligent smile, with a familiar hint of mischief. "Don't worry, nǔ ér. We'll make a plan."

DEMONS AND DEITIES THROUGH THE DYNASTIES

A Glossary

Hello! Author speaking. As I said in the last book, I drew the following definitions and interpretations of Chinese mythology below from my own research and experience, including the stories I learned growing up. Most of it comes from the classical Chinese text *Journey to the West* by Wu Cheng'en and the guidebook *Chinese Mythology A to Z* by Jeremy Roberts. There are other versions of Chinese folklore out there, so this is not by any means a comprehensive guide. But I do hope it will teach you a little bit about the mythology that appears in *The Fallen Hero*—and make you want to do your own research to learn more!

DEITIES

Dragon Kings: The Chinese believe in five Dragon Kings, four who rule over the seas and one who commands them all: the Dragon King of the North Sea, the Dragon King of the South Sea, the Dragon King of the East Sea, the Dragon King of the West Sea, and the Dragon King of the Center. Hmm . . . I'm seeing a pattern in their names. These beings live in crystal palaces beneath the water. The Dragon Kings don't just own pearls and jewels, they *eat* them. Sounds like an expensive grocery list. They're powerful enough that they watch over the seas, move mountains, and create massive tidal waves. Plus, the Jade Emperor relies on them for reports about the seas every year.

Erlang Shen: Erlang Shen's official title is "True Lord, the Great Illustrious Sage," which is pretty apt since he's an epic warrior. He's the god of war and waterways. He's also the nephew of the Jade Emperor. Erlang Shen has a third, truth-seeing eye in the middle of his forehead that can sense if a man is honest or not. The eye also gives him X-ray vision, not to mention a surefire way to mess with humans and demons alike. In many stories, his loyal dog, Xiao Tian Quan, never leaves his side. Don't mistake Erlang Shen for a dog-loving softie, though. Those two combined have and will really mess things up in Heaven. Xiao Tian Quan may be small, but he's fierce and powerful, and he helps Erlang Shen subdue evil spirits.

Guanyin: Guanyin is commonly worshipped as the goddess of mercy. In some traditions, she's considered male, but in others, she's considered female to better represent the qualities of mercy, compassion, and purity, traits customarily thought as feminine. Many pray to this goddess in the hopes that she will relieve suffering or provide help to others.

Jade Emperor: If you thought the Jade Emperor seemed intense at the Lunar New Year banquet, wait until you hear more about him. His full official title is "Peace Absolving, Central August Spirit Exalted, Ancient Buddha, Most Pious and Honorable, His Highness the Jade Emperor, Xuanling High Sovereign." The fancy title isn't just for show. He rules all of Heaven, Diyu, and Earth.

Becoming the Jade Emperor was no easy task, though. Once just an ordinary immortal, he hid in a mountain as he passed more than three thousand trials, each lasting three million years. There he cultivated his Tao—the Way, or the process of things coming together while transforming. Wild, right?

The Jade Emperor finally emerged strong enough to defeat the megapowerful demon that had been wreaking havoc on Earth. Everyone was in awe of the Jade Emperor, mostly because his beard had grown super long while he was busy passing all those trials. Anyway, after he got rid of the demon, the deities named him their supreme ruler.

Meng Po: Meng Po, or the Lady of Forgetfulness, serves Five-Flavored Tea to the dead in Diyu. She makes them forget the memories of their past lives. That way, spirits can reincarnate into their next lives without any burdens, like paying back student loans.

Nezha: Some of Nezha's many titles include "Third Lotus Prince," "Third Prince Lord," "Marshal of the Central Altar," and "Marshal Zhong Tan."

Basically, the story of Nezha goes like this: Nezha's mother was pregnant with him for three and a half years, which was understandably concerning. One day, she finally gave birth—not to an adorable Chinese baby, but to a lotus (or in some versions of the tale, a ball). So Nezha's father, Li Jing, like any good, gentle parent, whipped out a sword and sliced the lotus wide open to reveal a boy wearing a flaming bracelet on his right wrist. Totally normal birthing process in ancient China. A priest stopped by the family's house and told the parents to name the boy Nezha.

When he grew up, Nezha used two weapons: his spear and cosmic rings. They were so gobsmackingly powerful that when he swam in the sea with them, they shook the Dragon Palace of the East Sea. The Dragon King of the East Sea didn't like that, so he sent a messenger to wrestle the weapons away from Nezha. Well, Nezha didn't like *that*. He retaliated with one blow of his rings and defeated the messenger. The Dragon King liked that even less, and he sent his third son, Ao Bing, to teach Nezha a lesson. Once again, Nezha struck with his cosmic rings, and Ao Bing shrunk from a vicious dragon into a puny human. They had a giant battle, and eventually Ao Bing lost, because Nezha's just that epic. From then, Nezha was revered/feared as one of the strongest warriors in the land. So I guess the moral of the story is, really long pregnancies can give babies dragon-defeating powers.

Wenshu: Wenshu is known as the god of wisdom, and he speaks with a boom-y, echo-y, holier-than-thou voice. Don't think he's all brains and no brawn, though. Wenshu rides a big, fierce green lion and carries a double-edged flaming sword in his right hand that symbolizes wisdom's sharpness. In his other hand he holds a blue lotus flower that contains the Perfection of Wisdom Sutra, which he can also use to defeat enemies by reading from it and boring them to death.

Xi Wangmu/Queen Mother of the West: Xi Wangmu is the wife of the Jade Emperor. She is associated with the phoenix, the complement to the Jade Emperor's symbol of the dragon. Many stories depict Xi Wangmu as the guardian of the immortal peaches, which is no easy task, because everyone and their grandmother always tries to steal them. Sick of chasing thieves away for eons, Xi Wangmu was bound to grow cranky and kind of evil. Who can blame her?

DEMONS AND CREATURES

Bull Demon King: In *Journey to the West*, the Bull Demon King is the husband to Princess Iron Fan and the father of the Red Prince. Long ago, he also became sworn brothers with the Monkey King and six other demons. His true form is an enormous white bull. In *The Fallen Hero*, the Bull Demon King reveals himself to be the long-lost father of Ashley and Jordan. The siblings are less than enthused by this turn of events.

Dragon: Since ancient times in China, many Chinese have believed that they are "龙的传人" (lóng de chuán rén), which translates to "Descendants of the Dragon." According to this belief, the Chinese evolved from dragons. Pretty cool origin story, right? A dragon is thought to be a symbol of luck and wealth and is often associated with jade. They are also portrayed as powerful and mighty, which explains why thunder and lightning accompany them when they fly. Dragons can do pretty much anything: swim, fly, guard the gods and their treasure, make it rain (literally and figuratively), become a convenient form of transportation . . . you name it, they've got you covered.

Fenghuang/phoenix: Originally, the term "Fenghuang" referred to two divine birds who often appeared in Chinese mythology. "Feng" refers to the male, and "huang" refers to the female. In translations, "Feng" and "huang" became combined and known to some as a phoenix.

But while Fenghuang looks like a Western phoenix, it's actually a divine bird that symbolizes peace, prosperity, virtue, fortune, the harmony of male and female, and yin and yang. It's often paired with a dragon in Chinese mythology and imagery, with Fenghuang as the female and the dragon as the male. Fenghuang is also, of course, the name of the coolest weapon around: the Heaven Breaker's spear.

Horse-Face and Ox-Head: These guys are the two main guards of Diyu. They have animal heads and human bodies, which is just as demonic-looking as it sounds, and they bring souls down to the Underworld.

King Yama: The ruler of Diyu, the Chinese Underworld, King Yama's job is to sit at a desk all day in front of a line of recently dead humans, perusing his book of Life and Death. Based on how they lived their past lives, he'll sort them into the different parts of Diyu, like the Mountain of Knives, the Chamber of Mirrors, etc. He's like Judge Judy, only a lot uglier.

Monkey King: Honestly, this guy deserves a whole book all to himself, which is no doubt what he would tell me if he knew I were writing this glossary. Sun Wukong, or the Monkey King, is also known by other names, the most famous being "The Great Sage Equal to Heaven."

As legend goes, the Monkey King was born when he hopped out of a stone. He then went to live on the Mountain of Flowers and Fruit, where he reigned as king. The Monkey King's power (and ego) grew, until one day he dared to go up to Heaven to ask the Jade Emperor to grant him a title, just as he had all the great immortals. The Jade Emperor mocked the Monkey King, but instead of suffering a lesson in humility and returning to Earth like anyone else would, the Monkey King wreaked havoc on all of Heaven. Nobody could stop him—except Erlang Shen, who caught him and trapped him under the Five Finger Mountain, where he stayed for five hundred years. That's a *long* time to go without food, water, bathroom breaks, or Wi-Fi. Finally, the Monkey King was released—under the condition that he protect a monk on a dangerous journey to the west to obtain the Buddhist scriptures.

Special skills include shape-shifting (with seventy-two transformations); traveling 34,000 miles with a somersault; manipulating weather; using his hair to create copies of himself and save his master; and being the single most annoying being to ever walk planet Earth.

Nián: Nián means "year." It also happens to refer to a big, fearsome demon.

The nián plays a big role in Lunar New Year celebrations. The story goes that a long, long time ago, a bunch of scary monsters dominated Earth. Those creatures included the nián. Every Lunar New Year eve, the nián would do annoying things like mess up the festivities and eat humans, which made it kind of hard for people to enjoy themselves. One Lunar New Year, when the nián was doing its mass-destruction thing in a particular village, an old man came along. He saw the panic, and he asked why everybody was running around screaming. After the villagers explained, the old man showed the nián his red underclothes. For some reason this scared the monster more than anything the humans had threatened it with, like weapons, animal patrols, and mass pollution. (I'm kidding. It was actually the color red that had scared the beast.) The villagers took the old man's lead and flashed the nián with *their* underclothes, too. The nián stopped its rampage and ran away.

Red became the lucky color of the Lunar New Year. During every Lunar New Year since, people put red paper on their doors, and they beat red drums and set off red firecrackers to make a racket and scare off the nián. And in case you're wondering, yeah, the mysterious old man was probably a god in disguise.

Red Prince/Red Boy: Known as the "Red Boy" in *Journey to the West*, the demonic Red Prince has also been called the Boy Sage King and is the son of the Bull Demon King and Princess Iron Fan. He cultivated his fire-controlling powers for more than three hundred years, and he reigns over the Fiery Mountains. Like most demons, he's not exactly the biggest admirer of humans.

Yāo guài: The term "yāo guài" refers to demons in general. They're usually evil animal spirits or vengeful celestial beings that practice Taoism, a philosophy developed from Laozi's teachings centered on humility and religious piety, to hone their magical powers. With this power, they do fun stuff like plot total world domination. Usually, their greatest goal in demon-life is to achieve immortality and become deified into gods.

FAMILY TERMS/HONORIFICS

Ba (or bà ba): Ba means "father." Related: "dad," "paternal figure."

Dà shèng: Dà shèng translates to "The Great Sage, Equal of Heaven." It's the Monkey King's preferred title, and if you want to live, you should probably address him with that.

Dì di: Dì di is a respectful term for younger brothers that older sisters should use, unless those brothers are behaving badly.

Ér zi: Ér zi is a term of endearment for a son. It is also a term for less-than-endearing sons.

Jiě jie: Jiě jie is a respectful term for older sisters that all little brothers should use, with no exception.

Niáng niang: Niáng niang is a term of respect for mother figures, usually those who hold high status, like empresses and goddesses (yes, even the ones with evil tendencies).

Nǔ ér: Nǔ ér means "daughter."

Shī fu: Shī fu means "master."

Sūn nǔ ér: Sūn nǔ ér means "granddaughter."

Sūn zi: Sūn zi means "grandson."

Ye Ye (or yé ye): Ye Ye means "paternal grandfather."

OTHER TERMS

Diyu: The Chinese version of the underworld or afterlife, Diyu is ruled by a deity named King Yama. It's where both average Joes and bad guys go in the afterlife. So rather than being just a place of punishment, this realm is also a purgatory where souls await reincarnation into the next life. The capital of Diyu is Youdu. Imagine being in a waiting room for a really, really, really long time, listening to endless moaning and wailing, and eventually being greeted with scary demons wielding sharp, painful tools. Basically, it's like the dentist's office.

Hungry Ghost Festival: The Hungry Ghost Festival takes place during the Ghost Month, which is also referred to as the Seventh Month, since it takes place during the seventh month of the lunar calendar. People celebrate by burning incense and hell money and placing offerings to the dead on the altar. All the spirits come up from Diyu to eat, drink, have fun, and basically mooch off their living relatives on Earth.

Jiā yóu: Literally translating to "add oil," jiā yóu is a term of encouragement used to cheer on others as they undertake daunting tasks, like doing their laundry or saving the world from demons.

Lunar New Year: The Lunar New Year, or Chinese New Year, is just about the most important (not to mention longest) celebration in Chinese and other Asian cultures. It starts on the first day of the first lunar month and continues for fifteen days. During that time, everyone wears red and eats lots of traditional food, like dumplings, Chinese cabbage, and fish. It's also important to say nice things to relatives, friends, the weird barefoot uncle who's always sleeping through family gatherings, and everyone else who will stand still long enough to listen.

Huā Guǒ Shān: The Mountain of Flowers and Fruit, or Huā Guǒ Shān, is the peaceful place where the Monkey King reigns over his fellow monkeys with plenty of—you guessed it—flowers and fruit. The Water Curtain Cave beyond the waterfall is where the monkeys live.

Ruyi Jingu Bang: The Ruyi Jingu Bang, or Gold-Banded Cudgel, is the weapon of the Monkey King. It was originally a pillar of the Dragon King of the East's palace, but the Monkey King stole it. He can make the Ruyi Jingu Bang grow or shrink to any size. When he's not using it to slay demons, the Monkey King tucks it into his ear for safekeeping from the demons who are always trying to swipe it. Oh, and the Ruyi Jingu Bang weighs 17,550 pounds, so I wouldn't recommend trying to steal it anyway.

Shī: Shī is a form of classical Chinese poetry. It doesn't have to rhyme, but don't tell Erlang Shen, because we like giving him a hard time.

ACKNOWLEDGMENTS

I consider myself extremely lucky to type "The End" on a second middle grade fantasy adventure novel with a Chinese American cast. Getting to publish Asian American titles like *The Fallen Hero* is an honor that young Katie couldn't have imagined in her wildest dreams. As with *The Dragon Warrior*, writing the sequel, which you hold in your hands, was a massive journey that I couldn't have completed without the help of many wonderful folks along the way.

To my superstar agent, Penny Moore: thank you, as always, for passionately advocating for us #ownvoices authors, for seeing the heart of my diaspora stories, for finding the best homes for my books. Words can't express how grateful I am that we're on this journey together.

To my incredible editors, Sarah Shumway Liu and Hali Baumstein: Hali, thank you for championing my projects and editing them with such wisdom and love; I will never forget that you were the first editor to take a chance on this Chinese American author telling stories from her heritage. Sarah, thank you for enthusiastically picking up *The Fallen Hero* and my other works where Hali left off; your smart editorial vision has made the transition seamless, and I thank you for your tireless work in helping my stories shine.

To my hardworking publishing team at Bloomsbury: Alexa Higbee, Alona Fryman, Beth Eller, Claire Stetzer, Cindy Loh, Danielle Ceccolini, Diane Aronson, Donna Mark, Erica Barmash, Erica Loberg, Faye Bi, Jasmine Miranda, Lily Yengle, Melissa Kavonic, and Nicholas Church: thank you so, so much for shaping this book into what it is today, and for being endlessly enthusiastic about the Dragon Warrior series. Without you all, none of this would be possible.

To my talented illustrator, Vivienne To: thank you for the beautiful cover on *The Fallen Hero*, which is the perfect companion to the equally stunning *The Dragon Warrior* cover art. Your artwork makes my Chinese diaspora heart swell a million sizes.

To the marginalized bloggers in the bookish community, particularly Caffeine Book Tours, run by Shealea I: your support for my as well as other marginalized authors' stories means the world. Thank you so much for always championing authors of color and helping our books reach the readers who need them most. I am forever grateful to you all.

And finally, to my family and friends (you know who you are!): thank you for being by my side through the many ups and downs of my publishing journey. Thank you for keeping me grounded, for inspiring me, and for believing in the voice of this Chinese American writer. Please bear with me for a while longer, as I have many, many more stories that I hope to tell!